AKIKO'S QUIET HAPPINESS

THE JAPAN TRILOGY, VOL. 1

AKIKO'S QUIET HAPPINESS

JAN-PHILIPP SENDKER

Translated from the German by
Daniel Bowles

OTHER PRESS
NEW YORK

Daniel Bowles thanks the Hamburg Institute for Advanced Study for
its generous support of his work during his fellowship.

Production editor: Yvonne E. Cárdenas
Text Designer: Patrice Sheridan
This book was set in Berkeley Oldstyle and Agenda
by Alpha Design & Composition of Pittsfield, NH

1   3   5   7   9   10   8   6   4   2

Library of Congress Cataloging-in-Publication Data
Names: Sendker, Jan-Philipp author | Bowles, Daniel James,
1981- translator
Title: Akiko's quiet happiness / Jan-Philipp Sendker ; translated from
the German by Daniel Bowles.
Other titles: Akikos stilles Glück. English
Description: New York : Other Press, 2026. | Series: The Japan trilogy ;
Vol. 1 | Includes bibliographical references.
Identifiers: LCCN 2025010264 (print) | LCCN 2025010265 (ebook) |
ISBN 9781635425529 paperback | ISBN 9781635425536 ebook
Subjects: LCGFT: Novels
Classification: LCC PT2721.E54 A7613 2026 (print) |
LCC PT2721.E54 (ebook) | DDC 833/.92—dc23/eng/20250422
LC record available at https://lccn.loc.gov/2025010264
LC ebook record available at https://lccn.loc.gov/2025010265

Publisher's Note

FOR ANNA

AKIKO'S QUIET HAPPINESS

1

I RECOGNIZED THE COMPOSITION BY ITS FIRST NOTES: Chopin, a nocturne, the eighth. At the piano: an unassuming woman the age of my mother, to her left and right two shopping bags bulging at their seams. With her eyes closed, she played so well that passersby began stopping in their tracks. Although the piece was much too subdued for a public piano in a noisy shopping arcade, more and more listeners came under her spell all the same. Soon, not a footstep could be heard, not a cough, not a whisper.

The woman took her time.

Her upper body swayed slowly to the rhythm of the music. I couldn't believe how much this stranger was revealing of herself in public, couldn't believe the tones she elicited from the instrument.

Each one of them pierced my heart.

Right where it hurts the most, where no one else could reach.

Of all compositions, it had to be my mother's favorite. I hadn't listened to it since the day she was cremated.

I swallowed the lump in my throat and bit my lip.

After the final note, the woman let her arms fall to her side and remained motionless for a moment. Silence hung in the air. No one moved.

She opened her eyes, taking note of her audience. A wisp of a smile flickered across her face, uncertain and embarrassed. Hesitant, she rose, grabbed her shopping bags, and vanished into the crowd as if nothing had happened.

It took a while for people to continue on their way. I remained behind, alone.

My heart was pounding as though I'd been sprinting.

"So sorry I'm late." Naoko stood before me. She was out of breath. "What's wrong? Are you unwell?"

"No, why do you ask?"

"You're trembling!"

"Everything's fine. I'm probably just hungry." What was I supposed to say? Naoko had no interest in music.

She took my arm, and we entered an *izakaya* where we had eaten many times before. The food was good and cheap, as was the sake. We ordered edamame, sashimi, grilled fish marinated in miso, tamagoyaki, a few yakitori skewers, and two large glasses of beer.

I still could not get Chopin's melody out of my head.

"Is everything okay?" Naoko asked again.

I nodded.

After the waiter had left, she pulled a pink photo album out of her bag and laid it on the table before me. Glued to the cover was the photo of a radiantly beautiful woman in a white wedding dress, holding a bouquet. The picture was taken from the side, with the woman turning her head slightly and beaming at the camera. She glowed in a warm, soft light from the setting sun or from a spotlight. My eyes shuttled back and forth between the album and Naoko.

"Is that you?" I blurted out.

"Who else?"

Too astonished to reply, I stared at the picture. I had never seen Naoko look that beautiful. If I were being honest, it surprised me that she was even *able* to look that beautiful. Not that she was an ugly, plain woman—not at all. Naoko was half a head shorter than me, slightly stout, and had large breasts and robust upper arms and legs without seeming plump or fat. She had a round, somewhat flat face, full lips, and narrow eyes, and for as long as I had known her wore a pageboy hairstyle that looked fantastic on her. She had grown up in Osaka and was the only woman at the company who dared to wear bright colors: canary cardigans, floral blouses, scarves in rose, green, or pink. Whether on the street or at the train station, she was always recognizable from a distance in her red coat amid the sea of pedestrians wearing black, gray, and navy blue.

She had a certain effect on men. There was hardly a man among us in the department, I suspect, who wouldn't have wanted to visit a love hotel with her.

Impressed, I opened the album to its first page. She looked even more beautiful in the next picture. It was taken head-on, with the contours of her décolleté delineated at the neckline of her tight-fitting gown, the silhouette of a temple vaguely visible in the background. She was beaming, which was not a smile of hers I was familiar with.

I leafed carefully from one page to the next. The photos showed a happy Naoko trying on different wedding dresses, Naoko at the hairdresser, Naoko having her makeup done, Naoko at the florist—always at the center of a circle of laughing women who were doing her hair, tracing her eyebrows, holding a veil, or opening a car door. Naoko in a limousine, cheerfully waving from the open window. Naoko in a garden on a red bridge, a swan in the foreground.

What was missing was a picture of her with the groom, which came as no surprise. Naoko had married herself.

When she'd told me about her idea a year earlier, I'd thought she was joking. She said she was going to turn thirty soon and wanted to be married before then. Even as a little girl, she had dreamed about a wedding in white, about herself as a bride with a veil, wearing a crown in her hair and a dress that women only wear once in their lives.

But she'd never dreamed about a bridegroom.

Nothing about that had changed, she explained. She didn't want to spend her life with a man, or with a woman. She didn't want to fall asleep every night next to the same person and wake up next to them the following morning. She didn't want to share her breakfast with anyone. She wanted to go to bed when she felt like it, not when it was expected of her. She didn't want to have to wait for anyone, and, even more importantly, she didn't want to feel bad for keeping someone else waiting. She hated the smell of another person in her bed or in her bathroom, which was one reason why she frequented love hotels.

But because she didn't want to forgo a wedding, she had decided to marry herself.

Throughout the months that followed, Naoko would tell me about her wedding preparations every time we met up. She would describe in detail the kind of dress she was considering and how much fun she had at the fittings. She wanted me to tell her if she should wear a veil and where I would spend my wedding night if I were her.

I'd listened to it all and still hadn't believed she would really go through with it. Now I was clapping the album shut, speechless. "Wow" was all I could muster.

The waiter set our beers on the table. We raised a toast to the newlyweds.

"Did you ever think I could look so pretty?"

"No . . . I mean, yes," I stammered, slightly embarrassed.

"I didn't. I really didn't. At first, I thought it was just going to be a few framed photos and an album as a memento, but I was wrong. I look at the pictures and see how pretty I can be. Me, all by myself, without a man."

She raised her glass. "*Kampai.*"

"Kampai," I replied.

A server brought us a plate of raw tuna. We ordered two glasses of sake.

"Even my mother liked the album."

"You showed it to your mother?"

"And to my mother-in-law..."

"What did she say?"

"That I found a good match."

We giggled and laughed until the chef behind the counter shot us an inquisitive look. Naoko apologized, which we did several times more over the course of the evening, so loud were we. We pondered where the honeymoon might be, what a blessing it was that Naoko already knew her mother-in-law so well and liked her, and that presumably there wouldn't be any strife between parents and in-laws in this marriage, to which Naoko demurred that, with her parents, you could never be sure. I judged it to be quite an advantage that neither partner in Naoko's marriage could cheat on or lie to the other, but she took exception to this; there were plenty of people who cheated on and lied to themselves. After pondering for a moment, I agreed with her. What bothered us was a potential divorce: how does one go about divorcing oneself?

It had gotten late. We parted ways at Shinjuku Station; she was headed to Shibuya, and I continued on foot to the Odakyu Line.

While I was walking through the long corridors to the platforms, the pianist popped into my head again. In hindsight, I regretted not having followed her to offer my thanks. It had been a long time since anyone had given so much of themselves to me. I saw her before my mind's eye, with her stringy hair, that somewhat old-fashioned jacket, and her full shopping bags. She had looked like an ordinary housewife.

I thought of my mother. Tomorrow was the second anniversary of her death.

I don't believe in coincidences, she had always said. *Everything happens for a reason.*

At home, I cracked open another can of beer. *Fish will swim* had been one of my mother's sayings whenever she'd retrieve another beer or the bottle of white wine from the fridge during a meal.

My cellphone buzzed. Naoko sent me her wedding photo with a big fat heart and the words "say 'I do' to you" underneath. She'd noticed how much of an impression the pictures and their story had made on me. I surprised myself. Until this evening, a wedding had never played any part in my thoughts. Certainly not in my dreams. I didn't have a boyfriend and didn't want one. I'd never used a dating app. I took care to be as amiable as possible when I turned down the occasional invitation from a colleague to a meal, to coffee, or to the movies. Being with another person made me feel awkward unless I was meeting up with Naoko or Tomomi, and even their company was too much for me on some evenings. I didn't like answering questions from strangers about myself. I found it taxing to discuss what I thought about a film, a book, or a new manga series; who my favorite actors were; whether I preferred to eat fish raw, grilled, or fried; whether I'd ever been to Okinawa or Hawaii, or whether I dreamed of traveling there.

I felt more comfortable in groups than tête-à-tête. I didn't find it difficult to join in the laughter, to praise the food, to refill sake cups, and from time to time to nod approvingly at the right moments. That was enough not to attract notice among my colleagues and to give me the feeling, once again, of not being an outsider whom no one wants anything to do with.

When I looked at Naoko's wedding photo, something transpired within me. All of a sudden, I was imagining how I'd look in a white wedding gown with a veil and flowers. I envisioned myself posing in a park and holding a sprig of a blossoming cherry tree. What Akiko would I discover in photos of a wedding to myself?

Did I want to know?

Why didn't I?

•　•　•

I awoke with a headache. It was Saturday, the day I did little else but recover from the week. My office job wasn't especially interesting, but it was stressful, and the days were long.

Often I'd lie in bed on Saturdays until noon, run a few errands in the afternoon, do the laundry, watch a movie, read manga or a book, practice French vocabulary, and go to bed early. Every other weekend, I had an hour of French tutoring with Madame Montaigne.

I made myself coffee and heated up a croissant.

The longer I thought about Naoko's wedding, the more I liked the idea.

I found several million hits on Google for "solo wedding." There were agencies in Tokyo, Osaka, Kobe, and Kyoto offering all sorts of variations of such weddings. Some arranged two- to three-hour or half-day photoshoots in a studio, which included the wedding dress, makeup, and a hair stylist. Their websites featured photos of young women in bridal gowns with veils or a small tiara on their heads. Quite a few of them were younger than me, some of them grinning at the camera like schoolgirls. They looked like they were playing dress-up at a cosplay event. On other faces, though, I saw the same happiness, the same joy, the same pride, the same amazement I had seen in Naoko's pictures.

Other companies organized elaborate all-day events at hotels to which you could bring friends and witnesses, or even book a groom and guests in addition. There were all-inclusive packages or long price lists with extras like limousine service and hotel suites for the wedding night. That wasn't what I was looking for. I was fascinated by Naoko's pictures. I was fascinated by the fact that she was able to transform herself like that— from a friend and colleague into a beaming bride—and that she didn't need anyone else to look so beautiful.

I showered, got dressed, and cleaned the apartment. With its two rooms and kitchen, it was really too large and too expensive for just me, but I was attached to it, and my mother had left me what, for our standards, was a shockingly large life insurance policy. As a single mother, she'd presumably been afraid of what might happen to me if she were to die suddenly and, with that money, had wanted to make sure I could at least go to university and be taken care of for a while.

For the next few years, I wouldn't have to worry financially.

I swept the tatami mats and the kitchen, vacuumed the hallway, loaded the washing machine, and soon after hung up the laundry to dry.

While cleaning the bathroom, I caught sight of myself in the mirror, straightened up, stood still, and regarded myself. With no makeup, my skin was pale, almost white, and still wrinkle-free. My face was narrower than that of most women I knew, my nose longer and pointier, my eyes rounder and larger. I'd used to hate the small black birthmark on my right cheek, but now it didn't bother me. My lips were full and naturally red, so I only ever wore an understated lipstick. I brushed the hair out of my face and held it back in a ponytail, turning my head from one side to the other. My ears were too big, I thought, and stuck out slightly. That's why I rarely wore my hair in a ponytail. I used to be miserable about my looks, but now found myself neither particularly pretty nor particularly ugly. I was not a woman who attracted the gazes of men, and that was fine by me. Would I still transform in my wedding photos like Naoko had?

That evening, I went on a walk through Shimokita. It was a warm, early summer's day, the streets full of people. Ever since the train tracks had been routed underground, the neighborhood had changed. The large, somewhat chaotic market around Shimokitazawa Station, where my mother and I had often gone to eat and drink on weekends in those early years, was long gone. In the secondhand stores, next to the hand-me-down dress shirts, T-shirts, and jeans, there were now used clothes and shoes from Prada or Louis Vuitton bags. A big outpost of Muji had opened, a new hotel, an organic supermarket; thrift shops and smaller restaurants and bars like my mother's were rapidly disappearing.

Later, I bought another cold tea and a slice of *baumkuchen* at the Lawson at Higashi-Kitazawa Station. After exiting the store, I noticed a man on the opposite corner. He was conspicuously tall, had long, curly hair, and wore a dark-green hooded jacket. With his slightly slouching posture and his head somewhat drawn in, he looked like he wanted to make himself smaller than he was.

He looked toward me, and our eyes met. Immediately, he turned away again.

Without expecting to, I'd seen Kento-kun again. Kobayashi Kento-kun—for the first time in thirteen years.

2

IT WAS THE SECOND ANNIVERSARY OF MY MOTHER'S death, a Sunday.

On the day itself, I'd sat by her deathbed.

The first anniversary I'd spent at home alone.

For the second, I'd planned to consign her ashes to the sea.

On weekends in the summer, we'd occasionally take the train to Tsujido Beach to swim, since her bar was closed on Sundays. She loved the sea: the roar of the surf, the long beach. It was especially broad in Tsujido, and from it, you had an impressive view of Mt. Fuji. My mother would prepare the picnic, and I'd pack our swimming things.

The water was pleasantly warm. We'd spend a lot of time swimming alongside one another or sitting down in the sand and watching the surfers. I'd have a few magazines with me or read a book on my phone. She would just gaze off into the distance or stroll along the beach. Sometimes, she'd skip like a kid or spin around in a circle as if dancing. Late in the afternoon, she'd remove the food and beer from the backpack, and each time I'd be surprised she had managed to keep it cold in spite of the heat. We ate sandwiches with egg salad and ham, tamagoyaki, and strawberries for dessert. In silence, we'd watch the sun approach the horizon and sink into the sea. Over the course of those hours, my mother was surrounded by an ease I'd otherwise never witnessed in her.

A few days before her death, I asked her what to do with her ashes, and she asked me to spread them in the sea.

There was no place to do so more suitable than Tsu-jido. I'd intended to do it multiple times before and always postponed it.

Her urn had been perched on the little wooden sideboard beside the dining table for two years. I'd placed a picture of her next to it. It showed her on the day her wine bar opened in Shimokita. With a glass of red wine in her hand, she's standing outside the door beneath the red neon sign, beaming. She'd chosen it herself as her "official" obituary picture. Each morning, I'd set a small glass filled with red wine beside it or put a persimmon or a mandarin in front of it. In the evenings, I'd toast her in my thoughts and, if I was in the mood, would talk with her, tell her about work, about Naoko, about my excursions to the beach or to Inokashira Park, about the lessons with Madame Montaigne, my progress in French, and that we missed her. In those first months, the sight of the urn had given me the creeps. I didn't understand how this generic, plain white porcelain jar was supposed to contain my mother's remains. It was ridiculous to believe that something so wonderful, so special, could fit into something so modest, so inconsequential. Then I'd tell myself that it wasn't my mother, just her ashes. Over time, I got used to it. Now, I'd feel something missing if it were no longer here. There was no rule saying you had to scatter your mother's ashes on the second anniversary of her death. I could keep them as long as I liked.

A person dies as she has lived, I once read. I can't say whether that's true for everyone, but it was for my mother.

From the day of her diagnosis on, she bore her illness with great bravery. I'd insisted on accompanying her to the hospital appointment where the test results were to be discussed. Calmly, she followed the doctor's explanations, mutely nodding now and again. After his final sentence, he looked down at his desk with embarrassment. She remained still in her chair for another moment, swallowed, closed her eyes. I saw her lips quivering, her chin. The doctor squirmed around in his chair, fiddling with his pen. I think he was afraid my mother might lose her composure. He wasn't the type who could handle that well. I knew it wouldn't happen. In my life, I'd only ever seen her cry once.

In the two years before her death, she never once asked, "Why me? Why do I have to die so young? What did I do to deserve this?" She knew there was no answer to those questions.

She only accepted my help when there was no other choice. She spoke neither about her fears, nor about her pain, and I didn't ask.

She faced her illness with the same strength and discipline with which she had raised me as a single mother, with the same quiet resolve with which she managed her *sunakku* in Nara and had opened her French wine bar in Tokyo. And just as she would patiently listen to the advice of her customers and few friends and seldom follow it, so, too, did she deal with the doctors' recommendations. She kept drinking wine, sake, and beer, smoked, went to bed late, slept too little, worked instead of taking it easy. She hired a younger regular customer as a temp and reduced the open hours instead of closing. Not until a few days before her death did she ask me to put the sign "Temporarily closed for vacation" on the door. I'd added the word "temporarily."

I admired my mother for her courage.

Her body grew weaker, but not her spirit. She didn't gripe. She didn't complain, even when she kept getting worse. During those last weeks, I felt like Death was standing at her bed, and she was looking him right in the eyes—without blinking, without fear.

I don't know if there was ever anything that truly scared her.

And when she opted to die, it went faster than the doctor and the nurse who cared for her had thought possible. She refused food and water. My mother wanted to decide for herself when her time was up.

After her death, I wrote her parents a brief letter. I suspect my mother wouldn't have been okay with that, but I thought my grandparents had a right to know that the elder of their two daughters was no longer living. It was a polite, very formal note. I made an effort. They shouldn't think that my mother had raised me poorly. No reply from them ever came.

I wondered what I could do for her on this special day. Play her old Chopin playlist, even if it was hard for me? He'd been her favorite "French" composer, she would insist, regardless of how many times I told her he'd been Polish, not French.

"A Pole? With that last name? Not even you believe that," came her retort each time against her better judgment, just to annoy me a little. Chopin, she declared to me one evening after a few glasses of wine at her bar, expressed through music as no other what she'd felt throughout her life: an immeasurable, unfulfilled yearning. Neither on that evening, nor at any later point did I ask her what she was yearning for. I don't know if she'd have had an answer.

Hesitantly, I linked my phone to the speakers and searched for Nocturne no. 8 with Maria João Pires. My mother had worshiped the Portuguese pianist; to her mind, no one played Chopin with as much profundity and emotion.

I paused for a moment before pressing "play."

After a few bars, I began to cry. Tears streamed down my cheeks, and I was grateful for the comfort the music was able to provide.

3

THERE WAS EVEN MORE HAPPENING AT THE OFFICE than usual. There were problems with the books at our branches in Bangkok, and we were to check every statement from the past two years a second time: dull, monotonous labor. My only break consisted of a short lunch with Satō-san and Nakagawa-san. They worked in our firm's creative department and were looking for a slogan for a major client in the cosmetics industry. Their deadline was in two days; the campaign was prepared for the presentation, but what they were still missing was the headline, the main tag.

Ever since I'd casually helped them out with the catchphrase "We Connect People" for Japan Railways two years earlier, they would ask me for advice whenever they were stuck—which happened regularly. Sometimes I was able to help them, sometimes I wasn't. I was delighted whenever I'd later spot one of my short ad blurbs on placards or in a YouTube video and no one knew that it was by me. Satō-san and Nakagawa-san thought it wiser to keep our little brainstorming sessions to ourselves and always reciprocated with one or two bottles of particularly good sake. That was enough for me.

We met at a Korean restaurant near our office. Both were visibly tense and nervous; the client was important. Satō-san showed me two dozen photos of models from every continent who all looked different: long noses, short noses; big eyes, small eyes; white, brown, black skin; smooth hair, dreadlocks. The image of a young Japanese woman provocatively applying red lipstick to her lips came at the end, followed by the cosmetics firm's logo.

I pondered for a moment. Either something occurred to me spontaneously, or nothing did. "The world is changing. Are you? Say 'I do' to you."

The two looked at each other and nodded. They apparently thought it better than everything that had occurred to them so far.

I looked forward to the bottle of sake.

By evening, I was so tired I fell asleep on the train and didn't get home until after nine o'clock. I had just enough energy for a can of noodle soup or a microwave pizza, to drink a beer, perhaps two, and collapse into bed. In the morning, my phone woke me up at six. I could also have gotten up at seven, but this hour was the only time during the day I had to myself that I could spend in quiet and at my own pace without falling asleep from exhaustion. I'd make myself tea and toast, eat breakfast in bed, write a bit in my journal, or just enjoy sitting there and staring at the gray wall without having to add numbers, check statements, or answer questions.

On Friday, Naoko invited me to a *shabu-shabu* restaurant. I was delighted. After my mother's death, she was the person closest to me. We'd been working in the same department for five years, were among the first to return to the office after the lockdown because we both felt uneasy working remotely, and had become friends over time, despite being very different. Perhaps precisely for that reason. At first, I was a bit intimidated by her sense of humor and her openness. She had an opinion about most things and wasn't afraid to share it. I'd never met anyone like Naoko before. The more we got to know one another, the more I liked her.

She came from a family of midlevel employees; her mother was an accountant, as was her sister, and her father worked in the human resources office of a department store chain. She also had a younger brother who lived in a village near Nagasaki and, if I'm not mistaken, did something with music. The family didn't see each other often, but they spoke on the phone with one another a lot, and I liked listening when she told stories about her siblings or her parents.

We sat at the bar and both ordered the shabu-shabu lunch special. She was in a bad mood because she'd gotten into an argument that morning with a colleague who'd accused her of being too "dominant." Suddenly, she furrowed her brow, raised her eyebrows, and twisted her mouth into a derisive sneer.

"Men are afraid of women."

"How do you figure that?"

She shrugged slightly as though the question answered itself.

"I don't think you can make such a blanket statement," I objected cautiously.

"Of course you can."

"All men?"

"Some more, others less. Either way, though, none of them will acknowledge it. I think it's rooted really deeply in them somewhere. The vast majority of them probably don't even know it, and that's the worst part. If they'd at least admit it," she said with a sigh, "then we might be able to help them get over their fear. But as it is..."

A server set two pots with hot water on a hotplate in front of us. Floating in them were mushrooms, vegetables, and little cubes of tofu.

I thought about my mother. I'd heard this line from her several times as well.

Men are afraid of women.

Naoko jolted me out of my thoughts.

"Why do you think we've never had a woman prime minister? That no large firm is headed by a woman? Why do you believe not one department at our company is led by a woman? That Ibuki-san landed that position in Singapore last year and not Mikadori-san, despite her being three times faster, smarter, and more creative than that old snooze? Ibuki was at least smart enough to admit it himself. What do you think is behind the fact that among the thirty senior staff members there's only one woman—who, of course, has no children and who also looks and talks like a man? Because we're dumb? Because we unfortunately lack a few folds and ridges in our brains? Because we generously give up our careers for the benefit of men?"

She offered immediate answers to her own questions herself. "Of course not. They keep us down. They keep us down because they're afraid of us. Because we're faster. Because we can manage doing three things at once, and they can't. Because life grows inside us and not inside them. Because they can never be sure whether they're the fathers of our children or some other man is. And we're stupid enough to put up with it. We allow ourselves to be kept down. Honestly, though, I feel sorry for most men. It's got to be horribly stressful to always live in fear, don't you think? What a strain."

I couldn't imagine a man ever being afraid of me and rocked my head back and forth in doubt. I wanted to change the subject. Men and their fears did not especially interest me.

Naoko leaned over to me, her eyes wandering through the bar. "Just look at them," she whispered.

I looked around. Dozens of men were sitting around us, almost all of them our age. They were staring at their phones while eating their shabu-shabu, lost in thought. They wore ill-fitting suits, were scrawny and pale, and all gave the nervous and simultaneously exhausted impression of salarymen on their lunch break.

"I don't think this is a representative sample," I said with a laugh.

"It is," Naoko protested. "The older ones just wear more expensive suits, eat in fancier restaurants, and drive SUVs. Their fear is the same. Believe me."

As she was often wont to do, she spoke so loudly that nearby diners understood every word. The man next to us shot us a perturbed look. I turned away so that he wouldn't notice my laugh. I didn't want to antagonize anyone.

Naoko calmly dunked a slab of fish into her simmering broth. I asked whether she wanted to go with me to a flea market on Sunday. Weekends were long, and I thought it'd be nice not to spend every one of them alone.

Alas, she already had plans. "With one of these pussies," she whispered to me, grinning. "I can ask if he can bring a friend. Then we'll be a group of four and can really scare the hell out of them."

I shook my head, and we left it at that. My relationships with men were a matter we seldom discussed. Naoko couldn't understand that I wasn't interested in them or in women. Her persistent questions on the topic had irritated me several times before, and ever since, we avoided conversing about it.

It turned into another long day at the office. A colleague was out sick, so I handled her work as well and stayed at the agency until after ten. The lanes of Shimokita were deserted when I walked home from the train. Soft jazz emanated into the street from a few bars, and customers were still sitting over their sake and yakitori at two or three izakayas. Though I was hungry, I was much too tired to go get something to eat somewhere. I turned onto my street, and a woman walked toward me with her dog and just after her the man I'd noticed outside the supermarket. I recognized him from his height, his slouch, and the dark-gray jacket whose hood he'd pulled far over his head. Long curls hung out from the sides. He didn't notice me right away and started as we walked past one another. In the glow of the streetlamp, I saw his face. Kobayashi Kento-kun shot through my mind. His high brow, his unusually large eyes, his gait, his posture, his curly hair. It could be Kento, even if I had a hard time imagining him with shoulder-length hair. When I unlocked the door to the building, I turned around to look for him. The street lay empty.

The following evening, I ran into him again outside the *konbini* at Higashi-Kitazawa Station. I'd been at the movies in Shinjuku, it was midnight when I came out of the station, and he was standing half hidden behind a car, wearing the same hooded jacket with his back turned to the store. I gathered my courage, crossed the narrow street, and walked up to him.

"Excuse me."

Silence.

"Excuse me," I repeated. "Aren't you Kobayashi-kun?"

He shook his head.

"Kobayashi Kento-kun."

He cleared his throat a few times as if he'd swallowed something wrong. "You...you must be mistaking me for someone else," he replied softly.

The voice made me unsure. It wasn't as soft and high as I'd remembered, but flat, almost soundless.

"It's me. Akiko."

He didn't answer.

"Nakamura Akiko. From Nara."

For a moment, doubts crept over me.

"From junior high school. From 3b."

He acted as if he hadn't heard me. I briefly considered leaving him alone. "We were in the same *bukatsu*, the photo club. Do you remember?"

Instead of saying anything, he turned around and looked at me. He was wan and looked tired. A couple of whiskers sprouted from his chin and upper lip. His eyes, the expression on his face hadn't changed. He looked at me with just as much melancholy as he had thirteen years earlier.

"Do you live around here?"

He nodded.

"For a long time?"

"Hm."

"Me too."

He cleared his throat again. "I know." His voice sounded as if he had a cold.

How do you know that? I wanted to ask, but stopped myself.

Where and when had we seen one another the last time? After junior high school, Kento and I had switched to different schools. After that, we'd run into one another randomly a few times on the bus or on the street, say hello, but not speak with each other. I didn't have the guts to talk to him, and he presumably hadn't been interested. In Osaka, I watched him buy a half dozen books at a bookstore. We'd been standing in line at two separate registers, I said hello, and he either didn't notice or at least acted as if he hadn't.

A few weeks after my high school graduation, my mother and I moved to Tokyo. I hadn't been back to Nara since.

"Your long hair suits you," I said, just to say something.

We were facing one another, he'd lowered his gaze, and in the harsh light of the display window, I noticed for the first time how beggarly he was dressed. The sleeves of his hooded jacket were threadbare, his shoes were worn out, and he was wearing bleached-out sweatpants that showed stains large and small even in this light.

"Sorry if I bothered you. I'll get on my way. It was a long day," I said, turning to go.

"Where is your mother," I heard him ask abruptly.

I realized that he was missing his left canine tooth. "She...is dead."

"Ohhh," he blurted out loudly and in horror. He bowed his head, scratching at the asphalt with the toe of his left shoe, both hands buried in his jacket. "I didn't know. Sorry I asked," he whispered.

"It's fine." We stood there for a moment in silence. I wanted to say something, but nothing occurred to me. A profound heaviness came over me. My body felt as if someone had hung a lead vest over it. I wanted to go home. "I'm tired," I said.

He nodded.

"Maybe we'll see each other again. Take care."

"Hm," he replied without making any move to leave.

After a brief hesitation, I turned around and set off.

Kento. Of all people, Kento. During the three years of junior high school, we'd been in the same class and had sat next to one another in one of the back rows, separated only by the aisle. We'd even lived on the same street, he in a villa on the upper end near the forest, my mother and I in a small apartment on the lower end. His family's home lay behind a wall with neatly trimmed pines, cherry trees, bamboo, and a plum tree growing overtop. On my walks into the forest, I frequently passed by, imagining the sort of beautiful garden that might be hiding behind that wall.

For all intents and purposes, Kento should've been the stereotypical victim of bullying at school. When he first entered the classroom, he was so strange-looking most everyone giggled. His body's proportions were all off. He was the tallest one in the class but spindly as a rail; his arms and legs were too long, his hands too big, his fingers too thin. His head was really narrow and too big for his scrawny build. What was most striking was his face. It had delicate features, a high brow, large eyes, and full lips, almost like a girl's. He was one of the quiet boys, maybe even the quietest of them all. He often looked tired and regularly fell asleep in class. During recesses, he kept himself apart from the others, spending them in the schoolyard reading or sleeping in the classroom. In junior high school, he grew into his body, and in the last year of school, he had turned into a rather handsome boy. He was still the tallest in the class, but now his proportions fit. Kento was the only boy with curly hair, which he'd tried to hide in seventh and eighth grade by cutting it very short. In ninth grade, he let it grow out a bit, which I thought suited him well.

During class, we both rarely said anything. He never raised his hand; if a teacher cold-called him, he remained silent or gave terse answers that were even wrong sometimes. I suspected he did so intentionally because he didn't want to brag about how much he knew. In almost all subjects, we both were among the best in the grade by far; our written work balanced out our weak oral participation. He was especially good at music and math, I at Japanese and English. Gym was our worst subject, but unlike me, he improved from one year to the next.

I liked him from the start, even if we didn't speak much with each other. With his quiet manner, his always somewhat melancholy look, he wasn't like the other boys who got loud and boastful as soon there were no teachers around, bragging about achievements that didn't interest me and never at a loss for answers. Kento helped the weaker students with their work, and if anyone forgot his bento box, he willingly shared a slice of apple or a piece of onigiri.

The boys left him alone. Not a malevolent word was said about his appearance, his curls, or his high voice. At the time, I wondered why he was never bullied. He didn't have any friends who could have protected him. No one in our grade would have helped him, just as no one ever came to my aid. There was something else about Kento, something mysterious, an aura that intimidated the others. During recesses he would rarely say anything, never raised his voice, but whenever he did say something, he chose his words carefully, spoke softly and like a book, and everybody listened.

Sometimes, I felt like he wasn't even there, whenever he'd look at us in a weird way, as if he neither saw nor heard anyone else, as if he were completely indifferent to what was happening around him.

Once, two classmates claimed they'd heard from their parents that Kento was a musical prodigy. Allegedly, he could memorize long compositions at the piano and play better than any adult, and one day he'd be a famous pianist. A girl wanted him to tell her if it was true; he just ignored her question. He didn't participate in school orchestra, and when the music teacher once asked him to come forward and play something for us, he remained in his seat, silent, his head bowed. She asked him politely a second time, and again he neglected to respond. He was never among the students who had to play the piano in the auditorium for events. That's why we his classmates concluded that it was just a rumor.

At the beginning of our third year in junior high school, the teachers would frequently pair up Kento and me for work shifts. I didn't know if it was a coincidence or whether they thought we complemented each other well. Together, we'd sweep and wipe down the classroom, wash the steps, gather leaves and trash from the courtyard. All the while we'd say little, which suited me quite well.

For our afternoons, without realizing it, we enrolled in the same bukatsu: photography. At our junior high school, we had to participate in at least one school club, and for me, each of the sports clubs, which met almost every day and also on weekends, was out of the question. Calligraphy, flower arranging, Japanese archery, and tea ceremonies interested me just as little as chorus or orchestra. I wanted to be left alone. The photography club met only once a week and was supervised by an older teacher known for not being especially interested in student activities anymore. I chose photography, despite not even owning a camera. Each of the participants received one from school on loan. There were ten of us in our bukatsu, nine girls and Kento. We'd take photos throughout the week and meet every Wednesday after school to show one another our pictures. The others mainly took pictures of each other: wandering in groups of two or three through Nara, drinking boba, feeding the deer, eating ramen or crepes. Yet in every photo, they were grinning at the camera with the same dopey expression on their faces, giving the peace sign with their middle and index fingers. One picture looked like the next, and I yawned with boredom whenever they showed them.

The teacher insisted the group get to see Kento's and my pictures too, and it immediately became apparent that we'd chosen scenes without people. I'd concentrated on flowers, he on the sky. My photos were snapshots of roses, hyacinths, or plum and cherry blossoms. For weeks, Kento had photographed nothing but clouds or blue sky. He opened a folder on his computer containing hundreds of shots he wanted to show us one by one and which, at first glance, with few exceptions all looked alike. In some, the sky was overcast with grayish-white clouds, and in others, it shone a deep blue.

At some point, the girls realized that was all they were going to get to see, began to giggle stupidly, lost interest, and turned away. Even the teacher eventually shook his head wordlessly. After what felt like the hundred-fiftieth photo of clouds and sky, Kento and I were the only ones left sitting in front of the monitor. It didn't seem like that bothered him. With complete calm, he clicked on one picture after the other, we'd gaze at them for a long time, and the more I saw, the better I understood that each one looked different, that they were interchangeable only for the casual observer.

"They're really great," I said eventually. I wasn't sure if I'd spoken too softly or if he didn't care about my opinion—either way, he didn't respond.

Over the following weeks, he asked if he could photograph me. Just a portrait; I didn't have to do anything except look at the camera. But I wasn't supposed to smile. I felt my cheeks burning with embarrassment; I probably looked like a pimply tomato. Yes, I wanted to reply, yes, you certainly may, of course, as often as you like. But I couldn't utter a sound.

He misunderstood my reaction.

After a harrowingly long moment of silence, he apologized for asking, insinuated a bow, and turned away. Stop, please wait, there's been a misunderstanding, I should have called out at the time. I'm just shy. Very horribly shy. I think it'd be nice if you took pictures of me. I think it'd be nice if we spent an afternoon together, walked to the park, went to the cinema.

We could be friends.

But of course I said nothing.

At home, I sobbed in rage and disappointment. I was a whiny little scaredy cat. I lacked the courage to say what I felt, what I desired. If I'd had some, I'd be a different Akiko. Then I'd tell other people what to do and what not to do, like Eriko and Tomoko did. Then I might be the class representative, and no girl would ever think of ambushing me on my way home. Later I consoled myself with the thought that Kento might not even have asked this other Akiko, just as he wouldn't have asked Eriko or Tomoko.

That afternoon, I sensed that I felt something for him I didn't feel for any other human being. Since it was the first time, I had no words for it and didn't know what it meant.

Whenever he came close to me, my heart pounded. I would drop a piece of paper, my chopsticks, or a pen in front of him, knowing that he would pick them up and hand them to me. He did so with a great deal of patience. He probably figured I was a klutz. I took greater care of my appearance, frequently looked at myself in the mirror, and wondered what Kento could have seen in my face that would make him want to take pictures of me. I could hardly wait for the day the photo club met. Even my mother noticed the change in me.

Each week, I planned to tell him it'd be okay to photograph me, and each week, the dread was greater than my desire to spend time with him. Shortly before the end of the trimester, the teacher suggested we choose a partner for the following week and shoot portraits of each other. He would take care of procuring studio lights and a white screen. The others quickly paired off with one another, and Kento and I were the only ones left. For the whole week, I looked forward to the next meeting.

During the evenings, when I was sitting by myself at home because my mother was working at the bar, I'd think of him, imagine what he was doing in his room at the far end of the street. I'd dream he invited me on an outing, to get boba or at least to go for a walk in one of the parks, dream of visiting him at that beautiful villa. I envisioned sliding the shōji to the side, walking through the moss-covered garden with the bonsai trees. His mother would greet me at the front door. I'd bow politely and slip off my shoes, and she would lead me through a tatami room past a gleaming black grand piano to his room on the second floor. There he'd already be waiting for me. We'd sit down at his computer, and he'd show me the many portraits and photos he'd taken of me.

None of this happened, of course.

The next week, Kento didn't show up to the photo club, nor did he on the following week either. Instead, the teacher informed us that Kento had left the bukatsu officially and with permission. The club and its associated demands had grown too much for him and had become a burden.

Every time we saw one another in class, I would feel a pang in my body. Kento was like a mirror I looked into. And what I saw was a fearful little girl I couldn't stand on account of her cowardice.

That was one of the reasons why I started attending school less often. Also, I was bored and couldn't bear the others' hateful remarks anymore—regardless of whether they were directed toward me or whether I witnessed others being teased or tormented.

If the weather was good, I'd spend a lot of time in the forest, where I'd seldom encounter another soul. My mother was convinced there were spirits there, and I believe she was right. But I wasn't afraid of them, and they left me alone. I'd often sit on a mossy rock by the banks of a stream and watch the flowing water. It would burble and gurgle, and I'd imagine that the stream was endlessly saying something in a language I didn't understand. I could listen to it for a long time without growing bored. Or I'd roam around among the trees until I got cold.

During the winter, or when the weather was bad, I'd go to the local library, where the other kids who didn't want to go to school always were. We'd all hunker down in a corner and read. For hours. Without exchanging a word. We knew why we were there. There was nothing to say.

Books were our little getaways. For us, they served as the fortresses to which we'd retreat and where the world around us couldn't harm us. I admired the people who had created them for us with their imagination. The first thing I did when I opened a book was look up the author, where and when they were born, where they lived, whether they had a family, what other books they had written. They were mostly women, and I was grateful to each and every one of them.

As long as we weren't wearing school uniforms, the librarians would leave us alone, which is why we'd bring casual pants and sweatshirts or shirts hidden in our school backpacks and change clothes in the library bathroom.

There was a very friendly older librarian who would occasionally swing by and give book recommendations to anyone who wanted them. It was through her I found out about Yoko Ogawa and Banana Yoshimoto. We'd have conversations about books and about manga, and not once did she ever want to know why I wasn't in school or whether my parents knew where I was spending my time.

It was from her I learned that there are people who know the answers without asking questions.

My problem was homework. I didn't have a friend I could ask what was assigned, and that very first time, I got into trouble with our homeroom teacher because I hadn't done the work.

That didn't stop me from walking through the forest again a few days later instead of going to school. That afternoon, a slip of paper appeared in our mailbox. On it were numbers, with no note and no name. It took a while before I realized that they were the pages and chapter numbers for our homework.

From then on, every time I cut class, a note would be in our mailbox by early evening at the latest. Just numbers, never a word.

It was a mystery to me who helped me like this. Secretly, I hoped it was Kento. When I went to thank him for it, he had no idea what I was talking about. It was deeply embarrassing to me to have assumed he'd be interested enough in me to support my playing hooky in that way.

To this day, I still don't know who put the slips of paper in the mailbox.

After a few weeks, the school got in touch with us. My mother confronted me, wondering whether it was true what she had heard from my homeroom teacher.

I had never lied to her and didn't do so then either.

She admonished me and explained how important school was and that not attending class wouldn't solve anything and that I wouldn't pass the high school entrance exams if I kept on. She did not want to know anything about the reasons for my absences, or at least she didn't ask about them. But her words lacked insistence and conviction; say what she will, that much I could discern from her tone.

She didn't even demand I promise her never to do something like that again.

And since I was still among the best in the class and did my homework, the school never called us up again, despite my increasingly frequent absences. And my mother didn't ask any questions—for that I was grateful to her.

I feared the end of the school year because I had a feeling I wouldn't be accepted to the same high school as Kento because of my absenteeism. At the same time, I longed for the end because I hoped to be left alone by my new female classmates at the new school.

Ever since that time, my thoughts would inevitably return to Kento now and again.

Once, I was walking past a gallery in Roppongi with Naoko and through its large windows spotted an exhibition with photographs of various formations of clouds and sky.

I stopped, regarded the pictures, and pondered what might have become of Kento, whether he was doing well, had a family, whether he was happy—and what might have happened if I'd overcome my fear and shyness back then. One might also view life as a collection of missed opportunities, I thought, strung up on a necklace like pearls. Every now and again, another one would be added.

Naoko was surprised that the images fascinated me so. If I wanted to see sky and clouds, I could just look up outside on the street.

Kento was the only person from my school days I wouldn't avoid. He was the only person from my past I'd be happy to see again.

The next morning, I woke up with a stale taste in my mouth. My cell gave the time as 10:31; the sun shone into my room. I made myself tea and climbed back into bed, even though the apartment was begging to be cleaned. Dirty dishes from yesterday and the day before were piled up in the sink, the laundry rack was burgeoning with dry clothes, and a gray haze coated the windows onto the street.

I couldn't get the encounter with Kento out of my mind.

He came from a very well-to-do family; I couldn't understand why he'd be running around in such old, worn-out things, why he wouldn't have replaced the missing tooth, why he looked so unkempt. I'd imagined him as a doctor, like his father: medical studies at Keio University, residency at a hospital, his own private practice. Or he might have followed in his father's footsteps and become a surgeon. I couldn't square the Kento I'd met yesterday evening with the Kento I knew from school.

What had happened on the way from Nizaka-chō, in Nara, to Shimokitazawa, in Tokyo?

I googled "Kobayashi." The first thing shown to me was the ski jumper. Then came a race car driver. A soccer player. A musician. Anime characters. Students. The name was far too common for me to find anything out about Kento's family on the first go. There were a few hits for "Kento Kobayashi." He had in fact been a musical prodigy. At twelve years old, he'd won the prestigious Yamaha Prize—and never bragged about it in school, nor even mentioned it. At sixteen, the NHK Competition. At seventeen, the Suntory, as one of its youngest prizewinners. A bright future had been predicted for him in the world's concert halls. After that, there was no further information about him, just a note that entries had been deleted for data privacy reasons.

Among the videos, I found two films about him. The first was a short clip of a recital in a kind of auditorium, with shaky video and bad sound quality: Kento was playing a grand piano and looked as I remembered him from school.

The second was a twelve-minute recording of his performance at a famous competition.

At first glance, I wasn't sure whether it was really Kento. He appeared on stage in black pants and a white shirt, walked confidently and purposefully toward the piano, took a seat, adjusted the height of the bench, closed his eyes, and paused for a few seconds. Every movement seemed so self-assured, in a way I had never experienced from him in class. The cameras showed him from different angles and perspectives, now from a certain distance, then again in close-up.

His large hands flew over the keys at a rapid pace; his fingers moved so quickly that my eyes could hardly follow them. He made a face as though in pain, smiled, squinted his eyes, or gazed dreamily beyond the piano past the camera.

It was a complicated piece, and he played it without a score.

I felt the music throughout my entire body; I'd never heard or seen anyone play piano like this before.

After the final note, he let his arms fall to his sides as if in slow motion, remaining motionless on the bench for an eternally long moment with his eyes closed. Silence thundered in the hall. He stood up and bowed.

Only then did the audience burst into a raucous round of applause that simply would not end.

There was no trace of him on Facebook. His brother had a page, and so did his sister, but not him. In vain I scoured his siblings' posts for a picture or news of Kento.

Using the keywords "Kobayashi heart surgeon Nara," I found a short Wikipedia entry about his father Kenzo. He'd headed the Center for Cardiac Surgery at the university hospital in Nara, had studied in New York for a time, had been a professor, had received several awards, had been selected multiple times by a professional journal as one of Japan's best heart surgeons.

Kobayashi Kenzo came from a family of well-known physicians and had three children: Yuichiro, Kento, and Emi. He'd been a talented musician in his youth, had wanted to become a pianist, and had ultimately opted to study medicine after all.

He'd been born in Hiroshima on August 6, 1960, and had died in Nara on August 6, 2014. "Cause of death unknown."

A strange way of putting it. His date of death was listed precisely. How could the cause be unexplained for such a famous doctor? Maybe it'd had something to do with his birthplace, Hiroshima, a belated consequence of radiation poisoning perhaps. If his family was from that city, they were *hibakusha*, survivors of the atomic bombing. I knew this was a stigma many would rather conceal. In Japan after the war, people hadn't felt sorry for the hibakusha, but instead treated them like lepers. To this day, many families found it embarrassing to be connected to the atomic bomb and its aftermath. His birthday and date of death landed on the same day: August sixth—the anniversary of the day the bomb was dropped.

He'd been fifty-four years old, just seven years older than my mother. Not young anymore, but not old either. Although I'd seen Kento's father only once at a sports festival at school, his death moved me in an odd way.

I'd have loved to call Kento and ask what had happened to him, but for one thing, I didn't have his number, and for another, that would have been more than inappropriate. The circumstances of his father's death were none of my business.

4

I AWOKE IN THE NIGHT FROM AN INTENSE THUMPING sound and sat up with a start. The glasses were clanking in the cabinet. My heart was racing, my pulse irregular. An earthquake.

The light from a streetlamp shone into the room from outside. The shadows on the ceiling weren't moving, and it was silent in my apartment, in the building, on the street.

The earth wasn't quaking—I'd only imagined the sounds and must've had bad dreams without remembering what they were about.

In the kitchen, I heated up a kettle of water, drank half a glass, then another. I was freezing, though it wasn't cold. I was uneasy, afraid without knowing what of. The clock read 4:27.

I thought of Kento and his father. As if from nowhere, images flashed before me of a morning when I randomly found Kento behind our school's gym. He was sitting behind the ledge of a wall, crying, hugging his knees. His rumpled white shirt was untucked, and his pale-blue tie had a big fat black stain. It looked as if he'd been in a fight.

He gazed up at me anxiously. I remained there, uncertain. Eventually, I knelt down next to him, putting my hand on his arm. He didn't react.

Can I help you?

He only shook his head.

Gradually, his sobbing subsided. I stayed with him until the bell rang the hour. With his sleeve, he wiped the tears from his face and stood up. On the way to class, he disappeared into the gym and returned with a freshly washed face, a clean tie, and his shirt tucked back in to his pants. We both acted like nothing had happened.

Over subsequent weeks in class, he would often ask for permission to go to the bathroom and return with bloodshot eyes.

None of our classmates noticed, or none cared. Several times, I intended to talk with him but didn't have the guts to speak to him—another example of my cowardice, for which I so hated myself back then.

It was almost five a.m. In another hour or so, my alarm would go off. Going back to sleep now was pointless. As a diversion, I sat down at my computer, looked at pictures of "solo weddings," and considered which season might be best for a wedding. In April, I could pose beneath blossoming cherry trees—I really liked their pale pink—and in autumn, in front of the red glow of a maple, my mother's favorite tree. I liked both ideas; their common motif was the impermanence that lay in all true beauty. Impermanence and beauty are related, I thought—you can't have one without the other. Was there a more fitting symbol for a wedding?

Before I got ready for the day, I wrote a note to Tomomi. She'd invited me over to her house that evening. Her husband was in Sapporo on a business trip; I was to come by after eight p.m. when her son would be asleep, and we'd have time for ourselves. I wouldn't be home before midnight. I briefly considered canceling, but we hadn't seen each other in a long time, and I didn't want to disappoint her.

Tomomi lived in Sakuragaoka, a popular district among high-earning couples with children, where I'd otherwise have no business being. She lived in a narrow, three-story house without a yard, but with a tiny balcony on the second floor. Parked in front of the door was her husband's SUV, which I had trouble getting past.

Tomomi and I had gotten to know each other in college.

She liked to talk, and I liked to listen—we complemented one another well.

She'd gotten married six years earlier, and three years after that, she'd become the mother of a child and a housewife. We'd only seen each other infrequently ever since. She had no time on the weekends, and I was too tired during the week to visit her.

Tomomi opened the door before I could ring the bell. She was wearing a loose-fitting, dark-blue linen dress with a gold cross dangling at her breast, just like the one she had worn as a student because she liked the symbol so much. She wore a red velvet headband in her hair. She looked elegant as always and was obviously happy to see me. I had just taken off my shoes when her son called out loudly from upstairs, "Mama. Ma-Ma!" He'd just woken up again, she said and asked me to wait for her in the dining room.

The majority of the first floor consisted of an open-plan kitchen and a room measuring at least ten tatami mats—almost half the size of my apartment—divided into eating and living areas. A large television hung on the wall, with an animated film playing on mute, and toys were strewn all over the room. At the center of the dining table were a platter with raw fish, ginger, grated radish, and wasabi, a bowl with still-steaming-hot rice, and a bottle of sake beside them. A soft jazz trio emanated from the speaker on the kitchen counter.

Tomomi came down the stairs in quick steps.

"Excuse me for keeping you waiting. Yūma has been having trouble falling asleep lately. He's got a cold."

We sat down, and she passed me the fish. "It's nice you're here. We haven't seen each other in so long."

I nodded.

She placed a few slices of fatty tuna, salmon, and mackerel on my plate. We filled each other's glasses and made a toast.

Tomomi talked about her parents, who would soon move to Tokyo to be closer to their daughter, about an online cooking class she wanted to take, about Yūma's kindergarten, which was over a half hour away, yet was still among the most desirable and expensive in the area because it prepared its children for entrance exams to the best elementary schools.

I listened and praised the fish.

At some point she wanted to know how I was and what I'd been doing over the past few weeks, and I talked to her about my idea for a "solo wedding." She looked at me as if I'd told her I wanted to marry an octopus.

"Oh, Akiko," she blurted out. "You've got to be patient. You're still going to find a husband."

"I don't want a husband." I'd told her this before, but either she hadn't taken it seriously or she'd forgotten—likely the former, rather than the latter. It lay outside the realm of her imagination. One of the very first times we'd met, Tomomi had told me that she was looking for the right man. She wanted to get married at twenty-six, be a mother at twenty-eight, and stop working after that. For her, the "right one" meant someone who was willing and able to provide for the family. She found a life as a housewife and mother more worthwhile than one as an office lady. She didn't want to leave the house before eight, day in, day out, sit in an office for ten or more hours a day, and not come home again until after eight in the evening, only to be forced to watch a man be given preference for every job posting or promotion. For her, the only eligible husband was one who could afford that his wife not have to work. She'd found him in Ryo-san. He was six years older and managed some important division in Sony's marketing department. The fact that his wife didn't work was a status symbol for him, much like the SUV out front. Tomomi had a talent for finding people whose needs wonderfully complemented hers.

She set her chopsticks aside, incredulous. "What do you mean you don't want a husband?"

"I mean I'm comfortable being alone, that I don't need anyone, that I'm satisfied. I'd still like a photo of me in a wedding dress. Is that so bad?" The look on her face unsettled me. I sipped my sake.

Tomomi shook her head, stood up, and retrieved her wedding album from a drawer. The photo on the cover was also in a frame on the living room shelf. It showed her and Ryo beside one another, he in a tuxedo, she in a white wedding gown, her arm slipped beneath his. He was a head taller than her. "Look at our pictures. How would they look without a man?"

I paged through her album. It was even more lavishly produced than Naoko's. The couple had to have been traveling around Tokyo with a photographer, lighting technicians, a stylist, and a makeup artist for at least half a day. In most of the photos, he was looking at the camera and she up at him, or she laid her head on his shoulder with a gauzy expression on her face.

"Do you want to stand in front of a camera alone?" she asked. "How grim that would be."

I thought of Naoko's words: "...that I don't need a man to smile like that..."

Tomomi's wedding pictures told the opposite story. She and her husband were each the spotlight that made the other one gleam.

But that was probably the point of a marriage.

"A friend of mine had a solo wedding. Those pictures looked beautiful too," I demurred.

"I can't imagine. What could be beautiful about being photographed in a bridal gown without a groom?"

I had no desire for a lengthy debate, nodded noncommittally, and said nothing.

Tomomi put several more slices of fish on my plate. We refilled each other's sake and clinked glasses a second time.

I thought of my lunch with Naoko. "Do you think your husband is afraid of you?"

"You really have strange ideas this evening." She gave a diffident laugh. "Ryo? Of me? Why do you ask?"

"Oh, no reason."

Tomomi pondered. "I'm sure he isn't. But it'd be nice." She giggled again bashfully.

Now I was intrigued. "What would you like about that?"

"Then at least I'd have the sense that he's interested in me."

"What makes you think Ryo isn't interested in you?"

She shrugged. "We hardly see one another. He's never home at night before nine and is so exhausted that he passes out after a few minutes in front of the TV.

At least twice a week, he has dinners with customers or colleagues. Then he comes home even later, and drunk. If I want to seduce him, he's too tired. I don't even remember when the last time was we had sex."

I sat in anguished silence.

"Sometimes I wonder whether he has a lover." She drank a sip of sake and reflected for a while. "I can't really picture that though. He doesn't have the time or the energy."

Tomomi sighed. I poured us each more of the rice wine, the bottle nearly empty.

"I've been thinking about having a little cosmetic procedure," she said.

"Why? You look so good."

"I'd love to have rounder eyes, and this spot here," she pointed at a dark mole on her chin, "I've never liked. Doesn't yours bother you?"

"Uh...no, not really."

She shrugged. "I also want to see whether Ryo will notice the difference. Probably not. He also doesn't notice when I go the hairdresser."

Tomomi described exactly what the surgeon would do. Lift the eyelids a bit, round out and enlarge their shape a little, then remove the pea-sized mole. I was listening and also not. My thoughts wandered more and more. I thought about what Kento was doing at that moment, surprising myself. It was rare that I thought about another person during a conversation. I wondered what he would say about cosmetic surgery, whether he was afraid of women, whether he would react as dismissively to my idea of a "solo wedding" as Tomomi had. For some reason, I was sure he would get me. I'd had the same feeling thirteen years earlier; we could be friends.

Maybe I was kidding myself.

"...don't you?" Tomomi gazed at me expectantly.

I didn't know what she was hoping to hear from me and, embarrassed, said nothing.

"Were you even listening to me?"

I nodded.

"Don't you want plastic surgery at some point? Most of my friends have had work done."

"I don't know. Should I?" I'd never thought about it.

"I have no idea; that's for you to know. If you ask me, you could have your ears done."

"My ears?"

"Well, made a little flatter. Then you could put your hair up now and again or even wear a ponytail. That'd look good on you."

"Really?" I replied, at a loss.

"Absolutely. Don't misunderstand me. You look good. But you can always look better, right? Besides, we're not getting any younger."

"Hm." My ears were not a topic I'd recently concerned myself with. Sure, they did stick out a bit, but not so much that I'd thought of having plastic surgery. "You think?"

"I could recommend a top-notch clinic."

Instead of saying anything, I drank the last sip of my sake. It was an expensive brand that disagreed with me. It weirdly went straight to my head. I felt draggy, and I was slightly dizzy. Whenever I focused on the colorful plastic toys lying behind Tomomi, I felt like the colors were blurring together before my eyes. I felt like three people had talked at me all at once this evening.

Tomomi noticed my malaise. "Everything okay?"

"Oh, yeah," I immediately said in reassurance, "everything's fine. I'm well."

It was after eleven when we said goodbye. As tired as I was, I should have taken the fastest route home, but without much thought, I took a detour to Higashi-Kitazawa to see whether I'd run into Kento outside the supermarket. With every step I ascended the stairs, my tiredness vanished a little more.

5

KENTO WAS DRESSED ALL IN BLACK AND HAD TIED HIS hair back into a ponytail. He was standing outside the konbini, watching the train station exit.

I acted as though we'd planned to meet up and walked right up to him.

"Hello."

He avoided my gaze and greeted me with a nod.

We both stood there, hesitantly.

"Have you been here for a while?" I asked out of embarrassment.

He wagged his head faintly, which could have meant yes but also no.

"We could go have a drink. I mean, only if you wanted to of course."

Now he gaped at me as if I'd invited him to go dancing.

"It was just an idea," I added quickly. "It's too late anyhow."

"Hm. I...I mean...I don't really like going inside anywhere."

"Not at all?"

He shook his head.

"I get it," I said, although the opposite was the case. "I could buy us a couple of beers. Or do you not drink?"

"Rarely." He thought for a while. "Maybe, yeah, why not."

I dipped into Lawson briefly and returned with two cans of Sapporo. We crossed the narrow lane and sat across from one another on the train station railing. A woman out with her dog walked right past us, and the animal sniffed at Kento's legs, which was visibly disconcerting to him. She immediately apologized and pulled her dog onward. At almost the same moment, we opened our beers, drank a sip, and said nothing.

"You...you were at work for a long time," he said after a pause.

"I'm not coming from the office. I was at a friend's house for dinner."

He nodded.

I looked up and gazed into the night sky. The city lights illuminated it; only here and there did a few stars twinkle. The heaviness I'd felt at Tomomi's had vanished from my head. I thought of Kento's cloud pictures. "Do you still take photographs?"

He shook his head again.

"That's too bad. I really liked your photos."

I observed him from the side and thought I caught a glimpse of a smile on his face. I might also have been mistaken. He shot me a brief look as if wanting to ascertain whether I meant it seriously.

"Are you ever back in Nara?" I asked.

Again he shook his head.

"Have you been living here for a long time?"

"Ten years."

"Like us. Like me," I corrected myself. "You recently asked about my mother. Do you remember her?"

"I saw you together on the street one evening and would often see your mother by herself at night, but haven't for a long time now." Something wasn't right with his voice. He cleared his throat multiple times, and with quite a few words, the emphasis sounded a bit odd—like a piano that hadn't been played in a while, some of whose strings were slightly out of tune.

"She died two years ago," I said and couldn't help but swallow.

We both said nothing. I heard him sigh faintly several times.

"She had a bar, didn't she?"

"Yeah, La Grande Illusion."

We sipped our beers, watching the street and the comings and goings in the supermarket. It was a warm early summer's evening. I was surprised how many people were still out after midnight.

"We've been living in the same part of town for ten years. Weird that we haven't crossed paths before."

Kento pondered. "I don't know...I wouldn't call it weird."

"What would you call it?"

"I mean, I don't leave the house a lot."

"In ten years, though, you'd think we'd have run into each other, wouldn't you?"

"I'm really only ever out at night."

"Oh, you like the dark."

He ignored my remark.

I drank the rest of my beer. "Would you like another?"

"No, thanks."

"Would you mind giving me your phone number?"

"What for?" He sounded surprised, not dismissive.

"What do you need phone numbers for? To call somebody, maybe?"

"Why do you want to call me?"

You're being annoying, I thought, but said nothing.

"I don't have a cellphone." He took a pen and a little notebook from his pants pocket, tore out a page, wrote an e-mail address on it, and handed it to me.

I thanked him.

He handed me the little notebook. Except for the last few pages, it was filled with narrowly spaced lines of tiny handwriting, illegible to me. "There's room at the end."

Without a second thought, I noted down my cell number and "nakamura94@gmail.com" and handed it back to him. I saw his large hands and delicate, long fingers. They hadn't changed.

"You can play piano beautifully."

He looked at me, a bit shocked. "How do you know?"

"Google. YouTube. I saw a video. You were performing at a competition. Really fantastic." While still uttering that last word, I regretted having mentioned it. Kento grimaced. He closed his eyes and pursed his lips.

"That...was a long time ago."

He slid off the railing and walked a few paces toward the street. Suddenly he stopped and turned around to me. It looked like an invitation to follow him. We walked a big circuit through the neighborhood in silence and at some point ended up outside a little jazz bar I had never noticed before. Kento stopped. I understood that we had reached the destination of our walk.

Music poured onto the street from the open door. It was a little club with old guitars and posters of jazz concerts hanging on the walls. As far as I could tell from looking through the window, some of the tables were still occupied. A trio was playing, drums and bass setting the background against which the piano dominated. Kento leaned against the building on the opposite side of the lane, his hands buried into his pockets, his eyes closed, a foot tapping to the rhythm of the music.

It was soft, melancholy jazz, without sounding sentimental. I enjoyed the piano playing in particular. It suited this hour of the night perfectly.

For a while, I stood in the doorframe and listened. When I turned around, Kento was gone.

6

OVER THE FOLLOWING DAYS, I SAW AND HEARD NOTHing from him. I'd like to have known why he'd left me outside the jazz club by myself without a word. In the hope of running into him in front of the supermarket, I would get out at Higashi-Kitazawa, take detours on my way home, and sometimes walk through the neighborhood a second time late in the evening. Still, we did not run into one another.

His disappearance bothered me. I didn't believe it was a coincidence we didn't cross paths. He was intentionally avoiding me. I had done something wrong at our last encounter, yet no matter how long I mulled it over, I couldn't imagine what it might have been. There was also the possibility, of course, that he was lying in bed sick or had had an accident.

I wrote him a brief e-mail, a second one the next day, and received no reply to either.

A week after our meeting, I celebrated my birthday. I was turning twenty-nine.

That morning, my mailbox showed a message from Kento.

HAPPY BIRTHDAY

glowed on my screen in extra-large letters. Nothing more. Still, I was happy.

For my mother and me, birthdays hadn't played much of a role. We'd paid each other little courtesies and had gone out to dinner the following Sunday. If it was her birthday, I picked the place and treated; on mine, it was the other way around. We'd make a toast and wish one another many happy returns, and that was it. Even when I was still a kid, she'd never made a big deal out of it. I received two, maybe three presents, mostly things I needed anyway: a sweater or winter boots, books, a new bike (used). I didn't know any other way and didn't feel I was missing out on anything.

With my mother's death, the day took on another meaning for me—perhaps because the person who had given me life was herself no longer alive. I spent my first birthday without her alone at the seaside. I'd asked for the day off that day, traveled to Tsujido Beach, and walked up and down the beach for hours, until a surfer asked whether I'd lost something and if he could help me look. Aside from that brief dialogue,

I didn't exchange a word with another human being the whole day.

The year after, I opted to wish myself well. The evening before my birthday, I wrote myself an e-mail and wished myself the happiest returns for my new year. On the Internet, I found a picture of a birthday cake with a candle in the middle and a colorful twenty-eight in the background, downloaded it, and attached it to the message. The next morning, I opened it and was delighted. I'd bought myself a canister of black Chiran tea from Kagoshima and a new teapot as a gift and had them extravagantly wrapped. On YouTube, I found a video in which a young Japanese woman enters a room holding a cake and, with a friendly smile, shouts "Happy birthday." I watched it several times in a row.

For this year, I'd bought myself a new scarf and a pair of shoes, which lay wrapped on the table before me. I'd taken great pains with the gift wrapping; I loved unwrapping. My eyes remained glued to the screen, even if there were only two words in the message to be read.

HAPPY BIRTHDAY

I replied with my thanks and asked whether he wanted to go out to dinner with me that evening. After I'd clicked "send," I recalled that he didn't go to restaurants, bars, or cafés. I wrote a second e-mail, apologized for my carelessness, and invited him to drink a beer with me at nine o'clock outside the konbini.

OK, came the brief reply.

So that I could leave around seven o'clock in spite of all my work, I went without my lunch break. I wanted to have enough time to travel home, shower, and change clothes.

At just after six thirty, Naoko, Miu-san, and Eseru-san were standing at my desk. Naoko was holding a prettily wrapped present in her hands.

"Happy birthday," the trio said as if from one mouth.

"Thank you," I replied in surprise, very happy.

"We want to treat you to a drink," Naoko said.

"When?"

"Today. Now. Takahashi-san will also join us."

It was the first time they'd remembered my birthday; turning down their invitation would have been extremely impolite.

It was still not yet late. If we were to drink a beer in one of the bars near the office, it wouldn't be a problem to make it to the supermarket by nine.

I wrote another three e-mails, packed up my things, and a half hour later, we were sitting in an izakaya we occasionally visited after work. It was full of salarymen and office ladies like us who were exuberantly happy about the end of the workday, their laughter resounding all the way outside. It smelled of grilled meat and beer.

Three pitmasters stood behind the counter, enveloped in swathes of smoke, welcoming every new guest with a loud "*heeei irasshai*."

Naoko had booked a table and ordered large draft beers for us all plus something to snack on. We drank a toast to me, and I thanked everyone again for having thought of me. Naoko spoke at length about her wedding night, on which she'd had a lot of fun with herself. Judging from those descriptions, Miu and Eseru thought hers much more exciting than their own.

We laughed loudly and a lot, which didn't bother anyone here. The others told stories, and I listened.

When I looked at the time, it was eight. If I left in the next quarter of an hour, I wouldn't make it home, but I would at least be at Higashi-Kitazawa Station by nine sharp. Shortly thereafter, Takahashi-san, our department manager, showed up. He apologized for being late, we scooted together, and he sat down next to me on the bench.

Takahashi-san was ten years older than us and very well-liked in the department for his amiable, jovial manner. He congratulated me and ordered a round of beer and more yakitori, and we drank another toast to me, which made me feel uncomfortable. The others did not notice my unease.

Takahashi-san had recently become a father for the second time, and he complained about the abbreviated nights, how exhausted his wife was, and how difficult it had been agreeing on the first name Tetsuya. He had preferred Akira, after the manga author Toriyama Akira, but in the end had yielded to his wife's wishes. After all, it was she, not he, who'd brought the child into the world.

My cellphone displayed a time of 20:45. Getting up in the middle of his story would have been impolite and disrespectful. Kento was certainly on the way or already waiting for me outside the konbini. There was no opportunity to let him know I'd be late. I drank from my beer hastily and signaled that it was soon time for me to head home. Naoko protested. As the guest of honor, I could hardly be the first to leave, and no one was waiting up for me anyway.

Takahashi-san also thought it much too early to call it a night and ordered another round.

It was shortly before eleven when I got out of the train. I'd run the entire way to the rail station in Akasaka, and now I was scrambling up the escalator past the other passengers and running through the station's atrium. I exited the train station out of breath. Part of me hoped Kento was long since gone. The notion that I had kept him waiting for two hours was so unpleasant to me that I thought it'd be better to spend the rest of the evening alone.

He was standing in front of the display window in the garish light of the supermarket, as if wanting to be certain I wouldn't miss him.

I crossed the street at a brisk clip. "Pardon me. Excuse the delay," I said, bowing.

"It's fine."

"I am so terribly sorry."

"It's fine," he repeated calmly.

"Have you been waiting long?"

He nodded faintly.

"Oh dear, I'm so very..."

"It's not a big deal," he said, interrupting me with a calm voice. "Really it's not."

"You had to wait around here for over two hours."

"I could have left. You'll have your reasons for being late."

"I can explain."

"Not necessary."

I took a deep breath and looked at him. He had tied his hair back into a ponytail again and was wearing a black hooded jacket that looked like new and a freshly washed pair of pants. He'd shaved. I saw not a trace of irritation, impatience, or anger in his eyes. He honestly seemed happy to see me.

For the first time that evening, I relaxed.

"I'll get us something to drink," I said. "Sapporo?"

"No, thanks. I'd rather have some water."

"For a toast?"

"Hm, you're right. A small Sapporo."

In the konbini, I also bought a couple bags of shrimp-flavored rice crackers, potato chips, and smoked octopus, as well as two bottles of beer.

We sat down on a bench at the entrance to the train station. I tore open the bags with the snacks and handed Kento his beer.

We opened our bottles, clinked, and he wished me a happy birthday again. From his jacket pocket, he took a small package wrapped in red paper with a ribbon around it and placed it next to me on the bench. Judging by its shape and size, it was a CD.

"Thanks," I said, putting it away. "That's very sweet of you." The thought that I didn't even own a CD player made me sad.

"How did you know today was my birthday?"

He smiled sheepishly. "From school. In class I often had to collect the forms for the insurance policies before field trips. The date was on them."

"You still remember it?"

I considered whether I could recall his. "And yours? Let me think. September seventeenth?"

He shook his head.

"Eighteenth?"

"You're guessing, and with 365 days, the probability isn't high."

I grabbed a handful of potato chips and sat for a moment in silence, somewhat ashamed.

"Did I do something wrong when we last met?"

Kento scratched his forehead and sighed. "What do you mean?"

"I thought, maybe... because you left without saying anything."

"Hm. No, not really. I suddenly felt unwell and wanted to go home."

"I'm sorry."

"You were listening to the music. I didn't want to bother you." He lowered his gaze and shook his head gently. "I hope you weren't worried."

"A little."

"Oh... I really didn't want that." He sipped his beer and looked straight ahead. "You liked the music, didn't you?"

"Especially the piano. Didn't you?"

"I did," he replied, hesitantly. "I did, I did."

"Do you know the trio?"

"They play there a lot."

I'd have liked to know whether he usually stood outside the door and listened—and if so, what kept him from going inside and sitting down at a table. I'd have liked to learn what he'd been doing in Tokyo for the last ten years, how he spent his time during the days, why he no longer played piano, what had become of the prodigy. Part of me knew that these things were none of my business, but another part wanted to know more from him and urged me to ask. Maybe it'd be smarter, I thought, to talk about myself a little. That might prompt him to talk about himself.

"Did I already tell you that I'm getting married?"

He shook his head imperceptibly. It didn't look like that interested him especially.

"When?" he asked in a casual tone.

"Soon."

From the side, I couldn't tell from his expression whether the news moved him or not. Disappointed, I said nothing. After a long pause, I asked if he wanted to know who.

He nodded.

To heighten the suspense, I allowed myself a few seconds of time with my answer. "Me."

Kento turned around to me, honest astonishment in his eyes. "You...want to marry yourself?"

Apparently, he'd never heard of the notion of a "solo wedding." I explained the idea to him, and he listened attentively. When I'd finished, he said nothing at first, and I had the feeling I was able to observe him mulling it over. He tilted his head back and forth and emitted a quiet groan a few times.

"You," he repeated.

"Not a good match?"

Kento ignored my joke. "Have you really thought this through?"

I couldn't help but laugh. It sounded like a typical question that concerned parents or grandparents would ask, not someone my own age. I'd never heard it from my mother.

"I...I mean, do you know yourself? You don't want to marry someone you don't know, do you?"

"I've known myself for almost thirty years," I replied, without thinking about the deeper meaning of his question.

He, on the other hand, pondered even longer than usual before answering. "You've spent almost thirty years with yourself. That doesn't mean that you know yourself, though."

I fell silent. The discussion was taking a turn that I hadn't expected, but that I didn't find objectionable.

"May I ask you something else?"

"Of course."

"Do you like yourself? You can't possible marry someone you don't like, can you?"

I took several deep breaths. Did I know myself? Did I like myself? Two questions I had never asked myself so directly.

Kento waited. He wanted answers to his questions and wouldn't be satisfied with two or three terse sentences. Initially, I couldn't produce more than a long, drawn-out "hmm."

Who was I? Akiko Nakamura, born in Nara, living in Tokyo. Single. Blood type A. One hundred sixty-eight centimeters tall. Shoe size twenty-three. Slender. Twenty-nine years old. Half orphan. (Or complete orphan, who knows—I hadn't had any contact with my father for seventeen or eighteen years.) Accounts clerk in a prestigious ad agency. Unathletic. Hobbies: reading, journaling, visiting flea markets, drinking sake. (If you can count that a hobby.) Most of my colleagues would probably describe me as shy, even though I didn't think of myself that way anymore. I would say reserved. Favorite color: red. Favorite author: Mieko Kawakami. Favorite manga: *The Rose of Versailles*. Favorite instrument: piano. Deepest desire: none, at least none that came to mind now. As a teenager, I'd probably have answered this question with "to become an author." That was a long time ago. Biggest talent: nothing occurred to me right away for that either. Biggest weakness: my slowness—not in thought, but in action.

Did I like myself? Do you have to like yourself? Not so many things came to mind off the cuff that I liked about myself, but nor was there much I had to complain about either. Maybe, I thought, I just didn't take myself seriously enough.

Kento interrupted my thoughts. "If you don't know yourself and don't know if you like yourself, it might not be such a good idea to marry yourself, yeah?"

He sounded genuinely concerned.

"A lot of people get married without knowing each other well," I countered. "Or at least not as well as they should, don't you think?"

He shrugged. "Maybe. But…does that matter?"

I ignored his question. "What about you? Do you know yourself?" I replied. "Do you like yourself?"

He furrowed his brow pensively and began squirming back and forth on the bench anxiously. "Do you really want to know?"

"Sure, or I wouldn't have asked," I retorted, a little annoyed.

He reflected for a while. I didn't know anyone with whom a conversation was punctuated by so many long pauses. "To be honest, I don't know how well I know myself. What I do know about myself, I don't particularly like."

"What do you mean by that?"

Kento made no move to say anything in reply. Instead, he emptied his beer and looked around the square, ruminating.

His silence irritated me.

"What do you mean by that?" I repeated.

I could see in his face how difficult it was for him to answer my question and regretted having asked it a second time.

"Excuse me," he said quietly and after yet another long pause, "I'm really sorry, but I'm afraid I have to go home."

"Now? This second?"

He nodded. "I'm not used to talking so much."

"Why not?"

"I live alone."

"So do I." His answer made no sense. I didn't want him to leave and our evening to end this way.

Kento let out a long, deep sigh. He grimaced and wrinkled his brow. A minute passed, maybe even two, before he answered. "Do you remember the moment you spoke to me the first time outside Lawson?"

"Of course."

"You were the first person I talked to."

"That day?"

"This year."

We sat beside one another in silence.

I wanted so very much to say something but didn't know what.

At some point, Kento placed his empty beer bottle on the ground, leaned toward me a little, said goodbye to me with a few whispered words I couldn't make out, stood up, and left.

I remained behind, alone.

"This year."

I wanted nothing more than to scream.

7

MY KNEES SHOOK AS I ROSE FROM THE BENCH.

At home, I opened Kento's gift. It was a used CD by that jazz trio from the bar. Since I couldn't play it, I googled the band and found the video of a live performance two years earlier in a Nagoya jazz club. The sound quality was abysmal, the visuals shaky. Even the pianist sounded like somebody else. I clapped my laptop shut in disappointment. He probably could have sat here and played in front of me, and the music still wouldn't have spoken to me. My mind was elsewhere. What is life like for someone who goes six months without exchanging a word with another person? What has to happen to get so lonely?

The thought scared me.

In the kitchen, I drank a tall glass of *yuzu* juice, sat down, got back up, paced restlessly through the apartment. I thought I was hungry, made an instant noodle soup, ate a few bites, and shoved it away. For some reason, I felt guilty without knowing why, as if the loneliness in which Kento existed had something to do with me.

Eventually, I came to a stop before my mother's photo and urn. I picked up the picture and looked at it for a long while. Her exuberant laugh, her raised glass—it seemed as if she wanted to make a toast with me. How I would have loved to do so. I might even have told her about Kento now. "Oh, Mama," I sighed softly, replacing the frame. She was near me and yet at the same time so far away. I pulled up a chair and sat in front of the sideboard. With one hand, I gave the wood containing the urn a brief caress. It was warm, as if it'd been sitting in the sun all day.

I heard my mother's tender, high voice.

I heard her singing in the bath.

I heard her laughing.

I heard her scuffling steps throughout the apartment.

Her key in the lock.

Bit by bit, I grew calm.

Whatever was in that vessel was more than just the ashes of my mother.

After a while, I sat down at my computer and began writing an e-mail to Kento.

I am so very, very sorry . . .

I deliberated and deleted what I'd written. My sympathy was probably the last thing he wanted to hear.

Dear Kento, many thanks for the CD. I was very happy to ...

Again I trailed off mid-sentence.

I felt a need to write him without knowing what I wanted to say.

In the end, I typed just three words: **Please forgive me.** and pressed "send."

The reply came a few seconds later:

There's nothing to forgive.

Can we talk? I wrote back.

His answer appeared on my screen immediately: **No.**

Why not? I wanted to know and thought better of it. It would make him feel like he had to justify himself, and I didn't want that. He owed me nothing.

I'd have liked to write him something nice for the dawning day, something comforting, but nothing came to me, and even if it had, I didn't know whether he was interested in my comfort, whether he even needed it.

. . .

Something changed. My walks through Shimokita were no longer the same because I knew that Kento was living somewhere behind one of those building façades.

Alone.

In dead silence.

Whenever I opened my inbox, I first checked to see whether there was an e-mail from him.

In the evenings, I frequently walked to the konbini between ten and eleven at night, bought a few things I may or may not have needed, and waited. And waited.

One message from me to him remained unanswered.

I couldn't get Kento's questions out of my head: Did I know myself? Did I like myself?

The first I was forced to answer, after a great deal of thought, with a clear "I don't know," which logically meant I had to answer the second one in the same way. Someone who doesn't know themselves can't say whether they like themselves.

When I posed both questions to Naoko over lunch, she almost choked on her ramen. She threw me a scornful look over her soup bowl. What had gotten into me, she wanted to know, since when did I think such things? I didn't usually take myself so seriously. She herself didn't think she knew herself and, if she was honest, didn't have much interest in getting to know herself better either. There were certainly more interesting people out there. Besides, she was constantly changing; the Naoko of today was not the Naoko of yesterday or of tomorrow. How is someone supposed to know who she is if she's a different person the next day? Unlike me, she answered the second question with a definitive yes. She didn't think she had to know herself to like herself either. She just liked herself. Period. That was enough.

I wondered where I ought to begin my search, provided I wanted to know more about myself. With my childhood and youth in Nara, or in Tokyo? With my father, whom I'd last seen when I was twelve and about whom I knew virtually nothing? I could start with my grandparents, or with the argument that divided my family. Or with my great-grandfather, who was said to have been a notorious war criminal. He'd been dead for thirty years. Did I have something to do with him? How far back did my own history go? That was a question I'd like to have asked Kento.

Maybe it was the rice wine, or maybe at some point I'd have gotten over myself and mustered the courage to write him again sober. I'm not sure.

It was shortly before midnight, and I'd been walking through the neighborhood for a good hour in the hope of running into Kento. At the counter of a bar, I'd chatted a bit with the bartender and drunk a glass of sake. Then a second. It was like a fresh gust of wind blowing through my mind. I relaxed, felt lighter, my thoughts growing clearer and more alert with every sip. Why shouldn't I write to him? He didn't have to answer me.

I typed an e-mail on my cellphone consisting of just one sentence that had been on my mind for days:

When does one's own history begin?

The next morning, my inbox showed eight messages, all from the same sender.

The first he had sent at 2:14 a.m., the next ones in the few minutes after that.

If only I knew.

Why do you ask?

Why is it important?

Are you sure we even have our own history? Aren't we part of a bigger whole where stories have no boundaries because they flow into one another? Where one person's history can't be separated from another's because all of them are somehow connected and merge into something either sinister or beautiful, depending? A larger whole we're absorbed into, where we are as lost as we are protected, where the beginnings and endings of histories have no meaning?

In Hiroshima

Or Los Alamos?

?!?!?!?!?!?!?!?!?!?!?!?

The final e-mail was two hours old. He couldn't have slept much last night.

Never mind the previous messages. It's best you delete them.

Without giving it much thought, I wrote back:

They don't answer my question.

He replied promptly.

You're right. I can't seem to find the right words. I'd better not say anything so I don't use the wrong ones now.

The wrong words cause a lot of harm.

So can silence, I countered, spontaneously.

Less so

Are you sure?

No.

When does one's own history begin? I don't have an answer to that.

I don't even know if there is one that's universally valid.

Everybody probably has to look for the moment their history begins on their own.

With the first big disappointment?

With the first loss?

At birth would be one answer, as obvious as it is wrong.

At conception, because we can already hear and feel in the womb? Because that's the origin of our first fears and injuries we torture ourselves with unto death? Because that's where secrets and mysteries are bestowed upon us that a lifetime isn't enough to solve?

Earlier, I think.

With our parents' birth? Our grandparents'? How far back does our history go?

Anyone who starts thinking about it will find it difficult to stop. But that doesn't matter.

The search for the answer to a question is often more important than the question itself.

When did I become a *hikikomori*?

The day I first refused to leave my room in Nara?

The day I realized my only friend was an instrument with three legs?

Or the day that friendship fell apart?

You tell me.

I don't know.

That's always how it is when I look for answers.
In the end, I have more questions than I
started with.

Can you understand that?

I read our messages a second time in disbelief. Then
a third.

Kento, a hikikomori?

Inconceivable.

The good-looking, straight-A student with a brilliant
musical talent from a good family? Who'd been on a
path to a career as a concert pianist?

That might explain part of his behavior, but I still
couldn't believe it.

In my first year of high school, a boy joined my grade
who stopped coming to class around the end of the second trimester. He'd been a computer nerd and had no
contact with other students. He had a hang-up about
cleanliness; during breaks, even during class, he'd
compulsively wash his hands. After every lesson, he
would wipe down his desk until it gleamed. He always
sat by himself. During gym, nobody wanted him on
their team. From time to time, he had anomic aphasia;
I don't remember ever having heard a complete sen-

tence from him. One day they were saying in school that he refused to leave his room, and he stayed there until our final exams. Our class had taken note of it, but we weren't surprised.

That's how I imagined hikikomori: as outsiders, loners, victims of bullying, manic video-game players, nerds—but not like Kento.

No, as much as tried, I couldn't understand what he was writing me. He'd confided something in me, and I didn't know how to deal with it. I felt bad about it. I felt as if I'd even deepen his loneliness because of it. In my mind, I was walking through the neighborhood, trying to imagine where he lived and spent his time. Would I recognize his building if I were standing in front of it? Did he keep his curtains drawn even during the day, or did he let in the light? Was he a hoarder residing in his own filth, or did he maintain order fastidiously? Did he spend his days at the computer, did he read, or did he sleep most of the time? I was as little able to imagine his life as I was that of a tuna fish.

On the spur of the moment, I wrote him an e-mail.

Could we maybe get together? I'd like to talk to you.

He allowed himself a few minutes to respond:

Saturday, 10 p.m., outside Lawson. We can go on a walk together. Perhaps to Inokashira Park. If that's too far for your taste, we can turn around somewhere.

When I showed up at the konbini on Saturday a few minutes before the appointed time, Kento wasn't there yet. I'd worn my hiking shoes and long athletic pants and brought a backpack with provisions. The park was at least fifteen kilometers away; it'd be a long walk. In the supermarket, I purchased another two bags of trail mix and a large bottle of cold green tea, stowed everything in the backpack, and waited. The air was warm and humid; the weather app was predicting light rain for the period between one and three o'clock in the morning. I'd brought a rain jacket with me just in case.

After ten minutes, I grew restless. I'd never had to wait for Kento before. There was no message from him in my inbox, and none came either, no matter how often I checked my phone.

After twenty minutes, I sent him an e-mail asking if he was still coming.

No, he answered a few minutes later.

Tonight won't work.

A second message arrived right after:

I'm very, very sorry.

Disappointed, I pocketed my phone and grew annoyed—less at him than at myself. What had I expected of a hikikomori? It was a miracle he even dared leave his house.

I didn't feel like sitting alone in my apartment, and I set out to look for the little jazz club. As I walked past my mother's former bar, I paused. The door to La Grande Illusion stood wide open. I peeked inside. Three customers were sitting at the counter, a man and two women. A French chanson emanated from the speakers onto the street. The cover of *Paris Match* I'd given my mother on her grand opening was still hanging behind the bar. I was happy the bar still looked as she had left it, but at the same time, the sight of it hurt. For a moment, I considered whether I should have a glass a wine there, but I was afraid to and kept walking.

Too much history, even if it didn't begin there.

Not long after, I found the jazz club.

A different trio than last time was playing. The bar was full; some patrons were standing on the street drinking beer and conversing quietly. I leaned against the façade of the building across the street and watched the group. Three men, three women my age. They knew one another. I saw it in the looks they exchanged, in the way they laughed with each other. They liked one another. I'd have liked to walk up to them, join them, and just listen. At some point, I might have asked whether they knew and liked themselves, whether they knew when their history began. Or I'd have asked whether they knew a person who had exchanged his first words of the year on the twenty-ninth of June, whether they might be able to tell me how to help him, whether he even needed help.

One of the women looked over at me and smiled. I gave a fleeting hint of a reciprocation and closed my eyes.

At home, I found a story from Kento in my inbox, several pages in length. I read the first few paragraphs, grabbed a bottle of beer from the fridge, plopped down onto the futon, and started reading again from the beginning, my heart pounding:

From K.'s World

He knew something was off about himself without having any notion of what it might be.

He was different.

He had no friends. Not even in kindergarten.

When the other kids ran riot on the playground, he sat by himself on a bench and watched. Or at least made it seem like that's what he was doing. Secretly, his mind was somewhere else.

Whenever his siblings played together, he sat at the piano.

Or retreated to his room and painted or read.

Or lay on his bed and stared at the ceiling.

Whenever the other two traveled to Kyoto and Osaka with their mother, he would regularly throw up. He would have a stomachache and stay home. They didn't push him to come along.

He was grateful to them for that.

He wasn't interested in sports.

Or in video games.

Just in piano.

When his mother asked him why he spent so much time alone, he responded that it was too much for him otherwise.

That confused her. What is too much for you?

You, he should have said. My big brother and my little sister. Papa. School, in any case.

Of course he didn't say that. It wouldn't have been an answer she'd have understood. He didn't have another one. So he said nothing.

If he did come along, he would get tired quickly. All the people, the noise they made, the smells they gave off exhausted him.

On weekend family outings, his father would have to give him a piggyback ride at some point while his siblings ran alongside. Even his sister, three years his junior, had more stamina than him. They made fun of their slothful brother who was too lazy to walk. Only a harsh admonishment from their father made them shut up.

He felt, heard, smelled everything in an intensity he could hardly bear. He lacked a filter. A second skin that could have protected him from the many sensations. It cost him so much energy to regulate his senses, and in the end, he failed to do so.

He cried a lot. Not in front of the others, of course.

He was different. And he was ashamed of himself for it.

His parents were very worried and took him from one doctor to the next. They even took him to see a specialist in Tokyo. The doctors asked strange questions. They tested his blood, they tested his nerves, they shoved him inside a tube and tested his head, and not one of them could find a thing.

He was perfectly healthy, they said. Nothing was wrong with him.

How was he supposed to explain to them what he himself did not understand? He had no words for what went on inside him.

His parents were relieved, but the diagnoses changed nothing about his exhaustion.

He eventually knew that he was living in a world that wasn't made for him. Or vice versa. Either way, the result was the same.

8

I DOUBTED THAT KENTO WOULD COME THE FOLLOW-ing evening. I had written him that I'd wait for him at nine p.m. outside the konbini and that it would be no problem whatsoever if he didn't show. He shouldn't worry about me. Kento had answered me briefly and apologized one more time.

My behavior was and is strange, I know.
I am often a big, inscrutable mystery to myself.
And that means living with a stranger.
It means that I sometimes decide to do something and end up doing the opposite.
It means loneliness.
It means that I am never sure of myself. And if you aren't sure of yourself, then how can you ever be sure of someone else?

I try to accept it. Sometimes it works out for me for the better, sometimes for the worse. Mostly worse.

What choice do I have?

As I had the previous evening, I prepared for a lengthy hike and packed the backpack with two energy bars, a bag of nuts, and, just to be safe, two bottles of water.

It was a humid, muggy night. When I reached the supermarket, I hadn't been walking for even fifteen minutes, and sweat had already beaded up on my face.

Kento was already waiting for me. He was wearing his usual clothes and didn't seem like he was planning for a long walk. As far as I could tell, he wasn't even carrying anything to drink, in spite of the heat. He greeted me with an uncertain nod. We stood there in silence for a moment and, without exchanging a word, headed out.

Instead of taking the fastest route on Inokashira-dori, we wandered through a labyrinth of narrow, poorly lit residential streets. They lay there as desolately as if their residents had abandoned them long ago. Only the quiet whoosh of air conditioners indicated that people were living in these buildings.

It began drizzling lightly, and I removed my jacket from the backpack. Kento ignored the rain. I got the impression he didn't even notice it, so deep in thought was he walking beside me.

There was a lot I'd have liked to know about "K.'s World," but I'd resolved not to ask questions. Whatever he wanted to share with me he'd tell me in his own way and in his own time.

An hour might have passed before we spoke for the first time. My initial nervousness had subsided after the first few minutes, and in spite of our long silence, I felt no urge to say anything. I felt as if we were communicating in a different way.

It was Kento who broke the silence. "May I ask you something?"

I nodded, in eager anticipation.

"Did you find the moment you think your history began?"

"Um...not really. I wouldn't know where to begin looking."

"Maybe with your parents?"

"It's not that easy. They got divorced soon after I was born. I know virtually nothing about my father. Shortly before I started school, he suddenly showed up again at our house, and from then on spent four hours with me every other Sunday afternoon. He remarried, and when I turned twelve, he moved to Singapore with his new family. After that, we had no more contact. I don't have an address, a telephone number, or an e-mail address for him. I'm not even sure if he's still alive.

"My mother is dead, as you know. I don't have any contact with her family. They had a falling out when I still very little. I don't know why."

"I'm sorry."

"It's fine."

"Does that mean you're totally alone?"

I could have answered his question with a single word, but I still found it hard to utter it in that first moment.

"Hm," I said. After a while I added yes, and this yes, said aloud, sounded more forceful and more confident than it had sounded softly within. "Yes," I repeated, "yes, I am, and that's a good thing. I don't miss anyone, except for my mother of course. And I don't need anyone either."

He looked at me in surprise. "Then you do know something important about yourself."

"I did say I've known myself for almost thirty years."

It was the first time since our reencounter that I saw him smile, hesitantly.

"You've known yourself for just as long," I added.

Again, a smile flitted across his face, more reluctantly than the first one had. "I'm still a mystery to myself. Aren't you?"

I reflected for a good while. "No, not really. Should I be?"

"There's no law saying you have to be a mystery, is there?"

"I don't think so."

We crossed a street. Kento paused for a second as though he'd just thought of something important, then he walked onward, lost in thought. At the next traffic light, he turned to me:

"Do you sometimes intend to do something and then do exactly the opposite without knowing why?"

"Hm. I often do the opposite of what I'd like, but I know exactly why: because I have to."

The traffic light flashed green, and we continued walking.

"Because you have to," he repeated.

"Yeah. In the morning, for example, I'd like to lie in bed longer, dreaming the time away, drinking my coffee in peace, reading a book. Instead, I get up and go into the office."

"That's not what I mean. That's something different." He began almost imperceptibly walking faster. I had to make an effort to keep pace with him.

We walked on in silence. I no longer felt a trace of the calm I'd sensed before our conversation.

Eventually, we reached the beginning of Inokashira Park and sat down on a bench at the edge of a baseball field. I was exhausted and soaked in sweat. My feet hurt from all the walking, and I had a blister on my right heel.

I removed a bottle of water from the backpack and took a gulp. "Should we wait for the first train?" I looked at my phone. "It comes in an hour."

"I don't take the train."

"Ever?"

He shook his head.

"I could call us a taxi."

"I also never take taxis," he said softly. He was visibly uncomfortable.

"It won't be that expensive, and I am happy to pay for it, no problem."

"It's not about the money. It's . . . it's too much for me. But I can walk back by myself," he added quickly. "I don't mind. I really don't. Unlike me, you're probably not used to walking so much."

"Out of the question. I'll walk with you." I pulled off my right shoe and sock and examined the blister. It was as big as my thumb and was bleeding. "Do you have a bandage?"

Kento shook his head.

I stuffed a paper tissue in my sock, hoping it would reduce the pressure on the blister a bit.

"Do you understand what I mean when I say it's too much for me?"

It sounded like a request and not like a question.

I'd have liked to grant it. I'd have had to lie, and I couldn't do it at that moment.

"Maybe. I'm not sure. What exactly is too much for you?"

"Did you read the story I sent you?"

"Yes."

He pursed his lips, gazed into the overcast sky, and turned his head to the side. "The close confines of a car are too much for me," he explained so quietly that I could hardly understand him.

"The people in a subway car. Their smells. Their sounds. Their proximity. It's hard for me to describe. I still lack that filter, if you know what I mean. Not a lot has changed."

Kento got up. He stood before me, hesitant, and walked around the bench a few times before continuing on: "I haven't left my apartment in six years, aside from a few short shopping trips in the middle of the night. And it's not big. I'm still different. And I'm still ashamed of that."

He sat back down. I heard him breathing beside me and would have liked to touch him, to caress his hand or squeeze his arm, but I couldn't bring myself to do so.

His gaze was lost somewhere in the distance. "May I ask you something?"

"Of course."

"Didn't you find me odd in school? Didn't you ever notice anything about me?"

"Once I found you crying behind the gym, do you remember?"

"Yes."

"But otherwise? I don't know...I really don't. You were tired a lot, that's true. And sometimes I had the feeling you weren't really there. You'd look at us in this weird way. As if you didn't see us or hear us. As if what was going on around you left you completely indifferent."

For three years, we sat next to one another.

I hadn't understood a thing.

No one had.

Thirty young people who spent many hours together in one room, five days a week, for three years, and who knew nothing about one another, who didn't want to and weren't supposed to know anything.

Nothing important, at least.

The teachers had very meticulously focused on our exterior: that the length of our skirts, the color of our socks, the width of our ties conformed to the rules; that we didn't wear any jewelry and that our hair wasn't too long. Those who dyed it or added extensions were sent home.

As long as the external façade was okay, everything was in order; whatever lay beyond that didn't interest them.

I never liked going to school. Now I felt rage arising from that aversion.

Kento nodded wordlessly. "Pardon me," he said suddenly, "I don't know what's come over me. I'm talking way too much." He cast me a brief glance. "Sorry about that."

"You're not taking too much," I objected.

"Oh, I am. I've been silent for so long. I wasn't, I'm not...used to dealing with people anymore. I'd considered exactly what I wanted to tell you. I went over my story the whole day, and now everything has turned out differently..."

He turned away, and several minutes elapsed in which he sat beside me lost in thought. I wasn't sure he'd keep talking.

It was true: by his standards, he'd spoken a lot, more than he had at our previous meetings combined, and it almost made me uncomfortable—not because I wasn't interested. I had the feeling that words and sentences had broken out of him after those many years of silence. Now I was afraid that he had shared more of himself than he'd intended and that he would regret it later.

Out of embarrassment, I dug a bag of nuts and raisins out of my backpack and offered him some. He took a handful, yet didn't eat any.

Now I found our silence oppressive. "Do you still play piano?" I asked, just to say something.

"You already asked that."

"Oh...sorry."

"I haven't sat at a piano in almost ten years."

"I see," I said, although I knew that I wouldn't ever really understand any of it.

He stood up abruptly. "Do you mind if we go back?"

Every step hurt. I tried not to let my pain show. Kento would feel responsible for it, and I didn't want that. Eventually, I hardly felt my legs anymore. Taking a taxi or the train without him, however, was still out of the question for me.

Kento and I didn't speak much more; for tonight, everything had been said. He walked much more slowly than he had on the outbound journey, his gait grew more sluggish, and during the final hour, I had the impression that he was far more exhausted than I.

We parted ways without any big words. I felt that we both knew that we would see each other again. Perhaps I was just imagining that, though.

When I got home, it was shortly after seven. I undressed and examined my feet. Several blisters had formed on both, one heel was rubbed raw, the sock full of blood despite the tissue.

I showered, bandaged my wounds, took my last two painkillers, got dressed, and made my way into the office.

Outside the train station, I bought myself a cappuccino with a double espresso. I'd last pulled an all-nighter when I'd had to turn in a seminar paper during college. At the time, I'd gone to bed afterward; today my workday would last eight to ten hours.

By chance, Naoko and I ran into one another on the street outside the office. She noticed right away that I was limping and looked tired. I claimed I'd slept poorly and had just twisted my ankle on the stairs in the station. I wanted to tell her about Kento some other time.

Until lunchtime, it was more hectic than usual in the office, and I had no time at all to feel my tiredness. The afternoon was a slog. I grew unfocused, my eyes kept closing, I missed several receipts, and with each calculation became afraid of making mistakes.

On the way home, I ate some fish in a *kaiten-sushi* restaurant. There were only a handful of guests sitting at the conveyor belt, some of them busy with their phones, others staring off ahead in exhaustion; no one said a word. I watched the little plates of fish before me gliding past at the same speed.

The sushi chef was a young man. He looked over at me now and again, which I reciprocated with a noncommittal smile. He recommended some mussel specialty to me, and whether he mumbled or I was too tired, regardless, I didn't hear what it was. I took a plate of it and one each of tuna, mackerel, salmon, and tamagoyaki. The slices of fish were cut very thin, lying on a fat clot of rice, and tasted of nothing. I took an extra helping of wasabi; its pungency lent them some flavor. Naoko would have complained. For me, it was okay for the prices they were charging.

I ordered a beer and out of tiredness stayed in my seat longer than I wanted.

At shortly after nine, I was lying in bed and fell asleep immediately.

9

I DREAMED OF A GIGANTIC OCTOPUS. IT WRAPPED ITS long arms around me while I was swimming and tried to pull me down into the deep. The beach and the sea were full of people sunning themselves or playing in the water. I called out for help as loud as I could, but they couldn't hear me, or they didn't care. No one reacted to my cries. When I went under and my mouth filled with water, I sat up with a start. It took a long time before I fell back asleep.

In the morning, I was bothered by stomach cramps. I made myself a cup of tea and a hot water bottle and stayed in bed longer than usual. The warmth helped. After half an hour, the cramps subsided, and I went to the office with mild pain.

Shortly before my lunch break, I vomited for the first time. Naoko thought I had fish poisoning and should go home, but there was so much work piled on my desk, and my colleague was six months pregnant—I didn't want to burden her with my work as well. After I'd thrown up for the third time, I made my excuses to Takahashi-san and took a taxi. The whole ride I was afraid I'd have to barf in the car. At home, I brewed myself an herbal anticonvulsive tea, made a hot water bottle, and put myself to bed.

Neither the tea nor the hot water bottle helped. The pills were gone, and there was no one I could have asked to get me any. The nearest pharmacy was just a few minutes away, but in my condition, I wouldn't even make it to the nearest street corner.

That evening, I came down with a fever, my whole body hurt, and I was about to call for an ambulance. As soon as I'd made the decision to do so, I felt a little better and changed my mind.

Overnight, I lay awake a lot, thinking about my mother. She, too, had often slept little at night and had paced back and forth in her little room as long as she was still able to. For hours, I would hear her footsteps, which grew slighter and slighter week after week.

My fever rose. I shivered and suffered horrible headaches. I was probably dehydrated. I forced myself to drink a glass of tepid tea, but my body refused to keep anything down.

In the bathroom, I managed to find my mother's sleeping pills in the bottommost drawer. Without a second thought, I took two in the hope that they would remain in my stomach long enough to have an effect.

I realized too late that she had always taken half or at most one tablet. After a while, my eyes grew woozy, my limbs weak. The world around me said its goodbyes, and I fell into a comatose sleep.

I hardly remember the next day.

When I awoke the morning after that, I was terribly thirsty and felt somewhat better. I made it into the kitchen, drank two glasses of water, and prepared myself a cup of tea and rice porridge, then went back to sleep. My telephone showed a message from Naoko. She wanted to know how I was doing. "Better," I wrote back; she shouldn't worry on account of me.

I tried to fall back asleep, tossing and turning. I was exhausted but not tired. For a while, I stared at the ceiling and listened to the sounds from the street. Now and again, a car drove by. A dog barked, and somebody chided it. I heard two voices from the apartment below me conversing softly.

For the first time in a long time, I yearned for company, for someone near me, for someone who said nothing, didn't ask questions, and was just there.

I recalled my mirror from Nara. It was one of the few things I had taken with me to Tokyo. My mother had wondered why I was so attached to it. When we moved in, I had put it in the farthest corner of the hall closet without unpacking it and hadn't held it in my hands since.

I went to the closet, opened the door, shoved the jackets and coats aside, and took it out. It was two arm lengths wide and three tall, with a small white frame and a crack in the upper left corner. I leaned it against the wall across from my futon, went back to bed, and observed my reflection. The exhaustion of the woman lying before me was clear to see: dark rings beneath her eyes, unwashed, stringy hair hanging in her face. Not a pleasant sight. I winked encouragingly, and somebody winked encouragingly back. I smiled faintly, raised my eyebrows a bit, and studied exactly what my reflection did, just as I had done day after day, every evening, in my childhood and youth.

In Nara, this unremarkable mirror had been my constant companion. During meals, it stood in front of me on the table, and I watched my counterpart eat spaghetti with tomato sauce or *hayashi* rice. When watching TV, I sat it next to me. When I was sitting in the armchair reading or playing with my *Tamagotchi*, it stood against the opposite wall, and out of the corner of my eye, I saw the person in it observing me. Whenever I went to bed, I moved a chair next to my futon to lean it against. That way I never had to fall asleep alone.

There was always someone there listening to me.

Laughing with me. And crying.

Whenever I was teased during school recesses, I would disappear to the bathroom to see my reflection, to reassure myself that I wasn't alone.

I sat up straight, scooting closer to the mirror, and I was overcome by a feeling of deep familiarity. We looked at one another for a long time. I raised my hand and waved timidly. She waved back timidly. We stroked the hair back out of our faces and tied it back into a short ponytail. I stretched my arm out, running my fingertips over the cool glass, placed my whole hand against it, and pressed it gently against hers. We touched one another, the woman in the mirror and I.

I imagined Kento in a world full of mirrors. One hung on the ceiling over his futon. One leaned against a chair. One was in the bathroom, one in the kitchen over the sink. There might be two more large ones on the opposite wall so that they could reflect the room into infinity. How else could a person endure not leaving his room, his apartment, for five, six, seven years and not talking with anyone?

On Saturday, I was doing well enough to get back on my feet. I made tea and toast, and my body kept both of them down.

In the afternoon, I went shopping in the Ozeki supermarket for the *Obon* holiday that would begin on Sunday. I purchased a bouquet of roses, a few candles, two lanterns, a bottle of good sake, and a bottle of Bordeaux, a pair of persimmons, and bar of my mother's favorite chocolate. I really wanted to get an éclair au chocolat in Harajuku as well, but I was still too exhausted for the ride there.

At home, I dusted the urn, wiped down the picture frame thoroughly, and set a plate with fruit and a vase with the flowers beside it. That evening, I replaced the persimmons with a carafe of the French red wine.

So that my mother's spirit would feel at ease with me over the holidays, I lit a thick cream-colored candle that smelled like roses, a scent she had liked having around her.

I had only familiarized myself with these Obon rituals after her death; during her lifetime, we'd ignored the festival to the extent we could.

What use does a person have for holidays on which the spirits of their ancestors return if she doesn't have any ancestors she wants to be visited by? Why is a person supposed to clean gravesites at cemeteries if she doesn't have any relatives she wants to honor?

While the city prepared for the holidays, we would act as if nothing were happening. I nevertheless had the feeling that my mother was more stressed on these days than usual.

Instead of going to the cemetery, we would walk to one of the parks, meander around among the deer, and I would watch with envy the children who got ice cream or a mochi from their parents.

My mother's sunakku was even open during Obon because, as she explained it to me, there were many errant souls among the living, especially during the festival of the dead, who wouldn't find their way home and still needed one.

She was there for them.

For that reason, in the evenings, I'd have to walk by myself through the park, which was illuminated by many thousands of lanterns. It looked gorgeous and a little uncanny at the same time. At the sight of the lights meant to light the way for the dead, I was overcome by a profound sadness every time, without being able to explain to myself why.

I heated up water for an instant noodle soup and regarded my mother's photo. I loved the look on her face in the picture. She was looking directly at the camera, and her eyes expressed a great strength, almost a bit rakishly. Her smile: it wasn't put on. A genuine joy beamed from it. How young she'd looked when we had moved to Tokyo. Anyone who met us claimed not to believe that she was almost forty years old and we mother and daughter; most of them thought we were sisters. I closed my eyes, inhaled deeply and exhaled, and after a while, I had her very idiosyncratic smell in my nose. That wasn't something I often managed to do; her scent was the first of my memories to fade. It probably had to do with Obon that it suddenly permeated the whole apartment again.

My phone rang. An unknown number. I could hardly imagine who might want to reach me at this hour and on Obon, and I declined the call. Right after, it vibrated again. After a brief hesitation, I picked up.

"Hello?"

"Sorry, could I please speak with Nakamura-san?"

"Kento? Is that you?"

"Oh." He sounded amazed, as if it were a miracle to reach me if he dialed my number. "I didn't recognize your voice...Uh, is this a bad time?"

"No, not at all. What a surprise. I seldom get phone calls. Since when do you have a cellphone?"

"Since a while back, an old iPhone. I just didn't have a SIM card for a long time."

"How nice that it still works," I said.

"It's Obon today...so I was thinking...of you...I mean, because of your mother. I hope...I mean, I'm sorry if I'm disturbing you."

"No, no, you're really not disturbing me," I repeated.

It was nice to hear his voice. It gave me the sense of being somewhat less alone.

For a while we both said nothing. I heard his calm breathing and began to feel uneasy. When we saw one another, the breaks in our conversation didn't bother me. Over the phone, it was different.

"And you? What are you doing?" I wanted to know, just to say something. That was probably a strange question for a hikikomori, but he had to be doing something. Maybe there was an Obon ritual with which he remembered his father.

"Not much."

"I see."

Again, silence.

"Do you remember all the lights on Obon in the parks in Nara?" I asked.

"Yes. We went to look at them every year as a family. My little sister loved them, but they also freaked her out a little.

"Me too."

"Hm. I get it. You were there alone."

"How do you know that?"

"I saw you."

An ambulance siren sounded in the background, which was also clearly audible through my window. We lived just a few streets away from one another.

Kento cleared his throat. "I think I'll go now. I don't want to keep you."

You're not keeping me, you're not keeping me from anything, I wanted to reply, but instead I said:

"I was nice to hear from you. Can I pick anything up for you? Do you need anything?"

"Thanks. I visit konbini at night. They have everything I need."

"If I can help somehow anyway, let me know."

"Uh, thanks. Take care."

"You, too."

It took a few seconds before he ended the conversation.

● ● ●

Every year, our firm had a weeklong company closure over the Obon holidays. I wanted to use this time to look through my mother's last things. There were still some items in a moving box she'd culled and wanted to throw away. At the end, she didn't have enough energy to do so, or maybe she'd forgotten.

I retrieved it from the little supply closet and put it on the table.

There were three binders in the box. My name was on one of them, written in thick black marker. My mother had filed away a bunch of little drawings and notes I had given her over the years, all behind protective plastic. On the second, she had written "Family," and on the third, "Haruhiko-san," my father's name.

I flipped open that binder. Instead of keepsake photos and letters, I found neatly sorted bills, documents, and correspondence with an agency. "Smile Family" was printed on its letterhead, along with an address in Tokyo. The name didn't ring a bell. I paged through the papers, and nothing I saw or read made sense. The receipts were from between 2000 and 2006. To the extent I could follow everything, the agency had charged my mother for four hours of its services twice each month over a period of six years. The kind of service it provided was not evident from the documents. The only thing listed there was "HASHIMOTO HARUHIKO" in block letters, with a second name after it in parentheses: Taniguchi Tetsuya.

I took a closer look at the dates. Clearly, my mother had always engaged their services on a Sunday afternoon. It was probably a cleaning business that came to tidy up the sunakku every couple of weeks. Why, then, was my father's name listed on the bills? Why were they filed in this binder? And my mother had told me she cleaned the place herself to save money. I'd often helped her do it.

I googled the business. According to its website, it was an agency from which you could rent personnel for every occasion, by the hour, by the day, or by the week, and even on Sundays and holidays. Smile Family didn't offer cleaning crews, truck drivers, or waitresses, but brothers and sisters.

Aunts and uncles.

Husbands.

Grandparents.

Nieces and nephews.

And FATHERS.

I felt the blood draining from my head, I grew dizzy, and I lowered myself onto the tatami mats. My head hurt, as though I'd hit it on something.

It must be a misunderstanding, I thought. A big mistake. I'd understood something in the Hashimoto binder wrong. Maybe my father's name was just a synonym for a different service. Or my mother's name was accidentally listed on the bill. She never would have rented a father for me without telling me about it. Why should she?

She would never have betrayed me like this.

And kept it from me until her death.

She would never have put on such an act for six years.

Impossible.

Unthinkable.

Absolutely and completely unthinkable.

OR WAS IT?

Or was it? A voice inside me whispered this question and wouldn't stop, no matter how often I begged it to be quiet.

My mother would never have abused my trust like this.

Or would she have?

She'd never have deceived me like this.

Or would she have?

She would never have handed me over every two weeks for four hours to a strange, rented man.

Or would she have?

I wanted nothing more than to scream. WHY, MAMA? WHAT WERE YOU THINKING?

As if paralyzed, I lay on my bed and tried to remember. How and when exactly had my father, or the man I thought was my father, entered my life?

If I wasn't mistaken after such a long time, my mother had told me one morning that my father had gotten in touch quite unexpectedly and had wanted to see me again. He'd pick me up the following Sunday for a few hours. He'd gotten remarried and had a new family, but wanted to spend time with me every other Sunday afternoon from now on. It must have been before I'd entered school. I never got any other explanations.

Until that point, I'd never missed him. A person cannot miss what she doesn't know.

Our first meeting came back to me. I'd pleaded and begged my mother to join us, but she didn't want to. Without her, I'd felt very uneasy with him. He was tall and smelled odd. We'd only walked up the street into the park and fed the deer and hardly said anything. I think I was afraid of him.

Images of my first day of school surfaced within me: Haruhiko had picked up my mother and me, we'd gone to school together, and I still remember how weird I'd found it. I recalled us children walking across the big stage in the auditorium in alphabetical order, searching among the fathers and mothers for mine and being so relieved when I finally spotted her. He was sitting next to her and looking toward me with a grave expression. I didn't have the sense that he saw me. Most mothers cried. Mine didn't.

At the end of the school day, we took pictures beneath a blossoming cherry tree at the entrance to the school, several of my mother and me, one of me and him. There were none of the three of us, or at least I never saw one.

From then on, we got together regularly.

He brought me little gifts.

We went out for ice cream and to playgrounds, to the movies, to the zoo.

He picked me up promptly after lunch and dropped me off at the front door right on time for dinner. I don't think he ever even came inside once. Had he ever stayed longer than four hours? My mother rarely saw him and whenever she did, they'd only exchange a few words with each other. Like strangers.

Every year, during the autumn, he'd come to school for the field day.

There, he'd stand beside my mother along the Tartan track and cheer me on while I ran, jumped, threw— louder and more passionately than most other parents. Sometimes it made me uncomfortable, but secretly, I enjoyed having a father who supported his daughter. Once a year, there was a race that we children would run together with our brothers or fathers as a team. He had always been there for that too. Although we never won, it was fun to run with him.

Over time, I began to look forward to those Sundays. We did all the things my mother rarely or never had time for. Now and then, he would invite me on outings to Universal Studios or to the aquarium in Osaka. I recalled train trips during which we sat beside each other in silence. I recalled him picking me up and comforting me after I'd fallen from a jungle gym, buying me a new hat on a frigid winter's day because I'd left mine on the train. He held my hand when I got scared at the movies. We took pictures of ourselves in a photo booth. The strip of four photographs had stuck on the wall next to my bed for a long time.

He asked about my friends and how I was doing in school. I showed him my report cards—and my affection.

He was the only person to whom I let it be known how much I suffered in school.

He was the only person who could have had an inkling of how I was doing—if he'd cared.

He hadn't been an affectionate father.

He had been a loving one though.

He'd only been rented.

For four hours. Every other week.

Rented.

Like a car.

A bicycle.

A surfboard.

With these memories, images of our final reunion returned.

A few weeks after my twelfth birthday, he wanted to walk with me to the park to feed the deer. Like that first time, he said. I was surprised, but of course didn't suspect that I wouldn't ever see him again after that. We bought treats for the animals, wandered across the meadow, and held out the crackers to the deer, which they eagerly devoured. I liked feeling their cold, damp noses, glistening in the sun, on my skin. We sat down on a bench, and my father said that he would soon be moving to Singapore with his new family. His company had offered him a job there that was very interesting and well paid.

How soon, I wanted to know.

Very soon, he replied. In two weeks.

Can I come along, flashed through my mind. Then I thought of my mother and was ashamed at the thought. Instead, I said nothing. Eventually, I asked whether I could come visit him there.

Perhaps, he answered. First, he'd have to get settled.

I wept. Not in front of him, of course, but that evening, alone, in bed beneath the blanket, so that my mother wouldn't hear.

I'd liked him. After six years, he had long ceased to be a stranger.

He wrote me a few letters from Singapore, though I noticed that each of them was franked with a Japanese stamp and not bearing the name of the sender. He'd been in Japan briefly on business, he wrote, and had sent them from there. Sadly, his time was too short to meet me.

Next time.

That hurt.

And I believed him.

About the possibility of a visit from me he mentioned not a word.

When the letters stopped coming and I could no longer bear waiting, I asked my mother, after a long hesitation, whether she had an address for him, or a new telephone number. The old one to which I'd been allowed to send occasional messages no longer worked. She claimed she had neither the one nor the other. She was very sorry.

And I believed her.

They'd both looked me in the face and lied. For six years, each month, every other Sunday.

I hadn't grown wary. Not once had I had a whiff of suspicion.

How easy it is to abuse trust, I thought. How easy it is to exploit guilelessness.

Perhaps I'd been too gullible. Is it my own fault because I'd made it so easy for them to lie to me?

They'd deceived me. I felt tainted and exploited and sensed tears coming.

Maybe, it suddenly flashed through my mind, I wasn't my mother's daughter at all. We didn't even look especially alike. As an adolescent, I'd already been half a head taller than she, had thicker, slightly curly hair with a brownish tinge, while hers was straight, thin, and black. My face was rather narrow, hers rounder with high cheekbones. Maybe I was a foundling, and she'd adopted me, or the unwanted child of a cousin whom she had taken in.

I went to the bureau where I kept my personal documents and hastily opened one drawer after the other, in search of the old *koseki-tōhon* of my mother and me. I'd often held our family register in my hands and used it on many occasions. I'd read her and my names in it countless times, yet now I wanted to make sure that I hadn't deluded myself. When I found it, I read through it again thoroughly. My name, birthdate, and birthplace, our previous addresses, my mother's data—everything was correct.

My birth as the daughter of Nakamura Masako and Hashimoto Haruhiko had been registered by my father. Relieved, I returned the documents to their place.

I wondered whether my mother had separated out the binders to throw them away, or whether this was her way of telling me the truth. That wouldn't fit with my image of her.

What else might she have kept from me? This thought frightened me. The longer I reflected, the more question marks I saw in each of our lives. I didn't know anything about her divorce of my father and the argument with her family. How self-evidently I had accepted that there were good reasons for both.

And now?

I'd had a rental father.

A man who'd spent time with me for money.

I was too confused to formulate a coherent thought. I grew nauseated. Everything in my mind began spinning.

I couldn't stand it anymore in my apartment. It was hot and humid outside. Aimlessly, I walked through Shimokita. I perspired. My heart pounded such that I felt it in my throat.

At Sarutahiko, I bought myself a cappuccino to go, and while I was waiting, I watched the other customers. Young women like me, who were either preoccupied with their phones or deep in conversation. Are your fathers real? I wanted to ask them. Yeah? Are you quite sure about that? Do you have proof? Do they wish you well? Were the dead relatives you honor during this time even your relatives?

For a moment, I thought about calling Kento and telling him everything, but changed my mind. He lived in his world, and I didn't want to trouble him with my story.

I would very much have liked to meet up with Naoko now, but she'd gone to her parents' over Obon and wasn't coming back until the end of the week. I still dialed her number, but only her voicemail picked up.

Tomomi was visiting her husband's family over the holidays.

No one else came to mind as someone I could have talked to.

10

IT WAS A WEEK THAT WOULDN'T END. I AWOKE EARLY and couldn't fall back asleep despite feeling tired and worn down. The days seemed endless; I was happy about every minute that passed. To distract myself, I practiced French vocabulary, but forgot it again after a few minutes. I watched animal videos on YouTube for hours, read manga, went to the cinema and sake bars, but regardless of what I did, my thoughts were always with me and my mother.

The longer I thought about her, the more I got the feeling I'd hardly known her. Whom had I spent the first twenty-seven years of my life with?

Everything I knew about her I knew from her stories. There was no one who could have told me something about her, no one I could have interrogated to see whether what she'd told me corresponded with the truth.

From her stories, I knew only that she'd had me at twenty and had married my father shortly beforehand and was divorced again after not even a year.

From her stories, I knew that she came from Kobe and had fallen out with her entire family; that she kept us afloat with odd jobs during those initial years; that she dreamed of living in Paris with me; and that she had a weakness for everything French.

I had never doubted any of this. And why should I have?

But how credible had her stories been?

There was so much she had never spoken about. I knew nothing about her childhood, about her sister.

I didn't know who had taken care of me as a baby while she was working. I didn't know why my parents had broken up so quickly, why she'd fallen out with her family.

I didn't know how hard her life had been as a single mother, whether she'd felt lonesome, whether she'd had a boyfriend or occasional lovers. She'd never brought a man into our home and never mentioned one. I knew her only as a mother, not as a loving or desirous or love-sick woman.

I didn't know why she'd had a child so young, whether she even wanted me.

We didn't talk a great deal. I never questioned her.

Neither in Nara, nor later in Tokyo.

A few weeks after her twenty-eighth birthday, she had taken over a sunakku, a random, rare opportunity. She really was much too young to run a bar as a *Mama-san*. I was eight years old, and our life changed from one day to the next.

Her sunakku became my second home. It was located a ten-minute walk away from our apartment and fifteen minutes from my school. After class, I mostly walked straight to the bar, where my mother was busy preparing for the evening.

Her place was small, consisting of an L-shaped counter with seven barstools and two little tables. On the shelves behind the bar stood the bottles of *shōchū* and whiskey for her repeat customers. Beside them hung a large screen for karaoke. In the rear corner, there was a cooking nook where my mother made her little dishes like fried fish, vegetables pickled in vinegar, and cucumbers in miso.

I did my homework at one of the tables. The afternoons on which I listened to her clattering around with the pots and smelled the winter soup simmering down are among my loveliest memories. There weren't many moments when I'd felt this comfortable and secure.

My mother often asked me to help her, and I enjoyed doing so. Cleaning the bar while she prepared the evening's snacks in the kitchen was fun for me, and I spent time with her instead of sitting alone at home in front of a mirror.

As a reward, I was allowed to sing a few karaoke songs with her. For herself, she selected exclusively French chansons. Pictures of the Eiffel Tower flashed on the screen, of Notre-Dame, of couples meandering through the narrow lanes holding hands or sitting on the banks of the Seine in a tight embrace. As they did, my mother sang of love, disappointments, and unfulfilled hopes.

Every time, after a few notes, I'd get goosebumps and had the impression that she forgot everything around her. I found the sight of her beautiful and at the same time somewhat eerie and thought she should've become a singer, so lovely did her voice sound.

When I suggested that to her, she smiled and said she could only sing for me in that way. I knew that wasn't true.

Once, she told me that in a previous life she'd run a bistro in Paris on the Rue du Faubourg Saint-Antoine in the eleventh arrondissement. The whole neighborhood would gather in her bistro, the guests conversing, smoking, and drinking a lot until late at night, and now and again, Édith Piaf and Gilbert Bécaud would come by and sing chansons. As dawn was still breaking, when she was stacking the last tables and chairs and sweeping the floor, their songs had stuck in her head, which had made her very happy.

"You don't believe me?" she'd ask me with a wink.

"I do," I'd reply, "every word." And that was no lie.

In our karaoke, "Non, je ne regrette rien" was always her finale; I'd hear her hum the melody a lot at home.

Maybe it was her life's motto set to music. My mother had had to make many difficult decisions: divorcing early, raising a child as a single mother, not returning to her parents' home with me, and thus forgoing any financial support from them.

Not remarrying.

Renting me a father.

And she regretted nothing.

We were very different, my mother and I.

My mood in the sunakku changed as soon as the first guests arrived. From one moment to the next, I no longer recognized my mother. Suddenly, she would speak two registers higher. Her voice sounded fake, her smile was too garish, her gesticulations and expressions I found exaggerated—they were those of a different woman.

Most guests greeted me amiably, the odd one or the other even spared a few words for me, but I didn't like the way they spoke with my mother. The way they'd sit down at the bar, sending glances her way. The way they'd praise her food or her hairstyle or her blouse repulsed me without my being able to say why. Their stories, always the same, bored me to death, and later, I wondered how my mother had endured it, night after night. Still, I didn't want to leave. I found it hard to leave my mother by herself. I had the feeling I had to protect her without knowing exactly from what.

Only when she nodded at me, meaning it was time for me to go, did I reluctantly pack up my things and set out for home. Waiting there for me were an empty apartment, a cold dinner, and a mirror.

Outside of her sunakku, we spent little time together. Whenever I got up in the morning, she'd still be sleeping. I got ready by myself and packed the bento she had prepared for me overnight. Sometimes the food was still lukewarm, and I knew that she'd come home very late. As quietly as possible, I would sneak out of the apartment.

She did not know what I did on those many, many afternoons and evenings when I was by myself.

Before going to bed at night, I'd roll out her futon beside mine, fetch her blanket and pillow from the cabinet, and make her bed. Since she loved flowers, I'd place one blossom I'd picked for her on the way home on her pillow each evening. In the winter, it was sometimes just a leaf or a blade of grass or a snapped-off, half-wilted rose that the florist would give me. She never said anything, but I was sure she was happy about it.

On Sunday, her day off, she was often tired and would sleep until midday. Our only standing engagement during the week was our visit to a *sento* on Saturday in the early afternoon, our mother–daughter ritual. The public bathhouse was a neighborhood meeting place where the women all knew one another and exchanged the latest gossip. We belonged and at the same time didn't. The others weren't unfriendly, and yet even as a kid I felt, from the tone of their voices, from the manner of the smiles and looks they exchanged whenever we entered the bath, the distance they treated us with. As a young, single, good-looking mother who also ran a sunakku frequented predominantly by men, she was naturally suspect to the other women. If their mistrust bothered my mother, she never let on. She issued friendly greetings, laughed at others' jokes, and listened politely to the neighborhood gossip without ever participating in it.

I did not stray from her side. Fascinated, I observed the various forms of the naked female body. I was creeped out by the little old women with their sagging skin and their flaccid breasts, just as I was by the skinny ones whose skin stretched taut over their pelvic bones. There were the hefty ones, whose bellies bulged or hung over their hips in rings, and the young ones like my mother.

In the washing room, we always sought out the far corner. My mother sat me on a plastic stool in front of her, and I got to lather up her back and shoulders. This I did with great stamina. Then, she'd wash us both thoroughly. We slipped into the hot, steaming water and did not speak much. It was enough for me to be together with her. Although the water would eventually get too hot for me, I'd always wait until my mother rose and climbed out of the pool before me.

After bathing, we'd spend a lot of time blow-drying and combing each other's hair. In long, rhythmic movements, she'd draw the brush through my thick hair again and again and then braid it into a ponytail. When I took it out the next day to wash my hair, my heart would always sink a little.

At the end, I'd get a lemon soda, and she would drink an iced latte.

. . .

My mother and me.
Me and my mother.
We were alone.

Just *how* alone, I was long unaware. I'd taken the circumstances of our life for granted because I knew nothing else for us. I never once thought of calling it into question.

On the first school day of the new year after my "father" had allegedly moved back to Singapore, I was sitting in class, listening to what the others had experienced over the new year holiday. They spoke of aunts and uncles visiting, of playing with cousins, of the short trip to their grandparents', of eating together, of the *otoshidama* and how much money had been in the little envelopes and which relatives had proven themselves the most generous.

And you, Akiko, what did you do? How much money did you get and from whom?

Of course no one wanted me to share.

I was the one asking myself the questions.

Nothing, was the answer.

Like the year before. And the one before that. My mother's sunakku was one of the few that stayed open over the turn of the year because we couldn't do without the income.

In the afternoon, I'd gone to the bar with her and had helped with the preparations for the night: arranging bottles, chopping vegetables, washing glasses from the night before, sweeping the floor, wiping off the counter. When the first guests came, I went home. I sat there beside my mirror and watched TV until I fell asleep.

That night for the first time—why, I don't know—I became aware of the obvious; my family consisted of only my mother and me. Daughter and mother. What would become of me if something happened to her? If she got sick and died? There was no one who'd take me in, no one who'd be responsible for me, no one except my mother who loved me. Maybe my father, but he lived in Singapore with his new family. There was no place for me there.

When I realized that, a fear overcame me that was greater than everything I had hitherto known. A few weeks earlier, the mother of a girl from the parallel class had died. She still had her father and two siblings and presumably also grandparents, aunts, and uncles.

I was thirteen years old and alone in the world.

I'd have nobody.

Over the next few months, I often tossed and turned before falling asleep on my futon and wanted nothing more than to run to the sunakku every night, just to see whether my mother was still there. Once, when I did that and was suddenly standing in her bar, the guests laughed at me. That didn't bother me. I was just happy to see her standing behind her counter.

I never told her about my fear. And she never asked either.

It isn't that I kept secrets from her. There were just many things we didn't talk about. Which is not the same thing.

Out of boredom, I began thinking up stories for myself. If I were sitting at home alone, the hours passed more quickly if I daydreamed and wrote down what was going through my mind. More even than with reading, I lost track of time while doing this. Even my friend, the mirror, no longer played a role. The first stories were fairy tales of ghosts, storms, and speaking stones. One was about a bolt of lightning that didn't want to be sent to earth because it was afraid of wreaking havoc, and it didn't want to do that. Another was about a ghost who grew a half centimeter every week he didn't speak, and since he wanted to become the biggest and strongest ghost of all time, he kept his silence for many months. When he finally towered over all the other ghosts, he had forgotten how to speak. A third told the story of the friendship between a lonely little girl and a large stone that could talk. He had been lying on the same spot on a hill along the sea for thousands of years and dreamed of being in a different place. He asked the girl to help him, but she was much too weak to move the heavy stone even a centimeter.

She began scooping away the soil along the side of the slope beneath him with her bare hands until he started to slide and rolled down the hill faster and faster. With a loud scream, audible up to the top of the hill, he vanished forever into the sea.

A few texts I showed to my Japanese teacher. She liked them a lot, unlike my classmates. For them, my essays were just another reason to mock me.

Eventually, I began imagining what-if stories.

What if the old florist who occasionally gave me a flower for my mother could speak with his plants? I painted a picture for myself of him knowing each of his flowers by name and their keeping him company and comforting him after the death of his wife—how it grew harder and harder for him to part with them until he sold none of them at all and his customers collected money for him so he could still survive.

What if the unfriendly bus driver who gave me nasty looks every time I boarded one day grew into his seat? I imagined him at night twisting and tugging in vain and ultimately taking on the shape of his seat. The next day, a new, younger driver came who sat down on the old one and was friendly to the children.

What if a big, fat pimple grew on the face of every girl from my class who had ever said a bad word to me and these pustules eventually exploded?

I showed the stories to no one.

I imagined what would happen if I wrote books one day. I imagined children reading them in the city libraries, getting immersed in them, and forgetting the world around them.

I wanted to lead the life of a writer and yet didn't have the slightest clue how to become one. To be a doctor or a teacher you had to have gone to university. A bus driver needed a driver's license and definitely had to have passed some exam. My mother, in turn, had taken over her sunakku from one day to the next; as far as I knew, she hadn't had to take any test.

It was probably just like that for a writer; she just started doing it.

The idea that as an adult woman I could think up stories, write them down, and send them to a publisher, and that to do so I would need no license, no permit, no training, fascinated me.

What I didn't write about:

What if a daughter were allowed to visit her father in Singapore?

What if a young girl had the courage to invite the boy she liked for ice cream?

What if a mother were to watch her daughter fall asleep?

•   •   •

It must have been shortly after my thirteenth or fourteenth birthday—I'm no longer quite certain as far as the year is concerned—when my mother surprised me with the notion of going on vacation.

She had planned everything out exactly. Sunday was her day off, and she would close her sunakku for the first and only time on a second evening during the week. We would take the train to Kinosaki Onsen on Saturday as soon as we woke up, would be there around midday, and could spend two nights in a beautiful *ryokan*. She wanted to visit the seven famous public bathhouses with me and, if we felt like it, go on an excursion for an afternoon to the sea. Midday Monday we'd return, so that we'd had two full days, and she'd be back in town by late afternoon, in time to open her sunakku.

My excitement was great. For weeks in advance, I considered what I should pack. I went to the library and looked at travel guides on Japan's nicest and most famous thermal baths. In each of the books, I found a chapter or at least a few pages with pictures of Kinosaki Onsen. In all seasons, it was an especially pretty town with many old houses and a river right in the middle of it, with willows and cherry trees growing on its banks and a little bridge spanning it. I pictured every detail of the trip: my mother and I sitting next to one another on the train, looking out the window together, eating from our bento boxes. Me wearing a *yukata* for the first time and strolling through the lanes in *geta*, us drinking soda together and having all the time in the world. Us trying out one bathhouse after the other and, back in our room during the evening, enjoying a traditional ryokan multicourse meal, which I'd often read about.

On the night before our departure, I was so nervous that I couldn't fall asleep. I heard my mother's key in the lock. It was already getting dark. While she undressed and got ready, she was less cautious than usual and cursed once out loud.

On my arm, I felt her breath reeking of beer and whiskey, as I lay beside her. Shortly after that, she fell asleep. I did not.

When the alarm went off in the morning, she shut it off.

I got up, got dressed, made myself toast, packed my backpack, and waited for her to finally wake up.

While I observed my sleeping mother, my excitement mixed with an indeterminate fear. I wondered why she suddenly wanted to go on vacation with me. Was there something she had to tell me? Maybe she wanted to remarry? Or she had to close her sunakku?

She woke up late. We missed our trains and didn't arrive in Kinosaki Onsen until the early evening. During the train ride, my mother dozed the majority of the time. Occasionally, her head would fall onto my shoulder, she'd wake up briefly, and nod off again. I was sitting by the window, looking out, and with every kilometer we spent like that, I grew lonelier. I was overcome by a great melancholy I couldn't fight off. I hoped that it would dissipate as soon as we'd reached our destination—at the same time, I was tormented by a horrible fear that it wouldn't be the case.

When we finally arrived at our ryokan, it was too late for bathing. My mother promised we'd make up for it later, after dinner; the baths would be open until midnight.

The *nakai-san* served a meal like I'd never seen before. There was delicious vegetable tempura, tuna and hamachi sashimi, kombu in little bowls, radishes, and pickles. We were served miso soup, grilled fish, rice, and tamagoyaki.

My mother ordered a beer. She was very thirsty and quickly ordered a second. Her tiredness had faded; she giggled and was more chipper than I was used to. Her gestures and expressions reminded me a little of the moments when I'd watch her conversing with customers at the sunakku and she seemed to be a different person.

The click-clack of the wooden sandals in which the guests walked from bathhouse to bathhouse echoed up off the street.

We sat facing one another on the tatami mats. We had time together. The food was delectable. For weeks, I'd looked forward to this moment. I had every reason to be happy and yet wasn't.

We ate and didn't speak much. Now and again, my mother would ask whether I thought the food tasted good, and I'd nod. Several times, she began to say something; I had the impression that there was something she wanted to tell me, but that she couldn't find a suitable place to start or reconsidered at the last moment. Something was on her mind.

She accidentally knocked over the third bottle; the beer spilled onto the tatami mats. We called for the nakai-san, who attempted to wipe up everything quickly. The smell of beer still hung in the air. My mother apologized multiple times, and the server said it was no problem, it was no trouble at all, it could happen to anyone. Her expression conveyed something else.

The whole thing was infinitely embarrassing to me, and I was a little bit ashamed for her.

My mother drank another sake. She was in a good mood. It was her first vacation in she didn't know how many years. And she'd last been to an onsen as a child with her grandparents and her sister.

Her jollity depressed me.

After the meal, we went to a bathhouse, and there, too, she acted differently than usual. She talked more, conversed animatedly with women she didn't know, told jokes, which was otherwise not her style, and the chattier and louder she became, the quieter I grew.

When we returned to our room, our futons were rolled out and prepared for sleeping. I was bone-tired, my mother wide awake. As a night worker, she couldn't possibly go to bed now, she said, then went and fetched something to drink from the konbini across the way. The hot bath had made her thirsty.

I put on a nightgown, brushed my teeth, and crawled beneath my blanket. When she returned, I'd nearly fallen asleep. I heard the sound of her opening a beer, some game show on television, and then I fell asleep.

The next morning, I wanted to take an early bath with her, just as we'd planned, but she was too tired. I got up, slid into my yukata, crept out of our room, and wandered the streets alone. I wasn't used to walking on the wooden sandals and found it difficult at first. I was surrounded by parents with their children, by young couples, and a striking number of mothers with their daughters or friends on their morning walk to one of the bathhouses. I entered one of the onsens and followed our rituals: soaping myself up thoroughly, rinsing myself off, slipping into the hot pool, and closing my eyes. I heard birds and the rush of a waterfall. I missed my mother. I missed her so much it hurt.

Looking around, I was, as far as I could tell, aside from two old women, the only unaccompanied bather.

128

My skin had turned red when I climbed out of the pool, my heart thumping. The water was hotter than at home in Nara, and I'd stayed in too long.

I dried myself off, put on the yukata, and wandered aimlessly through town.

I looked in at the ryokan, but my mother was still sleeping. She'd probably stayed up late and wouldn't wake up until noon. We'd have only the afternoon together, I thought—our two-day vacation had shrunk down to one afternoon. Tomorrow, she'd sleep in again, and after breakfast, we'd have to return to Nara.

Eventually, over the course of those hours, I lost my voice.

I didn't notice until I came back to our hotel and the innkeeper asked whether everything was okay with my mother. The nakai-san had tried in vain to wake her at eight and hadn't been able to serve breakfast. Now it was too late, he said reproachfully and without any sympathy.

I had no desire to answer him and went to our room.

My mother was lying half naked on her futon, staring at the ceiling and humming a French chanson that I knew from her sunakku.

She wanted to know where I'd been, and I remained silent. She asked if I'd already had breakfast, and I made no reply. I felt as if my tongue were paralyzed. I had the words in my head, I saw the sentences spread out before me, and yet I was unable to say them aloud. Maybe there were too many of them. Maybe they made no sense, or no sense I could understand. Something inside me refused to utter even a single word.

I'd been left speechless.

She asked what had happened, whether I was feeling unwell, why I wasn't talking to her. Eventually, she gave me a look I hadn't seen from her before and that I found quite unpleasant. I turned away.

We walked to a bathhouse in silence, dipped ourselves wordlessly into the pool, and afterward mutely ate a bite for lunch. She asked if I wanted to have dessert. Ice cream. A mochi. I only shook my head.

When I still hadn't said a word by afternoon, we traveled to the nearby sea because she believed a walk on the beach would take my mind off things and render me talkative again.

We walked up and down the beach without speaking. The Sea of Japan lay before us, silvery gray and languid; there was no surf capable of drowning out our silence. It was awful. I felt like a prisoner, and the longer I sat in my prison, the more I made myself at home in it.

I hated myself for my stubbornness, and that only made everything even worse.

At dinner, she switched on the TV. *The Rose of Versailles* was playing, an old anime series from her childhood. She watched the episode, ate in silence, and paid no attention to me. After her meal, she declared that she had no desire to spend the rest of her evening with a mute person and was going to a sunakku. I could keep watching television, read, or visit a bathhouse, she didn't care.

I wanted to write her a note and ask her not to go, but I had no slips of paper and nothing to write with, and even if I'd had both, I probably would've lacked the words.

I waited until she'd left and the nakai-san had cleared away the food and rolled out our futons. Then I tried to remove the mirror hanging over the sink. I wanted to set it beside my futon, but it was firmly screwed in place.

I crawled under the bedspread, and I felt like crying. But I had neither words nor tears in me.

The next morning, we took an earlier train back.

It took three days for me to say something again.

My mother acted as if it were the most normal thing in the world that a daughter would stop speaking to her mother from one moment to the next. She didn't ask me what had been going on with me, nor did I speak about it anymore. We never mentioned our trip to the Kinosaki Onsen again—as though it had never happened.

The memory of it still plagues me; I dream about it regularly, even more often since my mother's death than I did before. I always see myself going down a long, narrow lane, with my mother walking ten, maybe fifteen meters ahead of me. I try to call to her to please, please, wait for me, but I can't make a sound. I try to walk faster, which doesn't really work in the wooden sandals. I take them off and start running, but no matter how fast I run, the distance between us always remains the same. At some point, I wake up and am totally exhausted.

My behavior from back then is inscrutable to me today. I am deeply ashamed of it.

I'd intended to apologize to her multiple times, but found neither the proper occasion nor the right words.

. . .

After graduating from high school, I absolutely wanted to attend university in Tokyo. In our final year of school, we'd taken a class trip there. On the first day, I'd still been overwhelmed by its size and the masses of people on the streets and in the trains. By the second day, I liked it more, and as we were driving back to Nara, I knew that I wanted to live there—a place where nobody knew me. I hoped to find a place amid Tokyo's anonymity without exactly knowing what it should look like. It was more like an urgent feeling, a certainty that I had to get out of Nara, combined with the hope that the capital city would be the right place for me.

Kyoto was too small, Osaka and Kobe too close to Nara.

When I told my mother that I wanted to study accounting in Tokyo, she was briefly taken aback.

I explained to her that I wasn't bad in math and found working with numbers easy, that there was nothing else that interested me, and that I had no talents I wanted to pursue, that starting salaries for accountants were substantial, and I wouldn't have to worry about finding a job. All big companies were looking for employees for their accounting departments.

She listened, nodded, and said nothing in reply.

Within a day, she decided to give up her sunakku in Nara and come with me.

At first, I was surprised. I hadn't suspected that she felt just as alien and unwell in Nara as I did. Then I was glad not to have to move to Tokyo by myself.

Our relationship changed. I became an adult, and my mother treated me like one. We selected an apartment together, furnished it jointly, shared expenses for shopping and groceries. Alongside my studies, I worked part-time at a 24-hour supermarket; if I hadn't, there were times we wouldn't have been able to make rent.

In a sense, she became the big sister I never had.

What didn't change was the fact that there was a lot we didn't talk about. The very fact that I was in my mid-twenties and had no marriage plans, indeed not even a boyfriend, she didn't mention with a word, nor even hint at. She didn't pressure me to find one as my unmarried coworkers at the office told me their mothers did. I didn't have the feeling that my mother worried about me. If she did, she didn't let on to me.

And I also respected her silence. I didn't know if she felt lonely, if she had a boyfriend or lover, if her bar was doing well. I suspected so because she looked much happier and more satisfied there than she had in her sunakku in Nara.

When she was still alive, we'd often have lunch together on weekends. She wouldn't get home from her bar until two or three in the morning, and whenever that woke me up, I'd hear her rustling around in the kitchen and drinking something before she went to bed. She slept just as long as I did. We'd meet in the kitchen around midday, sitting around the table in our pajamas, eating toast with egg salad, or noodle soup. Occasionally, I'd venture to her place in the evening—the bar was only a few minutes' walk from our apartment. If she was alone, I'd sit at the counter and drink a glass of wine with her.

. . .

At the end of the week, my need to talk to someone was so great that I wrote Kento a message asking if we could see each other that evening. He kept me waiting a long time with his response; he agreed in the late afternoon.

When we met up in front of the konbini, it thundered. The weather app forecasted a heavy thunderstorm. We set out on a walk anyway. After just a few hundred meters, it began raining buckets. I wasn't carrying an umbrella. The water pelted me in the face, streaming down my cheeks and neck. A few seconds later, my T-shirt and bra, even my pants, were clinging to my body.

I fled to the covered patio of the Mustard Hotel, and Kento followed me. We cowered on one of the wooden benches protected from the rain and said nothing, and for a few minutes, I enjoyed our silence and the pattering of the water around us. Suddenly, a clap of thunder rang out so violently that I started in fright.

"Do thunderstorms scare you?"

"Not really," I replied. "But that was loud. You?"

He shook his head.

A bolt of lightning illuminated the dark night sky, and just after, it thundered again. This time, we both flinched.

"Thanks for making time on such short notice."

Kento nodded. "I'd like to apologize to you one more time."

"What for?"

"On our walk, I talked so much about myself. I'm sorry. I don't know what got into me."

"I enjoyed listening to you." I thought for a moment. "*Enjoyed* may not be the right word for what you told me, but you understand what I mean, don't you?"

"Yeah...but I should have asked you if you were interested or if it was too much for you." He paused in thought. "The way I was behaving, I could have been speaking to a tree or a wall, but not to a human being."

"It didn't make me uncomfortable. It really didn't."

Our silence continued.

"Are you cold?" I asked after a while.

He shook his head. "Are you?"

"No." The air was very warm and humid. In spite of my wet clothes, I wasn't freezing; they had more of a pleasant cooling effect.

"I had a rental father," I blurted out.

"Hm," was all he said.

"My mother paid a man to play my father for four hours every other Sunday each month," I explained, in case he wasn't familiar with the term or didn't understand what I meant.

"Hm," he repeated.

"For six years. And she never told me about it. My own mother. Can you believe that? His real name was Tetsuya. I always thought he was my father...We were at playgrounds together, having ice cream...at the movies...I mean...that was his job, like other people go to the office. He probably even had other children. Who does something like that? That's, that's...." I talked and talked because I was more and more afraid that Kento wouldn't say anything at this point, and I feared the subsequent silence.

He said nothing.

The rain pelted down onto the asphalt. It was like a gray curtain behind which only the contours of the buildings on the other side of the street were visible.

The longer we sat beside one another in silence, the more a vague sense of disappointment grew inside me. What exactly had I expected of Kento? What did I want to hear from him? A few encouraging words? An explanation for my mother's behavior? Advice about whether or not I should look for my fathers?

I didn't know, and was now wondering why it'd been so important to me to tell him about my rental father.

Another blinding flash of lightning, followed by a crash of thunder. The storm was directly above us.

"No, that I can't imagine," was all he said. The rain almost swallowed his words. "No, I can't."

"I wonder what my mother was even thinking the whole time."

"Oh well...," he replied, sighing and shaking his head slightly several times. And again: "Oh well..."

I was too much for him, I thought. Of course. Betrayed, hurt, disappointed, furious Akiko was too much for him. I was overwhelming him. How could I believe, after all he'd told me about himself, that there'd be room in him for my story? That the relationship between a daughter and her rental father might interest him?

I'd have liked most to get up and run home through the rain. Who, aside from me, was so stupid as to look for a friend in a hikikomori of all people?

I wasn't mad at him. How could I be?

Kento suddenly arose and walked over to the large entrance doors, which opened automatically. He hesitated briefly, entered the lobby, and then walked over to reception. Through the glass façade, I watched him speak with the night porter. They were making some sort of deal; first he shook his head, then he nodded several times. A short while later, Kento returned with a black umbrella.

"I promised I'd bring it back tomorrow." He opened the umbrella. "If you'd like, I'll walk you home."

We plodded through the pouring rain. The umbrella was too small for the both of us. He held it over me and walked, unshielded himself, beside me. As we went up the street, he pointed out a brown multistory building and said he lived there. I knew it well. There was a secondhand store on the ground floor where I'd frequently shopped and a yoga studio on the second floor I'd been to before multiple times.

Only a wall had separated us.

At home, I flipped through the "Hashimoto Haruhiko" binder again. Four envelopes were filled with train tickets, from Tokyo to Nara and back. He'd come from

Tokyo every two weeks by the *Shinkansen*. The train tickets alone must have cost my mother a small fortune. In the very back, I found a few short letters that my rental father had written my mother. In the first, he asked for reimbursement of the expenses from his previous visit; there were two cinema tickets in the envelope and two bus tickets (each reduced price). In another lay the receipt for a kids' puzzle—his present for my seventh birthday, his handwritten note indicated. I closed the binder. For the first time, I felt something akin to rage.

Nothing had been real, I thought. Nothing was from him.

Nothing had been for me. Not even his smile.

Everything neatly accounted for and paid.

I took the mirror, placed it on the sideboard behind my mother's urn, and gazed at myself in it. I saw a young girl in a school uniform, her arms much too long and her legs much too skinny and peeking out from beneath a blue skirt that didn't even cover her knees. She was standing in a big, empty room, almost a hall, and it looked as if she was waiting for something, or someone. She trembled. She shivered from cold. The sweater was several sizes too big—she was almost swimming in it—and it was stained and had a few small holes in the middle. She slung her arms around her body and held herself tightly.

I wanted to take her hand and stretched out my arm. She didn't move.

She was afraid.

I could no longer bear the sight of her, closed my eyes, and counted slowly to sixty. When I opened them again, an adult woman was standing before me. She was my age, as tall as me, wearing the same things, and her nose, her lips, her narrow face—all of them resembled mine, but I was still unsure if it was me. She was also standing in a big, empty room, but it no longer looked as though she were waiting. We looked at each other for a long time. I took one step toward her, and she did the same. The similarity in the face was even more obvious now. The mole on the cheek, the large eyes. But she had clenched her hands into fists.

I swept a few hairs out of my face. She did not.

I cocked my head to the side and attempted a smile. No smile came back.

I raised my eyebrows. She remained motionless before me, staring at me.

Her expression scared me. Her eyes were hard, her lips tensed into a thin line.

"Hello," I said.

She remained silent.

"Is that you, Akiko?"

She nodded.

"I didn't recognize you."

"I didn't recognize you either."

She shrugged.

That's not me, I thought. This is a stranger.

11

I RECALLED A SUNDAY EVENING IN NARA.

The glasses in the cabinet began to rattle, scarcely audibly at first, then more vigorously. Before our eyes, the half-empty bottle of yuzu juice danced across the table like a marionette on invisible strings. A vase slid off the sideboard and shattered across the floor into a thousand pieces. For a fraction of a second, my mother and I paused and looked at each other—I saw the panic in her eyes. She'd lived through the Great Hanshin quake; I'd been too small to remember it. Later, she told me that one of my ancestors must really have been looking out for me that morning. Our neighbors' dog had awoken her with its barking. She'd been surprised because he was old and sickly and never really barked anymore. Seconds later, the earth shook as violently as it ever had before in her life. The whole house shook; the mirror in

the hallway came crashing down off the wall, the teapot and cups slid off the counter in the kitchen, glasses
toppled from the shelves, the bookshelf tipped over. It
fell onto my futon and would have crushed me to death
if my mother hadn't taken me into hers for a change before falling asleep; I'd been tormented by a throat infec-
tion, and my sleep was so restless that she'd wanted to
lie beside me and comfort me during the night.

In Kobe, her best friend from school had died beneath the wreckage of their home with her husband and
two children. Ever since, my mother had been afraid of
earthquakes, of any type of shaking. Even when a heavy
truck rumbled by our building, she would startle.

Come quickly, she called, leaping to her feet. We hurried to the door and ran down the stairs into the street.

We were the only ones there. Everything was quiet.
We heard neither anxious voices from neighboring
buildings nor the sirens of fire trucks or ambulances—
as if we'd only imagined the temblor. It was over as
quickly as it had come and, at least in our neighborhood, seems not to have caused any damage. My mother
was out of breath and grinned with some embarrassment. I took her hand and could feel how worked up she
was. I knew that she was afraid of aftershocks and suggested going on a little walk. Hand in hand, we slowly
walked up the street toward the forest. It was a warm,
dark Sunday evening in late summer, a sky full of stars
gleaming above us. At the end of the street, she paused,
looked up, and gazed into the night sky for a long while.
I followed her example. I had the feeling I saw a shoot-
ing star and made a wish.

Supposedly, she said softly, *there are more planets in space than there are grains of sand on earth. Did you know that?*

Yes, I answered.

Can you imagine?

No, I can't.

I can't either, she said, her gaze still directed upward. *Sometimes I wonder*, she said, *whether a being is sitting on one of those stars, controlling things here on Earth such that nothing happens by accident, that everything hangs together and makes sense. Even earthquakes.*

You mean a god?

We exchanged glances. *No*, she said, smiling, *not a god. More like a sort of administrator. As if we were part of a video game being directed from up there.*

We continued standing there for a while without saying anything and then made our way back. The earth did not quake again that evening or that night, but I still couldn't sleep well.

I couldn't get my mother's words out of my head. Maybe she was right, I thought. Maybe we were really only part of a simulation here. That would explain a lot of things I didn't understand, not just earthquakes and their victims. I was playing a role in a game that some being had thought up somewhere, at some point. My role was that of the outsider, for which the designers had given me slightly wavy hair with a brownish tinge, and made me more than a head taller that the other girls in my class, and made my parents get a divorce, and me have to grow up with a single mother who also ran a su-nakku, so that the other girls had a reason to shove me

142

around in the schoolyard or on the way home, or hide my school notebooks, my bento box, my rain jacket, my sports gear, and laugh when I couldn't find them, cut a hole in my sweater, smear dog poop in my school bag. Somebody had to be the victim. It didn't have anything to do with me, Akiko Nakamura; it wasn't my failure. It wasn't my fault. I hadn't done anything wrong. It was my role.

Shikata ga nai.

Suddenly that became more than just a saying. It was the answer to the riddle of my life. "There's nothing you can do. It can't be changed." As a character in the game, I had no influence on my fate. It was governed and controlled by another force unknown to me that had its own plans for me. It would be extremely dumb to want to rebel against it.

I was wide awake at the thought. It gave me courage. On the one hand, it wasn't a failure of mine that nothing would change, and on the other, there existed a game of variation. To torment the same victim all the time in a simulation was unimaginative and boring. After a period of suffering, a phase of quiet or of protest had to ensue. Perpetrators needed new victims or themselves became them.

It was not a question of justice, but of the logic behind every game.

What role was planned for me next? I wondered that night.

Or was I deluding myself? Didn't perpetual losers also exist in games, those for whom there was no hope, who suffered until they were removed from the game and replaced by new victims? It would've been easy to exterminate me. A bus driver who overlooks me. A leak in our neighbor's gas line. Sudden cardiac arrest, inexplicable to doctors.

One way or another, others would relieve me. It was only a matter of time.

From the streetlight outside the building, a sallow light was cast into our room. I sat up and looked at my mother sleeping. She was lying on her back, her mouth half open, breathing quietly, looking gorgeous. I was overcome by a great longing. I'd have loved to snuggle up to her like a little child, but I didn't want to wake her. Instead, I leaned over and gave her a kiss on the forehead. She briefly shook her head as if wanting to shoo away a bothersome fly in her sleep and turned onto her side.

The notion of being part of a simulation helped me through the last two years of my junior high school. I took the insults, hostilities, and bullying less personally. They weren't directed at me, nor could I do anything to stop them.

Shikata ga nai.

I often had the feeling I myself was a spectator in the game. I felt nothing when I searched the entire changing room for my things amid the others' laughter and found them in the trash can. I blamed no one, I reproached no one, and I did not report any of this harassment to my teachers. What would've been the point? My fellow classmates were also only playing their roles. They were the perpetrators. Or the followers. Or the indifferent ones. There were some of every type there, just as there should be in a good game.

Shikata ga nai.

Sometimes, I succeeded in viewing it all from above, as though impassively watching a film that didn't concern me. Then I'd slip out of my body like a spirit and float up to the classroom ceiling or over people's heads in the schoolyard. I saw Akiko suffering and felt nothing.

I only wondered at who'd thought out these perfidious tricks, which of the stars that being might be sitting on, whether it felt joy at having people torment one another. And if so, why?

In high school, at some point, the idea seemed to me too absurd. Maybe I also no longer needed it because my new classmates left me alone, making it lose its luster—though even today I occasionally think it might, though very improbable, still be the simplest explanation for a lot that remains a mystery to me. People are neither good nor bad. They do not lie and cheat purposefully. They do not torment anyone intentionally. They do not kill and murder of their own free will. They do not spontaneously start wars.

They are only part of a simulation and are carrying out the will of others.

They are playing their roles.

They have no choice.

Shikata ga nai.

I thought about that now. Maybe that was the answer. Someone had come up with the idea of adding a rental father to my role. It was nothing I had chosen for myself. But what in life do we actually choose for ourselves? No one had asked me if I wanted to enter this world at all. Two other people had decided that for me. One of them was dead, and the other wasn't interested in the result of his decision.

In games, there is a pause button, and I wished someone would press it now—and then the one to rewind. Wait, stop, only back to the point just before my mother fell ill. Or a bit further still? Back to my last meeting as a twelve-year-old with Haruhiko? But since I wouldn't know what I knew today, I'd be stuck in my role. I wouldn't do anything differently. So maybe just the restart button? Did I want an entirely different life?

No.

Who knows what role would be reserved for me in a new version of this game?

Things were as they were.

Shikata ga nai.

12

NAOKO WAS LESS SURPRISED BY MY RENTAL FATHER than I had expected. We were sitting in a bar in a tiny alley in Shibuya. She was listening to my story in silence, nodding from time to time or sipping her beer.

"And so," she asked when I had finished, "are you furious with your mother?"

I shrugged. Even if I were, it'd be hard for me to admit it. "I don't understand how she could come up with the idea of renting a father for me."

"It's very simple: she didn't want you to grow up without a father. She wanted you to be okay."

"With a rental father? You can't be serious."

"There wasn't anybody else, and she probably felt guilty about that."

"Why should she have?"

"Because all single mothers feel guilty, whether they admit it or not."

The certainty with which she said it annoyed me as much as the fact that she immediately sympathized with my mother. "Where do you of all people get off knowing that?"

"It's obvious. They want a family, so they get married and have a child or even several. Then the marriage fails, for whatever reason. The husband moves out, they stay behind with the kids, and deep inside they believe themselves to be responsible. Women always look for guilt in themselves first whenever something goes wrong in their family. It's in our DNA. It's. Always. Our. Fault."

I shook my head.

"You don't believe that? My grandpa left my grandma twenty years ago because he had another woman, whom he also walked out on a few years later. To this day my grandma believes it was her fault he left. If she'd been a better housewife, if she'd have treated him better and not disagreed with him so much and criticized him, he'd have stayed. 'Men don't like being criticized,' she would always tell me.

"Whenever my father used to be in a bad mood or angry, my mother always thought she had done something wrong. And whenever my sister's husband doesn't play with the kids, doesn't talk to her, won't sleep with her, or comes home drunk, she's firmly convinced it's because of her. Yet it's only because he's a complete idiot. Just like my grandfather was."

I shook my head again. "My mother could have told me afterward," I objected.

"She did, though. Do you really believe she neatly filed away those documents and kept them for years by accident, then sorted them, packed them in a box, and just forgot to throw them away? You don't really, do you?"

"Hm. I had already thought of that. That was really not her style."

"What do you mean 'not her style'?"

"Letting me know like that instead of telling me. I always felt her to be a brave woman."

"Then she definitely was too. Just because courage fails us once doesn't mean we're cowardly."

"Why didn't she say something to me sooner?"

"I suspect because it made her uncomfortable. Because she was afraid to admit it. Because, because, because...she'll have had her reasons. Why are they so important?"

"Because I'd like to understand."

"The reasons or your mother?"

"Both."

"How come it isn't enough for you in this instance to accept them both? I've long since given up wanting to understand my parents. They are how they are, and who knows why they're that way. Ultimately, the 'why?' isn't that important anyway."

"You think?"

She nodded.

Pensive, I played with my paper napkin. Naoko refilled our beer glasses and ordered two new bottles.

"Do you want to see them again?"

"Who?"

"Your fathers."

"Should I?"

She groaned aloud. "That's up to you."

I nodded. It was, but I didn't know. "Maybe, yeah," I said elusively.

Naoko took a big gulp of her beer. "If I were you, I'd very much want to know from this Hashimoto-san, or whatever his name was, what he was thinking the whole time he was pretending to be your father for six years. How many other 'kids' he had. I'd like to know why he never got in touch with you again. Whether he wondered for a second how you might be doing. Whether you meant something to him, or whether it was just a job, and if it was, what a strange line of work that is."

I nodded once more.

"And as for your real father, I'd want to know what kind of guy he is. He must've had something going for him or else your mother wouldn't have gotten involved with him, right? And fifty percent of your DNA comes from him."

I nodded again and envied Naoko her ability to express complicated matters so simply.

Yes, I thought, I wanted to see this rented Haruhiko again. I wanted to ask him these questions and likely several more.

About my real father, I wasn't so sure. I didn't like the label anyhow. What was a real father anyway? I could picture what a good father, what a bad father looked like. I could picture what understanding, absent, disinterested, or unkind looked like, but not real or pretend, genuine or fake.

Did I want to get to know the man who had fathered me and was indifferent to me afterward? My wits said a loud a clear "No." He was a stranger who did not hold my interest. At the same time, I heard someone inside me whisper the opposite. Thanks to my birth registration, I knew his name. With the help of our family register, I should be able to find out whether he was still alive and where he lived.

It would not reveal to me why he had no interest in his daughter.

13

THE OFFICES OF SMILE FAMILY WERE LOCATED ON THE ground floor of a nondescript office building in an equally nondescript side street in Harajuku. Through the windows, I saw two women working intently at computers; a coat stand stood against the wall with women's suits hanging from it. A third woman was on the phone. When she noticed my curious face behind the pane, she gave me an annoyed look. I quickly continued on. She didn't look as though she'd willingly give me information about my rental father. As a precaution, I was carrying a few old invoices with my mother's customer number. Even if seventeen years had passed since then, it shouldn't be much of an issue to find our account. I wanted to ask for the telephone number or e-mail address for "Hashimoto Haruhiko," and if she wouldn't give me his data for privacy reasons, which I'd understand, I'd leave my contact information and ask for a message from him. In my mind, it had sounded simple, a matter of a few minutes, but now I'd been pacing up and down the street for half an hour. It was oppressively hot and humid, even for a summer's day in Tokyo. I was sweating and pondered whether I ought to try this another day, accompanied by Naoko. I crossed the street and looked through the window again. A man was now standing behind the two women at the computers, looking over their shoulders. My heart recognized him right away. It pounded—I felt every beat. His distinctive head, his face with the robust nose, even the way he was standing there with his arms crossed were familiar to me. I turned away, walked to the other side of the street, and waited. After a few minutes, the front door opened, and "Haruhiko" stepped out.

He walked down the street. Without hesitation, I followed him at a few meters' distance. He went to Harajuku Station and took the Yamanote Line toward Shinjuku. I boarded the same car one door farther on. The train wasn't full. He sat down, removed his cellphone from his pocket, and began reading on it. The longer I watched him, the more certain I was that it was "Haruhiko." He was stouter than in my memory and had grown a touch of a little belly. He was wearing black trainers, lightweight black trousers, and a white T-shirt, and I had to admit that he looked pretty good. He got off at the next stop, rode the escalator up, bought a bar of chocolate and a manga in a Lawson, put the receipt in his wallet, walked to the Chūō Line, and rode to Kōenji.

I didn't let him out of my sight.

He took up position outside the train station exit and waited. After a few minutes, a young girl came toward him at a brisk pace. She was perhaps twelve or thirteen years old, somewhat stout, had a round, full face, long hair braided into a ponytail, and was wearing a school uniform. She was already smiling from afar, quite obviously very glad to see him. He smiled back, a warm, friendly smile. Even if it had been years since it was meant for me—I remembered it well.

The two hugged.

He gave her the bar of chocolate and the manga book. She beamed and thanked him.

From one second to the next, I felt sick. A dull, oppressive pain in my stomach. I turned away and was about to leave. Go. Just leave. A force from I know not where held me back. Unable to move, I remained rooted in place and closed my eyes. When I opened them again, I saw the two of them standing at the traffic light and then crossing the street.

I followed them.

They were not in a hurry. They strolled leisurely down the street, stopping outside a display window with stationery and school backpacks. She pointed at something, and he nodded.

A few blocks farther on, they entered a café. She wanted to sit in the window. A waitress pointed them to a table in the rear part of the room. I asked for a place at the counter, where I could monitor them well.

They ordered something, and presently a waitress brought a matcha latte over ice cream for him.

His tastes hadn't changed.

The girl got a soda and a slice of cheesecake.

They conversed. Most of the time, the girl talked. She was vivacious, occasionally bobbing up and down. He listened patiently. She giggled mischievously, and he laughed with her. He got a piece of her cake. At one point, he took her hand briefly and squeezed it.

Father and daughter. They were intimate with one another.

A raging fury rose up inside me. I didn't know this feeling, and it was so intense it scared me. I wanted to go up to him and throw his iced matcha latte into his face.

I wanted to take a swing at him.

I wanted to scream at him: You bastard, why did you do that to me? Why did you never get in touch again? Did you ever once ask yourself how I was doing?

The girl looked over to me, our eyes met, and I wanted to get up and go over to her table and introduce myself to her. Sorry to bother you, I wanted to say, I'm your sister. But it's not like you think. Nothing is as you think it is. This man is a thief. He robs children of their innocence. He robs them of their trust. Your mother is paying for him to spend time with you. Every minute. He'll be reimbursed for everything, even the bar of chocolate and the manga. Every scoop of ice cream. Every piece of cheesecake.

And one day, when your mother doesn't have any money anymore or thinks you don't need a father, he will vanish from your life.

Just like that.

From one day to the next.

You'll ask your mother where he's gone, and she won't answer you.

You'll wait for letters or a message from him and not receive any.

You'll cry, and it won't help.

He'll leave behind scars you know nothing about yet.

Have you been to the movies together yet? I wanted to ask her. Did he hold your hand when you were frightened?

I didn't know what was holding me back. Maybe the thought that she might be his real daughter. Why shouldn't a rental father have his own children? No, it was the weird feeling that sitting there, a few tables away, was really something like a little sister of mine. A little sister who needed my protection. We had the same father, even if he was only a rental. She was part of my family I didn't have. We weren't blood relatives. We were related in pain and in sadness, even if she had no clue whatsoever about that yet. She would learn of it soon enough. I didn't want to be the one to acquaint her with that.

How many little and big sisters and brothers did I have? Twenty? Thirty? Presumably dozens.

This sort of relation, I thought, is something special. We were bound together not by genes, but by the same experience of trust and his abuse.

Of loss.

Of emptiness.

Why shouldn't these bonds be just as strong as genetic ones, which were in fact nothing but coincidence?

The matcha and the soda were long finished, the cheese-cake eaten, when he looked at his watch and quickly asked for the check. They had forgotten the time and were in a hurry. That had never happened to him with me. At least, I didn't remember it happening.

They walked through the streets at a rapid clip. They said their goodbyes outside the subway station with a long hug. The girl turned around twice more and waved before stepping onto the escalator and slowly disappearing with it into the depths.

"Haruhiko" waved back, gazing after her. Then he left in the opposite direction.

I followed him.

His path led through a bustling shopping street. It was early evening, the businesses still full of people. We walked past a butcher, a bakery, several hair salons, a store with used household appliances, small restaurants, and bars. He strolled more than he walked and was easy to recognize because he towered a head taller over most passersby. He was in no hurry, looking into the display window of a bookstore, buying something in a drug-store. I didn't let him out of my sight. Several times I charged into people in passing and apologized. At one point, he stopped and looked around lost in thought. Eventually, he turned down a side street and disappeared a few buildings on into an izakaya. I wanted to go after him but couldn't bring myself to do it. Maybe he was meeting someone, now sitting at a table with a woman, and the opportunity wouldn't arise to talk to him. And even if it did: would I muster the courage to ask him all the questions I'd been carrying around for days? My body trembled with agitation. I paced the street and a few minutes later, my heart pounding, entered the bar.

It consisted of just one room with a U-shaped counter in the middle, a grill behind that, and three little tables that were all occupied. The only empty seat was at the corner of the bar at a right angle to my rental father. I stood in the doorway, irresolute. The barkeeper welcomed me with a friendly nod and gestured to the open seat.

After a brief hesitation, I sat down.

"Haruhiko" nodded at me casually, and I greeted him in return. He had a beer and a bowl of edamame in front of him he ate calmly one after the other, while watching the barkeeper at work. A younger couple was seated next to him, occupied with themselves and immersed in conversation.

I ordered a beer and acted as if I were looking around. It was an old joint with dark walls, the ceiling covered in soot from the grill's smoke. The weekly specials were listed on a couple slips of paper. The paper was wavy and yellowed. It must have been a long time since the weekly menu had been changed. An impressive selection of large sake bottles were stored in a refrigerator, next to which were stacked several crates of beer. The barkeeper took care of the guests by himself. I guessed him to be around the age of my rental father; he already had graying hair and a gray goatee. He brought me the beer and a warm, damp cloth so I could daub the sweat from my forehead.

"You have to try the tamagoyaki," said "Haruhiko," suddenly directed at me. "It's the house specialty."

His voice. A shiver ran down my spine; my hands began to tremble. I could have picked it out from among thousands. It sounded as it did then: engaging and approachable. A voice you wanted to trust, by which you could feel safe and secure.

Hello, Akiko, I'm happy to see you. Are you doing well? What are you in the mood for today? What would you like to do? Take good care of yourself. We'll see each other in two weeks...

"It's an old family recipe. Isn't it, Yagumo-san?" The barkeeper nodded, visibly flattered, and waved him off modestly.

"Believe me: you'll find no better in Tokyo."

I offered casual thanks for the recommendation and regretted not having ordered any shōchū. Something with a high alcohol content would have taken away some of my fear and agitation. Or at least I wouldn't have felt them as strongly.

"Is this your first time here?" "Haruhiko" turned to me.

You liar, I wanted to respond. You miserable fraud.

You bastard. How had you been able to lie to my face like that? But I could hardly get out a sound and only replied with a quiet yes, more aspirated than spoken.

159

"Good choice." He smiled at me, and for the first time, our eyes met. He had developed little wrinkles around his eyes. They looked sadder than I remember, and he still had that friendly smile that I knew all too well.

It made the rage inside me all the worse. Whatever you say, I thought, whatever you do, I won't believe a word.

"You're sitting in the oldest izakaya in this part of Tokyo. Yagumo-san's grandfather opened it before the war. It's a miracle the building survived the bombings nearly unscathed."

Again the barkeeper nodded, placing "Haruhiko's" omelet on the counter and asking what I wanted to eat. I ordered agedashi tofu and a few skewers.

For a while we sat in silence beside one another. I tried to concoct the lines word for word that I wanted to say to him, but the words got all mixed up on me. I couldn't manage to formulate a coherent sentence in my thoughts. Everything inside me began to blur. Images. Memories. Sentences. Kanji.

"Haruhiko" raised his glass and toasted me.

I wanted to say something. "Do you come here often?" was all that occurred to me.

"It's my second home. Whenever friends want to see me, they just come here. Except on Tuesdays. Then his sister is here, and neither the omelet tastes good, nor..."

"Don't believe a word he says," the barkeeper interrupted him, laughing. "He and my sister are best friends. She just wants nothing from him." He laid my skewers onto the grill and sprinkled seasoning overtop. It smelled good.

"Are you from Tokyo?" "Haruhiko" asked me.

"No, from Nara."

"From Nara," he repeated slowly, and then fell silent for a moment, pensive. "A beautiful city."

I nodded. "You've been there before?"

"A lot. In the past, quite a lot." He turned toward me and looked at me inquisitively. I evaded his gaze. The barkeeper set a plate with a small serving of tuna tartare before me to try and wished me bon appétit. I stared at the plate, not knowing what to say. "Haruhiko" wanted to know what had brought me to Tokyo.

"University," I replied.

"Do you work here in the area?" He did not seem as though he noticed any of my tension.

I shook my head. "In Akasaka."

"Let me guess. You work in television?"

"Wrong."

"For a lawyer…"

"Wrong again," I cut him off. "I work in the accounting department of a large company."

"You like numbers?" "Haruhiko" sounded quite shocked.

"Why does that surprise you?"

"I…hmmm…," he replied, embarrassed. "I mean, at first blush I wouldn't have pegged you as a numbers person."

"I'm not."

"Oh. In that case, it's an interesting choice of careers."

I shrugged. "It just turned out that way."

"Do you enjoy going to the office?"

"Hm. The work isn't particularly complicated. My colleagues are nice, so is my boss. So I don't have to hold my nose, really. What about you?" My counter-question was supposed to have sounded casual, but my voice had quavered.

He inspected me, ruminating. I could no longer bear to look him in the eyes and lowered my gaze.

"On some days I do, on others less so."

"What does that depend on?"

"On a lot of factors," he answered vaguely.

I waited in vain for further explanation. Instead, he snapped an edamame and shoved two beans into his mouth.

"What do you do, if I may ask?"

He took a large gulp of his beer, regarded the glass in his hand, as if the answer to my question lay within it, and remained silent for a while. When I was no longer expecting an answer, he said: "People can rent me." "Haruhiko" looked at my face and added: "Not as what you might be thinking right now. I'm too old for that."

I acted as if I didn't understand what he was talking about.

"Many years ago, I founded an agency where you can rent people who act as acquaintances, work colleagues, friends, or relatives for certain occasions. For funerals, for example. Or birthdays."

"I'm sorry, but I don't understand. Who gets the idea to rent relatives for a funeral?"

"In most instances, we go to funerals as friends or colleagues of the dead person because families don't want other mourners to learn how lonely the deceased were. They don't want to burden them with such negative thoughts, if you know what I mean. It's similar for birthdays.

"Personally, I mainly play roles having to do with families. Tomorrow, for example, I'm invited to a wedding. A single woman has rented me as her companion for three hours. She's in her mid-thirties and would prefer to stop being asked why she doesn't have a boyfriend, when she's getting married, and whether she doesn't want kids. It's very unpleasant for her that people worry so often on her account. She has the feeling she's becoming a burden for her family and friends. I'm playing the part of her new partner. I'll smile amiably, make small talk, and no one will worry about her anymore, and she'll feel under less pressure, if you know what I mean. A few days ago, I played this role at a funeral. Same story, different woman."

"And that's not obvious? I mean…don't people get suspicious?"

"Why should they? Nobody is interested in me or my story or the truth. We talk about the weather, about baseball or soccer, the food—the sorts of things you talk about when you don't want to say anything. People rarely listen and even more rarely ask serious questions."

"Haruhiko" ate a piece of his omelet. He seemed a bit more tense than he'd been a few minutes earlier.

I tried to imagine him as a rental guest at a wedding or a funeral. I couldn't. In my imagination, he was a (rental) father; no other part was intended for him.

"So really, you work as an actor, or am I wrong?"

"That's not how I'd put it."

"Why not?"

"An actor speaks lines he's learned by heart and that someone else has written. He's got a script or a play and always knows how the story ends. He's got a director at his side telling him what to do. I don't. I never know how the story ends. There's no one telling me what to do."

I nodded although I wasn't sure I understood exactly what he meant.

"Recently, I had to step in as a husband. A woman's brother wanted to get married and had invited his future in-laws to meet his parents and his older sister. The sister was divorced, and that was so awkward for the bride that I was rented to act for the evening as if I were the husband of her sister-in-law. That was very stressful."

"How come?"

"I'd invented a biography for myself and introduced myself as a doctor. No one told me that the father-in-law was a cardiologist. We were sitting at the table catty-corner from one another, and the whole evening he was trying to have a conversation with me about the pros and cons of a new cardiac catheterization. Do you know anything about heart catheters?"

"No."

"Me neither." He grinned.

I tried to reciprocate his smile. "You must be a good improviser."

"Hm."

I instinctively held my breath before asking the next question. "Do you also take on the role of fathers?"

His eyes narrowed as though he were scrutinizing something in the distance. The barkeeper had overheard my question and cast a glance at "Haruhiko" I couldn't construe.

"Haruhiko" took a deep breath. "Yes." He emptied his beer and ordered a second and one for me as well.

"For a long time now?"

"For almost twenty-five years. I was one of the first. If you look on the Internet today, the selection is bigger."

I had to have been one of his first children. I was about to take a piece of my tofu, but my hands lacked the strength, and I put the chopsticks back down.

"How does someone get the idea to become a rental father?" I said in a low voice.

"I know it sounds odd to most people. For the mothers, it's a big relief." He paused briefly before continuing. "I began when an unmarried friend had a child. When she wanted to register her for kindergarten, they wouldn't even give her an appointment for an interview as a single mother. In her distress, she asked me to play the father. We looked at kindergartens as a couple, and her daughter got a spot without a problem. A little after that, a friend of that friend, a divorced mother, asked me if I'd accompany her to a parents evening at her son's elementary school. The teacher and the other parents weren't to learn that she was living apart from her husband. That'd have cast the family in a negative light. She didn't want her child to be bullied for it. That also worked out well. Shortly afterward, then, I founded an agency: Smile Family. From us, you can rent whatever you need. Grandfathers. Small children, even babies. Work colleagues."

He drank from his beer, pursed his lips briefly, and turned toward me. There was a trace of melancholy in his eyes. "At first, I didn't how I was supposed to behave as a father, what was expected of me. I read books, copied things from movies, and watched families at playgrounds. Since then, I've had over three hundred children. At the moment, it's thirty-three. Twenty girls and thirteen boys. I've known most of them for many years."

THREE HUNDRED.

I was one of them.

I excused myself and stood up, intending to go to the restroom. I almost fell over. My knees were trembling; I briefly held on to my barstool. I was dizzy, my breathing heavy. Did I need to know all this? A part of me wanted to leave, not hear another word about rental uncles and aunts, fathers and grandfathers. The other part wanted to know everything: every detail, every story about every child, about every mother.

Every present he had given someone else.

One of three hundred.

I didn't even feel rage anymore now. This number was too gigantic. At least he never called me Mariko or Ayumi, I thought. Instead, on my eleventh birthday, he'd written the wrong date on the birthday card and couldn't locate me in a class photo. At our first field day together, he'd mixed me up with a classmate until my mother made him aware of the mistake. I'd been surprised but thought nothing of it. We didn't see each other often after all. In a peculiar way, the knowledge that I wasn't alone had something comforting about it. At the same time, it made the whole thing even more egregious.

When I returned from the restroom, we sat in silence for a long time. "Haruhiko" told the barkeeper a story. I didn't listen.

"How can someone be father to more than three hundred children?"

"Not at the same time. Spread out over the years," he explained, as though I'd misunderstood something—as if it would make the matter more understandable.

"Don't you ever get anything confused?"

He smiled bashfully. "I do my best. Every child has their own file where I note down after our visits what we did and what we talked about, whether they were sick or got an award at school. Before our next meeting, I review it."

I saw him filling out my index card:

Akiko, Nara, June 2001.

Doesn't like strawberry ice cream. Sprained foot (gym class, gymnastics).

Wants a pet (cat, color and type don't matter).

Loves jigsaw puzzles, especially ones with animals on them.

How could you?

"And they all think you're their father," I said softly. It was a realization, not a question.

"Haruhiko" nodded anyway.

"Don't they ever get suspicious?"

"What child ever thinks their father could be rented?"

The barkeeper set the skewers on the counter before me. I didn't touch them. I felt sick again, even more than before at the café. I was afraid I might have to vomit and thought of little Akiko.

I'd have liked to give her a hug now.

"Haruhiko" ate the rest of his omelet and glanced over at me now and again without smiling.

I wanted to ask why the mothers deceived their children like that, whether they knew the harm they were causing, and couldn't get out a sound.

"You're not eating at all." He looked at me, worried. "What's wrong with your hands?"

Without noticing, I'd balled my hands into fists so tight the knuckles had turned white.

"Are you unwell?"

"No, no, I'll be fine. I'm not very hungry."

"If you're not feeling well, you should drink a shōchū. Yagumo-san, bring us two shōchū please."

The barkeeper set glasses on the counter in front of us and gave us generous pours.

"Haruhiko" raised his, wanting to clink glasses. I hesitated. He was holding out his glass toward me.

The warmth of the alcohol spread through my throat and stomach. It went straight to my head and calmed me down a bit.

"Haruhiko" exchanged a few words with the barkeeper about the food and ordered several *kushiyaki*. "You're starting to look better," he said and ordered a second round of shōchū.

"You know, a lot of single mothers feel overwhelmed. Or they're ashamed. The end of a marriage is always a kind of failure too, and they feel responsible for it. They believe their children need a father, and when contact with their biological father has been severed, which happens frequently, I'm the substitute. An offer. A kind of service provider. You know what I mean?"

He was waiting for my answer. I nodded weakly.

"There's a demand for this service, and I fulfill that. Now, whether this need is good or bad is another question. But we can't deny it. It's there. That's not something I can change. I try to help."

I was only half listening. In my thoughts, I was with me and my siblings and the guilelessness that connected us. "Does no one tell the children the truth?"

"That's the mothers' decision. I do what they want. They're my employers. In many cases, they prefer me to say I've got a new family and am moving to America or Singapore. Then I write the children a few more times, and the contact trails off. These children don't learn until they're adults, or even never, that I was a sort of rental father. Maybe that's the best solution. But almost no mother wants to live with this lie forever. We tell her children at some point. In most cases when they are sixteen or seventeen."

He fell silent for a moment and took a deep breath before continuing.

"You can imagine that those aren't easy conversations. A lot of kids want nothing to do with me afterward. I can understand that. I'd probably feel the same way. Some get in touch again later. I still see a few today as an adult. They now pay me themselves—and insist on calling me Papa." He paused again briefly and reflected. "It's difficult to untangle yourself from a lot of these affairs. Whenever our wishes and desires coincide with the lies we hear, then deception suddenly becomes truth, if you know what I mean."

"Haruhiko" looked at me. His voice had changed. It had grown quieter and more hesitant. No less engaging, but more querying, it sounded almost a touch fragile. It was no longer the one I had in my memory.

"How do you do it?" I asked cautiously.

"How do I do what?"

"Play father to the children for years at a time."

"Hm...well. Sometimes, I doubt whether I'm doing the right thing. But then I think these children at least had a father who visited them regularly and that I was there for them whenever we saw each other, even if I was only rented. Still better than nothing, right?"

"And then from one day to the next, you have to leave them."

He furrowed his brow. "It's not as easy as you might imagine. Every child matters to me. But I knew beforehand that the day would come. It's my job."

"Your job?"

He nodded.

"Is it that simple?"

He said nothing.

"Isn't it ever hard for you to say goodbye?"

For the first time, he owed me an answer.

"You said you're not an actor."

He swayed his head from side to side and continued saying nothing.

I waited.

"Do you have children of your own?"

"No. Then I presumably wouldn't be able to do this work."

"Did you not want any?"

"I'm not married. It just never worked out."

"Haruhiko's" eyes grew smaller, the crow's feet around them larger and deeper, and his shoulders drooped. He sat hunched before me; the weary sight of him disconcerted me. I excused myself once more and went to the bathroom. In the mirror, I saw that my neck was covered in red spots. I thought of Kento and wished he were here with me now. He wouldn't have to say anything, just sit next to me. As if paralyzed, I remained sitting on the toilet for a few minutes until startling up upon hearing another guest waiting outside the door. I apologized multiple times and returned to the counter. The place beside me was empty.

"Taniguchi-san asks for your pardon. He received a call and had to leave unexpectedly," the barkeeper said. Embarrassed, he slid a piece of paper toward me. "I am to give you this."

I held the paper in my hands and didn't know what to do. For a moment, I wanted to grab my things and run after him. In the end, I unfolded the note. He still had the same beautiful handwriting.

I thank you for not saying anything to little Kanahi at the café. She has a difficult enough time of it.

Unfortunately, after so many years, I do not
remember your name, but I do remember you. You
and your enchanting mother from Nara. Even if you
find it hard to believe me, I would like to tell you that I
enjoyed every hour with the little girl you once were.

Everything was paid—nothing was faked.
Try to forgive your mother. She wanted only the best
for you. We do not always achieve our aims.
> *You know where to find me.*
> *I wish you all the best.*
> *Taniguchi Tetsuya*

Even his name had been fake. "Coward" flashed through my mind. You recognized me and said nothing. You could have apologized—or at least explained yourself. You've abandoned me a second time.

For a long while, I held the note in my hand and stared at its lines. I wanted to get up, but I lacked the strength. I was stunned. I no longer even felt much of my rage; it had yielded to a profound sadness and endless exhaustion.

Too much. It was all too much.

Mostly, I was too much for myself. Me and my history—when and where it began I did not know.

The barkeeper could see I wasn't doing well and offered me a shōchū on the house. I was already tipsy enough, mumbled "no thanks," and asked to pay. My bill, he replied, had been settled by Taniguchi.

Numb, I crept back through the shopping street to the train. I discovered red spots on my upper and lower arms, and my skin burned as though I'd lain in the blazing sun all day. My limbs ached. Every step hurt.

I didn't understand where my profound rage at my alleged father had gone, why I hadn't screamed at him, how it could have dissipated so quickly. Instead of denouncing him, I'd inquired how he'd felt when he had to say goodbye to a child. I'd shown empathy with him instead of with me.

Did I like him more than I wanted to admit to myself?

Or was it little Akiko coming forward and not allowing me to rage against her (rental) father? He was the only one she knew.

Little Akiko, for whom rage had always been creepy—her own and that of others.

I wanted to protect her.

I'd have liked to take her by the hand and start racing, past the amazed pedestrians, all the way to Kōenji Station. There, I'd have run up the stairs with her and boarded the next train and ridden off. Far away.

Just little Akiko and her older self.

All the way to France.

To Paris.

To the Rue du Faubourg Saint-Antoine.

We'd visit our mother there and at daybreak, after all the guests had left, sweep the bistro with her while humming "Non, je ne regrette rien."

Or while singing it—singing loudly.

I saw ten-year-old Akiko standing an arm's length before me, with her pigtails and long skinny legs.

She watched me, and whenever I took a step toward her, she retreated back one. The sight of her was so familiar to me I wanted to scoop her up in my arms and hug her, feel her child body pressed to mine.

I reached out my hand, but she didn't want to be touched by me. She didn't want to ride away—not with me. She wanted neither my protection nor my comfort.

She circled around and turned her back toward me.

Akiko, why are you turning away?

She didn't answer.

We were more estranged than I thought, she and I. Why?

14

THE DAY AT THE OFFICE HAD BEEN LONG. IT WAS JUST after nine when Naoko and I were packing up our things. She asked me if we were still going out for drinks together; I looked as if sake would do me some good. I declined, with thanks.

I wanted to be by myself.

Although I was dead tired, I didn't want to go home. The idea of sitting in front of my mother's urn was distasteful to me. There were too many questions she couldn't give me answers to. I also didn't feel like going out to eat and drink at a bar or restaurant.

Instead, I strolled aimlessly through the train station in Shibuya. All around me, weary passengers were hustling to their trains, couples were meeting up for dates, friends or colleagues were parting ways, exhausted salarymen were eating late noodle soups at one of the food counters.

I felt alone amid the throngs of people who all clearly had a place to go or something to do. I wanted to talk to someone and called Naoko. She didn't pick up. I tried Kento but only let it ring twice. How was he going to be able to help me at a time like this? Not long after, my cellphone vibrated in my purse. It was Kento.

"Did you call me?"

"Um…yeah. I hope I didn't disturb you." I took refuge behind one of the wide pillars to be able to understand him better. "Can you hear me alright?"

"Yes, very well. What are you doing?"

"I'm in Shibuya."

I briefly considered telling him about my meeting with my rental father, but I cast the thought aside straightaway. First, it'd be entirely the wrong moment, and second, I wasn't sure whether it'd even interest him or whether it wouldn't be too much for him.

"Have you already eaten?" I inquired instead.

"Yes…by which I mean no. I…don't have very regular meals."

Again, we said nothing for a while. I noticed a woman my age standing alone a few meters away anxiously waiting for someone. She kept looking at her watch. Her hands were clutching a purse. She looked pale and was nervously looking from left to right and back again. For some reason, I felt sorry for her.

I didn't want the conversation with Kento to end.

"Can you tell me a story?" I asked softly.

"What would you like to hear?" he asked in surprise.

"Uh…it makes no difference to me."

"Hm. I don't know…not much has happened with me today."

"You could read something to me."

"What should I read to you?"

"Anything."

"Hm."

"A newspaper. A book, perhaps."

I heard him standing up, walking a few paces, leafing through something.

Then he cleared his voice:

"Carpets on the grass,
One whole night without a home—
Yet rich in moonlight"

He flipped some pages.

"Oh, butterfly, oh!
If you could sing like a bird
You'd long have been caged"

"Did you write them?"

I could hear his smile. "I don't write haiku. These are by old masters. I recently got my hands on a haiku anthology and have been reading it since."

He could read aloud very well; I'd have liked to ask him for a third and fourth haiku.

I waited to see whether he'd read another unprompted, but he remained silent. Only his quiet breathing was audible.

"Thank you, they're very nice," I said eventually. "I'm afraid I have to go. Take care."

"You too."

I wandered through the train station without knowing where in fact I was headed. It was unpleasantly hot. I was sweating. The brief conversation with Kento had distracted me; now I was feeling as forlorn as I had before. At some point, I ascended the stairs to the Yamanote Line. It ran in a circle above ground, and since our move to Tokyo, I'd ridden on it fairly frequently just to see something of the city.

The train wasn't full. After two stops, I managed to snag a seat and looked out the window. Tokyo rolled past me as in a film: broad streets on both sides, intersections lit by brightly flickering neon ads, dark storefronts, illuminated windows behind which I could make out the outlines of human bodies, an impenetrable web of thick and thin cables and wires, approaching trains, more neon signs.

Interrupted every two or three minutes by announcements for the next stop: Ebisu – Meguro – Shinagawa – Tamachi. People got off; people got on. Train wheels rattling over the tracks.

At first, the monotony calmed me. I decided simply to remain on board until Shibuya; the circuit took the better part of an hour. It was Friday evening; if I felt like it, I could go around a second time.

I looked around the train car. Most passengers were either busy on their cellphones or reading manga. Others slept, their heads had slumped to the side, onto their chest, or back, their mouths open slightly. This was how I imagined the victims of knockout gas.

Sitting catty-corner to me was a middle-aged man. Dark patches had formed on his white shirt underneath his armpits. He'd draped his suit coat over his knees. His beet-red head revealed to me that he had drunk too much alcohol. He stared straight ahead, his eyes glassy.

No one paid any attention to me, just as I paid none to anyone else. We were completely indifferent to one another, I thought. Happenstance had brought us together on this evening in Tokyo, and happenstance would lead us apart again over the next few minutes— as if we'd never crossed paths.

I let loose a loud whistle just to see what would happen.

No one reacted.

I inhaled deeply and exhaled while emitting a sort of grunting and groaning sound.

Nothing.

Perhaps I was too quiet.

I groaned louder. Once. Twice.

The drunk man gaped at me, nodded, and grinned lewdly.

Beside him was a man my age who looked up from his phone. Two earbuds protruded from his ears, he wore his hair short, a white shirt, a dark blue suit, and he looked as if he were on his way home after a long day at work.

Our eyes met and did not look away. I winked at him. Nothing about his expression changed.

I winked a second time.

Nothing.

We just looked at one another. I was suddenly not at all sure whether he even saw me or was staring right through me. After a few seconds, he lowered his gaze as though nothing had happened.

At the next stop, the seat next to him became free. I stood up and sat down beside him. Without looking up, he scooted a few centimeters to the side. Presumably, I weirded him out. Maybe he was even afraid of me. Still, I didn't want anything from him except his attention. I wanted to be seen. I wanted someone besides a drunk man to finally react to me and prove I existed, that I wasn't imagining everything here as I'd imagined having a father.

I wondered what I'd have to do on this train car to attract others' attention, to provoke some sort of reaction, to be seen and heard.

Call out for my father at the top of my lungs?

Sing "La vie en rose"?

Stand up and dance?

Walk on my hands?

The sleepers would awake, briefly check and see what was going on, and close their eyes again. Everyone else, I was sure, would continue acting as if I weren't there.

It was all a charade, it suddenly occurred to me. The equanimity, the patience, the calm with which they endured or ignored and would continue enduring and ignoring my escapades—what of it was genuine and what was faked?

What in life was genuine? What was faked?

How was I ever supposed to tell those things apart if I hadn't even noticed that my father had been rented?

I want to tear down the façade, I thought, I want to destroy it, to smash every last piece of it to bits so that no one ever even thinks of rebuilding it!

A painful twinge shot through my head, and I winced.

I could sit here with a drum and bang on it loudly, I thought. I would bother and annoy them, I would unsettle them, maybe even frighten them, and they would show me none of that, just as my (rental) father had never shown me what he really felt.

I'd been his job.

10,000 yen per hour.

Not including expenses.

Minimum of four hours.

Every other Sunday.

"Everything was paid—nothing was faked," he had written.

I didn't believe a word of his. Otherwise he wouldn't have said goodbye to me like he did: with a couple dishonest letters and consoling words. (*It is very beautiful in Singapore . . . I am sorry we were not able to see one another on this visit . . . next time for sure.*)

If I'd meant even the slightest thing to him, he would've sought out my company. No longer every other week, nor every month, but maybe every second or third one. A card at the beginning of the school year. A hello on the new year. A message on my birthday.

I wouldn't have been hard to please.

Everything was faked.

Now I was again feeling the unbridled rage at him that had vanished in the izakaya from one moment to the next.

How had he managed to do that?

I didn't understand myself.

Try to forgive your mother. She wanted only the best for you. We do not always achieve our aims.

Am I able, am I allowed to be furious if someone only wants what's best?

What had been my mother's aims?

To spare me the disgrace of being a fatherless child at school? Everyone knew that my parents were divorced and that my mother ran a sunakku and was a single parent. Whether my father showed up for field days or not didn't matter much anymore.

What exactly had the abuse of my trust been worth to her?

I could no longer confront her, and the fact that she'd left me alone with so many unanswered questions I found unfair of her.

She'll have had her reasons.

I'd like to know them, at least a few of them.

The young man beside me exited the train. For a moment, I considered following him, down the platform, up the stairs, through the streets, until he turned around and asked what I wanted.

A woman boarded and took a seat across from me. She was about my mother's age and certainly no office lady on her way home. She had too elegant an appearance for that. She was wearing golden earrings, a loose-fitting, black linen dress, a light linen jacket overtop that looked very expensive, and a dark-red scarf.

The woman didn't immediately retrieve her cell-phone from her bag. Having placed her hands in her lap, she sat perfectly erect and looked down at the floor, immersed in thought. Even before the train began moving, I clicked my tongue twice loudly, following it with a growl. She looked up with a start and scrutinized me thoroughly. All of a sudden, she stood up and sat down beside me. She was head shorter than me.

"Are you unwell?" she asked.

"Why should I be unwell?"

"I don't know. You seem like you're not doing well."

"Where do you get that idea?"

"It's written on your face. Has no one told you that?"

"No."

She shook her head as if she found that hard to believe. "Then no one has offered you help either, I suspect."

"I don't need help," I countered.

"Are you sure?"

"Yes."

The train abruptly came to a halt on the open tracks. The conductor apologized on behalf of Japan Railways for the resulting delay. The journey would continue in a few minutes.

"You are tired," the woman said.

"Hm."

"It's late, but you don't want to go to bed yet, and no one is waiting for you at home. That's why you're riding the Yamanote Line in circles around the city."

"How do you know that?"

"I can tell by looking at you, and you're not the only one."

We said nothing for a while.

"I had a rental father," I said.

"How lovely," she said. "I didn't have any sort of father."

"How come?"

"I don't know. I never asked. He wasn't there, and nobody ever mentioned him either."

"I see."

"Was your father good to you?"

"I didn't see him very often. He was only borrowed: four hours every other week, for six years."

"Oh. Was something off about him? Did you give him back?"

"No. I suppose my mother couldn't afford more time with him. Rental fathers aren't exactly cheap. But I don't really know. My mother never told me anything about it. Now that I've found out, I'm not sure what I'm supposed to believe and what I'm not, what I'm imagining and what corresponds with reality. Are you able to understand that?"

She nodded knowingly. "Of course."

"I don't know if I can trust myself anymore."

"Be afraid of those who trust themselves too much."

"A little bit might help."

She nodded again. "I feel the same way. It doesn't feel good."

"You know this feeling then?"

"Yes, of course."

"Have you known it for a long time?"

The woman pondered. "Ever since I spoke with a spirit for the first time."

"You believe in spirits?"

"It's not a matter of belief."

"You're right." I reflected. "With whose spirit did you speak that first time, if I may ask?"

"With the spirit of my dead little sister."

"Oh," I blurted out a second time.

"For over forty years, she's been coming by at least once a week. And people regularly visited by spirits know that this reality is only one of many, if you take my meaning."

"I think I do," I said pensively.

We were still stopped. This was more than unusual. I couldn't recall the last time I'd been on a train idling on the open tracks. The conductor apologized again and promised we'd continue onward after a brief period of waiting. He was sorry for the unpleasantries it would cause us. The other passengers took no notice of it, or at least they showed no signs of doing so.

"How sad," she said.

"What's sad?"

"We're probably stopped because somewhere along this stretch someone laid down onto the tracks."

"Where do you get that idea?"

"It happens on this line from time to time. I believe it's the spirits of the dead growing bored and calling to other spirits. Don't you hear them?"

At that moment, the train jolted forward and came to another abrupt stop a few meters on. The lights went out for a minute, then came back on. I still didn't detect any restiveness among the other passengers. They were sitting there, looking at their phones or sleeping as though nothing had happened. I briefly wondered if they were even still alive. Perhaps this strange woman and I were surrounded by people whose spirits had long left them: lifeless puppets, shells with a human countenance, façades. The conductor apologized another time and asked for our patience; for the moment, it was sadly unforeseeable when we'd be able to continue our journey, and naturally there was not the slightest cause for worry.

"Or an earthquake," I said.

"Or an earthquake," she said. "Shikata ga nai."

"Shikata ga nai," I repeated.

We waited patiently for what might come next.

"Do you ride this line often?" the woman asked.

"No, not really. What about you?"

"Yes, regularly. It's the line with the most spirits of the dead."

"I didn't know that. I thought that was the Chūō Line."

"You're never alone on the Yamanote Line."

"I see."

"I'm very tired," the woman said. "Would you mind if I leaned my head against your shoulder for a moment?"

"Not at all."

Her head was so light I hardly felt it. We sat like this beside one another and waited. Gradually, I felt the warmth of her body on my arm and shoulder. Her breathing became steadier; I suspected she'd fallen asleep. I, too, was overcome by a great exhaustion. My body grew heavier and heavier, and eventually my head fell forward.

I awoke just as the train was pulling into Harajuku. My neck was stiff and tight and painful.

The seat next to me was empty.

I regretted not having asked her for her phone number.

Another pearl on my necklace of missed opportunities.

The next day, I could picture the woman with the scarf as clearly as if we'd spent the entire night together. Still, I was unsure whether I'd really met her on the train or whether I'd dreamed it up. On my dark jacket, I discovered a thin red thread that matched the color of her scarf.

I was still not sure.

But maybe it wasn't so very important after all.

Maybe, I thought, it was a mistake to believe we always had to make a clear distinction between the real world and the world of fantasy—or that one was even possible.

Maybe what we call reality is only a product of our imagination, not that of an administrator or game inventor on some distant planet, but our own. And since no two people are alike, but each of us is unique, we cannot even occupy one and the same reality. There are as many realities in the world as there are people and their imaginations, and they all exist parallel to the same time, united in the erroneous belief that we share the same world, speak of the same things, see the same sights, hear the same sounds, smell the same odors, when in fact they are at most the same words we use to talk about those things and ourselves.

We say the same thing and mean something different.

From the first day on, life is full of sophistry and errors in judgment, I thought, a constantly expanding, unresolvable, perpetual misunderstanding.

It could only lead to unhappiness and discord, to disappointment and contention.

Strictly speaking, it was a miracle there wasn't more of that.

15

THE WEEKEND HAD ARRIVED. ALTHOUGH I COULD'VE slept in, I was already awake shortly after eight o'clock. During the night, I'd had the nightmare about my mother and me at Kinosaki Onsen again. I was running after her, calling out over and over. She acted as if she couldn't hear me. Passersby paused and watched us, but no one stopped her. I tripped and fell onto the pavement, which is what woke me up. After that, I had trouble falling back asleep.

From downstairs, I heard the muffled voices of neighbors.

I was due to meet Tomomi in the morning, and in the afternoon, I had French lessons with Madame Montaigne, as I did every second Saturday each month. I checked the weather on my cellphone and saw a voice message from Kento. Instead of getting up, I placed the telephone on the pillow beside me, rolled onto my side, and pressed "play":

"Hello...good morning...It's me...again...Hope I'm not disturbing you...I found two more haiku...which you might like..."

He spoke so deliberately that I could've listened to the message at double speed and still understood everything. But I didn't want to. I enjoyed the way he talked, how he'd insert pauses between words, as though giving them air to breathe.

"The first goes like this:

"In a former life
I once appeared as a whale—
Lonesome it was, lonesome"

He waited a few seconds before continuing:

"It's by a contemporary master, a woman...the second is by a man:

"Father, mother – dead
the rear door standing open
to hills of bare trees"

Kento fell silent. I could hear him breathing and shutting a book.

"When I read them, I couldn't help but think of you. I don't know why...I think they're well done...I'll be glad if you also like them...Uh...I'm going to bed now...Hope you have a nice weekend...Goodnight."

He'd sent the message three hours earlier. I listened to it a second and a third time. I hadn't read any haiku in years. They'd been required in school, and at the time, I'd found most of those short poems boring and vacuous. The ones Kento sent me I liked a lot. I wrote him a brief text:

Thanks for the haiku. I think they're really very lovely.

I'm glad, he replied immediately.

Are you up already or still awake?

Awake again. I only sleep two or three hours a night. Mostly from around 5 a.m. to 7 or 8. Then at some point during the day I'll go back to bed.

Gotcha. I'd be dead tired if I only slept two or three hours.

I am. It's not a good rhythm, but I don't have another one.

Did you already eat breakfast?

No

What are you up to?

Taking some notes.

You're writing?

No, I'm just noting down a few memories from back when.

From K.'s World?

In a manner of speaking, yeah

Could I read some more?

Instead of another text, I received an e-mail with an attachment and no explanation.

From K.'s World

His siblings love birds.
  So does he.
  They want to keep a budgerigar as a pet.
  He does not.
  Locking an animal you love into a cage makes no sense to K. It is a contradiction in terms.
  Their parents say No.
  Then they say Maybe, and finally they say Yes.
  The children get a blue parakeet and call it Toru. The cage alternates between his brother's room for a week and his sister's for a week.
  The bird is not skittish. It doesn't take long for the children to be able to hold a finger inside the cage, for

it to jump on and nibble away. Toru is allowed to fly around their rooms, and if Emi stands still for long enough, it will sit on her shoulder.

On the afternoons K. is alone at home, he sits before the cage and gazes at the animal. Sometimes it stands on one leg, cocks its head, and leers back from its tiny, dark eyes.

The cage is small; the bird cannot do much more than hop from one perch to the other or cling to the bars of the cage with its claws. It spends most of its time cooing and tweeting in front of a round mirror hanging in the middle of the cage. In its image, it must recognize another bird. Eventually, it will peck at the mirror, as if enraged at the deception.

Toru is lonesome, K. thinks. It yearns for company. He feels sorry for the animal.

One afternoon, he opens the window in his sister's room and then the door to the cage.

His siblings will be very sad if they discover the empty cage, but that is of no concern to him at that moment. Birds want to fly. Birds belong in nature.

Twittering, Toru hops from perch to perch but will not come out.

Come on, he says, taking the cage and setting it on the windowsill.

Fresh air pours in. It is an unusually cool spring day.

All of a sudden, Toru grows very quiet.

Birds are chirping in the garden. Toru looks like he is listening to them.

K. wonders whether they are telling him something, whether they are encouraging him to flee his captivity or warning him of the perils of a life lived in freedom.

He waits.

He flicks the bars of the cage.

The bird's passivity annoys K. He lifts up the cage and shakes it gently. Go, fly already, he commands.

Toru remains sitting on the perch and does not move.

What a stupid, stupid animal, he thinks, closing the window and returning the cage to its place.

From now on, he ignores the bird.

Later, when K. himself is sitting in a cage, the bird frequently comes to mind.

What could have been going through that little head back then, what had kept it from leaving its prison and flying away? Perhaps some caprice, or the strangely cool air intimidated it.

Or the song of the other birds.

What would he do, K. thinks, if someone came and opened the door to his cage for him?

The probability is exceedingly low, yet the very idea scares him.

He sees Toru sitting on his perch, the opened door before him and the wide-open window, and suddenly understands what a clever animal the parakeet had been. In freedom, he would likely have survived only a few days.

K. hopes to be just as clever.

Those who know no freedom will perish in it.

I wondered whether this was Kento's way of telling me that I'd never understand what was going on with him, just as he had never understood the bird—or that it would never suffice simply to open a door.

The more I learned from him and the more he told me about himself, the more enigmatic he became to me.

I tried to imagine how Kento spent his days.

What would I do if I didn't leave my apartment for a while?

Sleep, sleep a lot. Read. Watch a few movies. Browse videos on YouTube. Journal. Cook, maybe. Watch tutorials and take an online sewing class. How long could I keep that up? Two weeks? Three? Four? Certainly not a quarter of a year. How had Kento survived this for almost a decade now? What did he do with his time?

I'd have liked to wish him a nice day, but instead sent him a friendly waving emoji.

I received no reply.

Tomomi and I met in front of the Kaminarimon Gate in Asakusa. She had asked me whether I'd go with her to Sensō-ji temple; her father was gravely ill, and she wanted to pray for him. Afterward, we could go get something to eat.

I arrived a few minutes too early, and Tomomi was already waiting for me. She was wearing a lightweight, loose-fitting dress in dark blue, her hair tied back into a ponytail, and she smiled when she spotted me amid the crowd. From looking at her, I didn't notice her grief. Even in this oppressive summer heat, she seemed elegant. While sweat was running down my entire body, she gave the impression of having just gotten out of a well-air-conditioned car.

For a few seconds, the sight of her was unfamiliar. Her eyes were rounder and larger, the lids lifted slightly, the birthmark on her chin gone without having left a trace. I pointed to my chin and eyes inquiringly; the reply came as a nod.

"You look good," I said. "Your new face suits you." Tomomi smiled in relief.

"Are you satisfied too?"

"Yes."

In spite of the heat, there was quite a large thronging crowd. We squeezed our way through the masses down the long path toward the temple, one business after the other lining each side, selling souvenirs, snacks, and devotional objects. "How's your father doing?" I asked.

"He's alright. Slowly improving a bit. At least I hope he is." She stopped at a kiosk and bought an *omamori* for him, one for her son, and one for her husband's car so it would shepherd him safely through traffic.

I recalled the time shortly after my mother's diagnosis:

We had gone to Sensō-ji together, reluctantly on her part though: Didn't I know that she didn't believe in such things? she chided. Ghosts and gods couldn't help her. At most, the right medicines would.

It'd been even more packed than today, and my mother was very tense. She'd been doing more poorly than I'd wanted to admit. I'd bought us good luck charms, we'd burned incense sticks, let the smoke waft over us, donated money, bowed before Buddha, and softly murmured our prayers. I offered up my fervent wish for my mother to get healthy again.

What she wished for I don't know.

Tomomi and I each lit a bundle of incense sticks, waved the smoke over us, and stuck them into a large bucket of ashes. She closed her eyes and certainly prayed for her father's convalescence. I had no sudden impulse for what I might wish for, so I prayed for world peace.

At a stand selling *omikuji*, we each tossed a hundred-yen coin into a slot and drew a stick with a number from one to a hundred. Our fortunes lay in the corresponding drawers. Mine promised me *daikichi*, "the greatest happiness." Cares and potential worries would vanish. I'd become famous if I wanted to; any financial woes would soon be consigned to the past. If I should desire to move or travel, it'd be a good time to do so, and everything would turn out well in my marriage or relationship too. The sun was shining upon my house.

With a faint smile, I folded the slip of paper and put in it my wallet.

Tomomi's fortune portended the opposite: *daikyō*, "terrible unhappiness." The person she was waiting for would not appear. Whatever happiness and contentment she had would last only briefly. She should not undertake any travel whatsoever. In certain instances, imminent death was waiting for her. Only with great humility and modesty could disaster be averted. She stared at the prophecy, raised her eyebrows, and eyed me as though I could tell her what to make of this. In her expression lay a mixture of irritation and a trace of uncertainty. At length, she tied the slip of paper to a wire for such things, with dozens of other bad omens already hanging from it, and repeated the ritual. The next number augured "average happiness." She tried it one more time, and now the prophecy promised her "the greatest happiness" in all areas of life, just as it had me. Satisfied, she dropped the slip of paper into her handbag.

We proceeded to the main temple and carved ourselves a path through the crowd to the counters where visitors could request special prayers for themselves or their relatives. Tomomi wanted a monk to pray for her father's health. She wrote his name, her address, and her request on a form and paid three thousand yen. In exchange, she received another wooden amulet for her home with a gold ribbon around it bearing good wishes. We removed our shoes and took our seats on the benches in the waiting area at the rear section of the hall, where a dozen visitors were already sitting.

There, an older man caught my eye—he may have been around seventy, short, and obviously alone here. His suit was shabby, yet he seemed as if he had donned something special for this occasion. He looked around solemnly, our eyes met, and I gave the merest hint of a smile, which he did not reciprocate. I wondered whom he wanted to ask Buddha's assistance for. Perhaps for his daughter or a grandchild? Or his wife was lying at home or in the hospital, and something was growing within her that would kill her, and the doctors had tried everything and told him, her husband, that there was nothing more they could do for her: only a miracle would help now. And he, despite not really believing in ghosts or gods and having always looked down a bit on those who did, set out for Sensō-ji, full of sadness and rife with fear, but still with just enough hope that he didn't despair. Here he sat, waiting patiently for his turn and thinking of his wife, who was a few centimeters taller and had actually been much too beautiful for him, who had, for reasons he could not fully grasp to this day, chosen him in spite of it all. He thought of her lovers, whom he had tolerated because this woman was the love of his life, and he didn't want to lose her.

I began imagining his story in more and more detail and recalled earlier days and how much it had helped on those never-ending afternoons and evenings to think up stories for myself and write them down, how much faster time had passed when I was lost in my reveries.

And why I didn't do that anymore.

How hard it was to do what was good for you.

To even know what that might be.

A young monk roused me from my thoughts. He led us into the area in front of the gold-gleaming, flower-adorned altar, where an older monk was waiting for us. We sat on the ground, and he took time until everyone had found their seats. A hefty strike of the drum sounded, and he began to recite. His voice sounded scratchy and not especially mellifluous; I didn't enjoy listening to him. Accompanied by monotonous, dull drumbeats, he chanted a sutra in a loud singsong. When the ceremony was over, Tomomi was the first to rise.

"My knees," she groaned, "I can't sit a second longer. I hope it at least helps."

With both of us hungry, Tomomi suggested a *soba* joint nearby that she'd found on the Internet. It had the best ratings by far; its noodles were supposed to be freshly prepared and, according to several portals, were said to be the best in the whole area. A long line snaked in front of the restaurant.

In heat like this, I'd rather have found a quick seat in some air-conditioned restaurant, but Tomomi obviously thought it important we eat here, and so I said nothing.

While we were waiting, she sent several messages to her husband with suggestions for what he could do with their son. The two seldom spent time together.

I watched her as she did it and wondered what she would say in reply to Kento's questions: Do you know yourself? Do you like yourself?

When I told her about my thoughts, she looked up from her iPhone briefly and then continued typing.

"Of course I know myself," she eventually said. "I'm thirty years old. It'd be awful if didn't know who I am and what I want at my age." She paused for a moment in thought, wrote something, and turned to me. "You also know me, though."

I rocked my head back and forth vaguely, so as to mean both yes and "I'm not sure."

"I'm a daughter. Mother. Wife. Sister. What else about me can you think of?"

We inched forward in the queue, and I reflected. "Friend."

She nodded.

"University-trained accountant."

She nodded once more. "There's nothing else about myself I need to know."

"Hm. Maybe I put it the wrong way. I didn't mean the roles you have but the qualities you imbue them with."

She shrugged as if she didn't understand why I was drawing a distinction there.

"Do I like myself?" Tomomi pursed her lips as though for a kiss and considered this. "I cannot think of a reason why I shouldn't like myself. It's much more important whether others like me. My parents. Yūma. My husband. My sister. You."

We'd reached the entrance to the restaurant, and a server ushered us to our table at the window on the second floor. I was relieved finally to be in a cooler space.

Tomomi ordered tea and warm noodles for herself and cold soba with tempura for me. I dabbed the sweat from my forehead with a damp cloth and wiped my hands clean.

"Could you imagine, purely hypothetically of course, renting a father for Yūma?"

She looked at me, puzzled. "Where did you come up with this weird question?"

"Just, uh...wondering." In that moment, I didn't feel like telling her my story. I hoped she could help me better understand my mother.

"Why in the world would I need to rent a father for my son?"

"Assuming you and Ryo were to separate, and Ryo wouldn't take care of Yūma, that they'd lose touch."

"You mean that he'd remarry."

"For example."

Tomomi took an unusually long time to ponder this. Normally, she was quick to offer an opinion about everything and everyone.

"I don't think I'd wanted to remain single for long. I imagine life as a single mom to be sad, lonely, and difficult. It's hard for you to find a job because you've got a kid to take care of. Everywhere you go, people look at you. In kindergarten and later in school. The neighbors. My parents. They'd be terribly worried and would pester me to find a new husband every time we saw each other. Or even worse: they'd start looking for one for me. And then, at every opportunity, they'd tout the example of my married little sister with her two children. No, thank you."

A server brought our noodles and tea. Tomomi's broth smelled delicious, but she paid no attention to it; with her chopsticks, she stirred the noodles around absentmindedly without tasting them.

"I could imagine there being a number of men who'd still find me attractive even though I'm thirty years old and have a kid. Maybe I'm deceiving myself though. It'd probably take a while to find someone. What man wants to raise another man's child?"

She set down the chopsticks and drank some tea in short sips. A trace of melancholy darkened her expression.

I shouldn't have asked her these questions.

"That's why I'd never split up with Ryo either, even if he only sleeps with me twice a year and hasn't noticed that I had cosmetic surgery..."

"He hasn't?"

She shook her head sorrowfully. "The saddest thing is it didn't even surprise me. He's always elsewhere with his thoughts. At the office, with his clients, wherever." She bit her lower lip. "If need be, I'll eventually take a lover. I wouldn't ever have to tell *him* that I had a kid, and whenever he bores me, I'll find a new one." Tomomi stood up, excused herself, and disappeared off to the restrooms.

I felt very sorry for putting her in this situation. After the stories about her marriage from our last dinner together, I could—no, should—have predicted that her answers to my questions would take this turn.

Why hadn't my mother gotten remarried? She'd been a very attractive woman. And young. Twenty-one when she got divorced. Should she have not wanted a new husband, I wondered, then why not? For my sake? I had to admit that I was grateful to her for not having allowed a strange man into our lives, despite knowing how selfish this thought was.

Perhaps there'd been lovers she'd have liked to marry who ran off after learning about me.

Lovers afraid of women with children.

Likely.

Tomomi was gone for a while. When she returned, I apologized for my questions. She waved me off as though she'd already forgotten about it. Still, I felt I owed her an explanation. For a moment, I hesitated, then said: "I had a rental father."

She looked at me in astonishment. In a few words, I told her about "Haruhiko" and how I'd found out about him.

"Hm." Tomomi reflected. "Was he nice to you?"

"Uh...yeah," I replied in surprise.

"Did you have a good time together?"

"Well...I think...mostly we did."

She nodded in relief, as though doing so answered all major questions. "I'm sure your mother probably gave it a lot of thought."

"You think so?"

"Of course. Why not."

"I guess so." Her reaction disappointed me although I couldn't have said what response I'd expected or hoped for.

We silently avoided eye contact with one another, then took our chopsticks and tried our noodles. They tasted wonderful, weren't too thick, and had just the right consistency.

Tomomi's face squinched in indulgence. "Aren't they delicious?"

"That they are."

"Our waiting paid off, didn't it?"

"Absolutely."

"Good choice, don't you think?"

I nodded.

She took another bite and smiled contently.

And I thought about my mother.

And about my rental father.

About the old man at the temple.

About Kento.

And about how life consists only of stories, and not until the end do we know which were made up and which were true, which were the important ones and which insignificant.

I doubted whether we might even ever be sure.

After our meal, Tomomi suddenly found herself in a big hurry. We parted ways outside the restaurant. I watched her vanish into the crowd without really knowing what to do with myself in the remaining time before my French lesson.

The person I'd have liked to see didn't leave his apartment, or did so only late at night.

I strolled aimlessly through the streets around the temple and bought two teacups I didn't need at a housewares store, plus a new bamboo whisk for foaming my matcha, even though I seldom drank it at home and the old whisk was still in perfectly good condition.

I found a seat at a café and was about to message Kento, but all the questions that came to mind—"What are you doing?," "Where are you?," "Are you doing okay?"—made no sense in relation to him. Instead, I sent him a picture of my purchases together with a waving emoji and the question whether he liked drinking matcha. When he didn't answer, I recorded a voice message for him.

"I just wanted to say hello. I'm sitting in a café in Asakusa. I was with a friend at Sensō-ji. Have you ever been there before? We prayed for her father who is pretty sick. I hope it helps ... I was there with my mother too. It didn't help her ... but that doesn't necessarily mean anything ..."

I listened to the message and immediately deleted it.

How hard it was to find the right words.

How hard it was to say what I really wanted to say.

Afterward, I set out for my French teacher, Madame Montaigne.

She'd been among the first regulars at my mother's bar. Over time, the two got to talking, got along well, and when my mother decided to fulfill a dream and learn French, Madame suggested she give her lessons. A few months later, my mother wanted to stop because it'd become too much for her and too expensive. I offered to take lessons with her; we could split the costs and motivate each other and quiz one another on vocabulary. That'd been six years ago. After my mother's death, I rather wanted to quit but changed my mind. I liked Madame, her lessons were fun for me, and she claimed I had a special talent for her language. At her request, we met every other weekend either at midday or early evening so we could drink a glass of wine together at the end of the hour.

Madame spoke perfect Japanese. She was in her mid-sixties, came from Bordeaux, and had fallen in love with a Japanese man in Kyoto on a world tour almost forty years ago and had stayed.

Today, she opened a bottle of white wine right at the beginning of the hour and poured us each a glass. It was her daughter's birthday—she worked for a cultural foundation in Paris—and we made a toast to her.

"How do you say 'rental father' in French?" I asked without giving it extended thought.

Madame shot me a puzzled look. "You mean 'adoptive father'?"

"No, 'rental father.'"

"I don't know the term. I've heard of 'surrogate mothers.' But 'rental fathers'? What exactly is that?"

"A man mothers pay to pretend to be the father of their child or children for a certain period of time. He visits them regularly and joins them at school for field days and parent evenings so that no one finds out the mother is single."

"But the children know he isn't—how should I put it?—their 'real' father?"

"Uh...well...I'm not sure. I don't think so."

"What mother would do that to her children, *ma cherie*? I can't imagine anyone using a service like that."

"In Japan they do."

"Are you sure?"

"I...I've read about it. You'll find a lot of stories about it on the Internet."

Madame shook her head faintly. "I've been living in this country now for so long, and it never ceases to amaze me. If there are 'surrogate mothers,' though, then why shouldn't there also be 'rental fathers'?" She pondered. "Anyhow, as far as I know, there is no word for that in French. We call a rental car 'la voiture de location.' A rental father could be called 'le père de location,' but that doesn't make any sense. In France, they'd declare you mad if you asked about that. Why are you asking?"

"Oh, no reason."

16

I FELT UNWELL IN MY OWN SKIN. I COULDN'T BEAR being in my apartment for any length of time, which from one day to the next had grown too small and cramped for me, and the sight of the urn containing my mother's ashes weighed on me. I felt as if we were two silent people living together in the same room who could no longer maintain their silence, but who lacked the words to express what they wanted to say.

Every evening after work, I dined alone at one of the cheap conveyor-belt sushi, curry, or ramen restaurants in Shimokita or Shibuya and took long walks afterward, but even in my own neighborhood, so deeply familiar to me, I felt oddly out of place. Only when I could barely walk from exhaustion would I go home, collapse into bed, and fall asleep at once.

On the train rides to Akasaka and back, I observed people all around me pushing and shoving their way into the train cars without any display of emotion, staring at their phones with expressionless faces as though nothing else in the world existed. They endured the cramped quarters on the trains in silence and without complaint. I'd never noticed that before.

I'd been one of them.

At the office, I did my work and, as often as practicable, kept to myself.

During the meeting with my rental father, I felt I'd abandoned the old me I'd known and trusted, and now I couldn't find a path back—not because I didn't want to and repudiated that self. I'd gotten lost. I was straying through the days and through my routine, looking in vain for the entrance to Akiko's former world.

I was walking on thin ice. Maybe we all were. Probably I'd been doing so before too and just hadn't noticed. Now, with every step, I heard the cracking and crunching.

Something inside me had been thrown off kilter.

I considering seeking out Tetsuya, aka "Haruhiko," again, but what did I want from him? Would it help me to make a scene in front of him in his izakaya, to show him my rage, my disappointment, in view of others?

I doubted it. It'd only be proof of my weakness.

Besides, I was afraid I could be forsaken again by my courage when face-to-face with him.

Nor were there any questions I still had to ask him, at least none he could have answered for me, and none for which his answers, I thought, would help me move forward.

A deep mistrust was growing within me, of myself and of the way I viewed the world. If for six years I hadn't noticed that my father was merely rented, I wondered what all else I'd missed and was still missing.

I felt an increasing aloofness from everything and everyone, including—or perhaps especially—from myself.

Naoko was the only one who noticed. Eventually, she asked what was going on with me.

"What do you mean?" I replied.

"You're different than usual."

"Different, how?"

"Absent in some way. You don't go out drinking with us anymore in the evenings. Every day, you bring a bento box with you for lunch that you prefer to eat by yourself at your desk, as if you had a doppelgänger and were sending her to the office."

I understood exactly what she meant. "I don't know what you mean," I said.

"You look like Akiko. You talk like Akiko. You do your work as conscientiously as Akiko. And yet I've got the feeling there's a stranger before me."

"I'm sorry. Don't take it personally. It's got nothing to do with you." My reply was a covert admission that she'd been right, but this nuance was lost on Naoko.

I took detours with the train or sat in restaurants and bars just to watch people and think up a life for them, variations on what-if stories.

At Tokyu Hands, I bought myself a notebook and began writing these down.

At a bar in Ginza, I noticed a woman sitting at a table by herself, as I was. A few years older than I, she was wearing her hair in a pageboy cut like Naoko's, a tight-fitting black dress that suited her well, and a matching ring and necklace. She'd made up her lips in a tantalizing red. A small black handbag lay on the table before her, a clear cocktail with an olive in it to the side, presumably a martini. Although she wasn't looking at the clock, she seemed like she was waiting for someone. She came across as mildly impatient and tense.

I imagined her working for an insurance company or a real estate firm in a position that was higher and well-paid for her age. Her dress and jewelry hadn't come cheap. She was waiting for her boyfriend. He was in his late thirties, tall, good-looking, and worked in a similar job at a bank. They'd been together for eight years, and for the woman, it was only a question of when they would marry. Only in allusions had they discussed it, but she loved him, and he gave her every reason to assume that he reciprocated her love, so what was there to discuss? It was his job to propose, and she'd expected him to do so in the autumn at the latest, when, as they did every year in October, they planned to travel to a beautiful seaside resort for a long weekend.

By some coincidence, the woman had learned a few days earlier that the man had married a colleague the previous year. He'd been dating her for five years, and according to everything she'd been able to find out, they were a happy couple and had been planning the wedding for a long while.

Her love transformed into a hate so profound that she herself marveled at its intensity.

Inside the clutch on the table beside the cocktail glass was a pointed, sharp folding knife.

I imagined her boyfriend arriving at the table, greeting her tenderly, telling her how good she looked, imagined them having a drink together, then perhaps another, imagined him paying and them looking for a nearby hotel to make love, just as they had done countless times in previous years.

I imagined him lying next to her later, a bit worn out, his eyes closed, dozing languorously. I imagined her reaching for her handbag, producing the knife, and stabbing it into his chest with all her might where she suspected his heart to be.

The woman cast me an interested glance, wondering perhaps what I was writing down so assiduously. In an unpleasant way, I felt caught, clapping the book shut and sipping on my "Blues on the Beach," which sounded better than it tasted.

A short while later, the man she'd been expecting arrived. He was tall and good-looking. He greeted her tenderly, ordered a drink, and paid her compliments. I couldn't hear what he was saying but read it in her face.

I paid for my cocktail and left.

Or the couple at the kaiten-sushi restaurant: they were sitting directly across from me at the other side of the U-shaped counter. I could see only their heads and their hands whenever they took a plate of sushi from the conveyor belt. The man had a somewhat gruff face, with scars on the skin of both cheeks and a large nose. By contrast, the woman's face was pretty, almost delicate, with pale skin. I figured them both to be in their early sixties.

Every now and then, the man would say a few words, his loud, coarse voice traveling all the way to me. The woman nodded. I couldn't tell from her facial expressions whether she was agreeing with him or of a different opinion—or even listening.

I imagined her to work in the housewares department of a large department store; Takashimaya was too expensive, perhaps at Seibu. Her husband was a delivery driver and loaded new products into the beverage machines on every corner. They'd been together for over thirty years and had a daughter who was already married and living with her husband's family in Kagoshima. She only rarely came to Tokyo. It'd been two years since they'd last seen their daughter.

The pair lead a routinized life.

They get up together, eat breakfast together, say goodbye for the day, eat dinner together, watch TV together afterward until they head off together for bed around eleven p.m.—in separate rooms for a few years now.

Occasionally they visit a cheap sushi restaurant; they both love fish.

They don't do much talking—they never have. Life is the way it is.

Once a year, they go on vacation together for three days. Either they visit their daughter, or they travel into the mountains.

I imagined the wife waiting for her husband one evening over the coming winter. The day before, she'd made a sukiyaki and now she is sitting at the set table, worrying. It will be eight o'clock soon, and he's normally home a few minutes before she is. She calls him, but he doesn't pick up.

She waits without touching the food.

She phones her daughter to ask whether her father might have contacted her.

No, he hasn't.

At around ten o'clock, she's about to call a colleague friend of her husband's, but she can't muster the courage. How would it look for a wife to cause a ruckus because her husband comes home a few hours later than usual?

Time ticks on.

Around midnight, she goes to bed, but she can't fall asleep.

The next morning, she calls her husband's company.

He had duly parked his vehicle in the lot yesterday at four thirty in the afternoon and said goodbye in the office.

They do not expect him today; he took the day off.

I imagine her going to the nearest *koban* with this information. The police officers show no particular interest in the case. Every day, for a broad range of reasons, people in Japan are reported missing and show up again after a short while.

Only in rare cases do they actually disappear.

She waits for a sign of life from her husband. A call. A message on the Line app.

When she wants to initiate a bank transfer the next day, she notices that there are only a thousand yen left in their joint checking account. The savings account has been closed, the sum of three million yen withdrawn.

For the police, this is a positive development in the case. It suggests this is neither an accident nor a crime, but a planned, voluntary disappearance, an internal family affair—for which they are not responsible.

The husband remains fully AWOL.

Despite the evidence, the wife assumes there was an accident or a crime.

She couldn't bear a different truth.

She becomes a grieving widow, embittered at the disinterest and inaction of the police and the authorities.

OR

After a long hesitation, the wife concludes that her husband has left her and had been leading her on for years.

She wonders about the man she spent the previous thirty years living with, why she let herself be deceived like this.

After the initial shock, an unbelievable rage seizes her. He's stolen not only all of their savings, but he's also robbed her of her trust. How will she ever be able to believe anything of anyone again?

She packs his things into two suitcases and takes them to an organization that helps the unhoused. His books, manga, CDs, and his collection of model cars end up in the garbage. She expunges every trace of him from her life. She's too old for a new beginning, but still young enough for a life without him.

I noted down detailed versions for the two variations. That was the advantage of made-up stories, in contrast to those that life wrote. I determined which turns they took. I decided who pretended what to whom and how and when they met their end.

My fantasies gave me stability. They distracted me. With them, I created worlds I controlled, where only what I wanted is what happened.

True, these were strange stories I dreamed up. It was a mystery to me where the ideas came from or what they meant. They were quite atypical for me and didn't really match my interests. I was neither a reader of crime novels nor fascinated by horror stories. Whenever it got too suspenseful or violent in a movie, I'd close my eyes.

But what did I know about myself?

On several occasions, I took the Yamanote Line in the hope of running into the woman with the red scarf again. I don't know why, but I was sure she'd understand how I felt. Unfortunately, I encountered neither her, nor one of the spirits she'd told stories about.

I'd have liked to talk with them.

One morning, for the second time, I found a thin red thread on my jacket that matched her scarf, as if she'd been sitting next to me somewhere without my noticing it.

There wasn't a single place in the whole huge city where I could find peace of mind.

Among its forty million inhabitants, there was not one person with whom I could have found peace of mind.

I sent Kento a short message that he didn't answer.

On one of my late-night wanderings, I ran into him randomly near the jazz club. His hands buried in his pockets, he was wearing a thin, gray sweatshirt jacket and track pants of a kind, with numerous stains.

Tonight, the sight of him saddened me.

He smiled, a bit embarrassed. I sensed that he was happy to see me.

"Hi," he said. "Sorry I haven't been in touch."

"No worries."

Whenever we met, we'd remain silent for a while.

"The band you like is playing in the jazz bar," he said at last.

With a glance, he asked me if I'd like to go see. I nodded and followed him.

There were even more people standing outside the club than there were last time. They looked younger than us, were drinking beer, and conversed with one another in hushed voices. Inside, the upright bass was in the middle of a solo, just after which the pianist and the drummer joined in.

We took up position on the opposite side of the lane. I'd have liked to drink a beer, but couldn't be bothered to go get one.

"Are you doing alright?" he asked, interrupting my thoughts.

"Why should I not be doing alright?" I answered, surprised at how irritated I sounded.

"I don't know."

I let out a soft sigh.

"Yes, I'm doing okay. I might look a little worn out, but everything is fine," I replied, without conviction. "Thanks for asking."

I lied without intending to, and I knew I was lying, which made it worse, and to judge from Kento's expression, he also knew I was lying, which made it a bit worse still. I felt rotten and would've loved to leave.

For a while, we listened to the jazz trio. Then, the piano was playing, unaccompanied. The soft piece reminded me of the quiet compositions by Ryuichi Sakamoto, which I listened to from time to time. The music began to calm me down.

With Kento, I had a feeling he was elsewhere in his thoughts.

"Is there any news about your rental father?" he asked suddenly.

I regarded him with surprise. "What makes you ask?"

"When we saw one another last, I got the impression you were planning to start looking for him."

"Uh...yeah...that's right."

"Did you find any trace of him?"

"I met up with him."

He furrowed his brow and nodded contemplatively. "You met up with him," he repeated, drawing out each word a bit as though wanting to be sure he'd understood me correctly.

I expected the obvious question about how the reunion had gone, but he said nothing for a long time.

I, too, remained silent, less because I didn't want to tell him anything about "Haruhiko," than because I didn't know how to describe our encounter and what had happened with me since.

I thought of the trip with my mother to Kinosaki Onsen, of how I simply went mute at the time. My feeling was similar now. I wanted to say only what was absolutely necessary, if anything at all, and suddenly understood why; I mistrusted every sentence I said.

I didn't believe myself.

We exchanged glances, and the longer we stood facing one another like that, the more I felt that he could read my thoughts, that he knew exactly what was happening within me.

"I'm thirsty," I said when I became uncomfortable. "I'm going to get a beer. Would you like one?"

"No, thanks."

"Something else?"

He shook his head.

"Will you still be around?"

A fleeting, apologetic smile flashed over his face.

When I returned, Kento was rubbing the palms of his hands together and then putting the left hand on the back of his neck. This was an odd habit of his I had observed before rather often.

"Did you get bitten by something?"

"I don't think so. If I leave the house, I sometimes get headaches. Putting a warm hand on the back of my neck helps. At least, I imagine it does."

I took a swig of my cold beer.

Kento was pondering something. "If you like, I could send you another story."

"Yeah, sure...why not."

He winced briefly. I shouldn't have said that.

"Of course," he quickly added, "only if it isn't too much for you."

"Not at all. Don't worry."

"It's about two episodes with my parents. I couldn't help but think of them after you told me about your rental father, and I wrote them down."

The following evening, I was eating a pasty, boring-tasting vegetable curry in Shimokita, sipping a beer, and killing time watching cat videos on YouTube. Cats were among my favorite animals, and since my mother's death, I'd often considered buying myself one. I enjoyed their noiseless, sleek movements, their looks which I could never figure out. That's likely why the little film clips were so good at distracting me.

My phone vibrated. An e-mail from Kento, containing nothing but a text file.

17

From K.'s World

Once, his father takes him along to the Festival Hall in Osaka. A large orchestra from Berlin is in town performing a program of Johannes Brahms' violin concerto and his second symphony. It would be a change of pace from the solo and chamber concerts they had attended before, his father said, and K. would like it. Both compositions were very romantic, each in its own way.

A trip with his father is a special occasion for K. During the week, they do not spend much time together. Whenever his father comes home late from the hospital, the children are usually already sleeping. In the mornings, they do not see much of one another and are too busy to exchange more than a few words.

He misses him, even if he would never put it that way.

Their primary one-on-one times come while playing piano, which K. perceives more as time spent in a triad. They practice pieces for four hands together. He enjoys sitting with his father at the grand piano and yet is always slightly tense and nervous because he does not want to make any mistakes.

K. greatly looks forward to the concert and at the same time is afraid the many people and the stimuli in the large Festival Hall or the music might overwhelm him. If that turns out to be the case, he must not under any circumstances let it show. Not for all the world does K. want to disappoint his father.

They depart in good time, there is little traffic, and during the ride, one of their infrequent conversations unfolds.

K.'s father expresses how much he enjoys his son's piano playing and remarks on what progress K. is making and that he should continue to practice so diligently. His talent was a gift, and with this gift, as with any gift, comes a responsibility. No one has the right to squander it.

His father speaks about the famous orchestra they are about to hear, and he enjoys listening. He likes his father's voice.

They talk about school briefly and then a bit about baseball; for whatever reason, his father believes it interests his son. Maybe he thinks it must be of interest to a young boy.

K. would like to ask his father something, about his job, for instance: whether he has seen many of his patients with heart conditions die, but he knows that he does not like to talk about it and lets it be.

After they have ridden about halfway, the breaks in conversation grow longer, which does not bother K. Their quiet togetherness in the car is enough for him. If he had his way, they could also drive all the way to Tokyo.

At the concert hall, his father leads them to their seats in the eighth row.

So as not to be overwhelmed by the people and the many stimuli, K. closes his eyes.

The first sounds in the strings are not loud, yet they seize him with a force he was unprepared for.
    Nothing is safe from them.
    Then the entire orchestra joins in, and he clenches his seat's armrests with both hands.
    The violin resounds; he hardly dares to breathe.
    Upon looking at his father from the side, he sees a tear streaming down his cheek.
    He senses why his father is crying, though does not know what to do.

So he closes his eyes again and acts as if he had not noticed anything.

During intermission, father and son remain in their seats.

They exchange glances.

Never before and not ever since has K. felt so close to him.

On the way back to Nara, his father hardly says a word, nor does he ask any questions.

For this, K. is grateful to him.

He would not have known what to say in reply to anything.

He is so full of music that there is no more room for words and sentences.

In lieu of thoughts, he has the first bars of the concert in his head.

The first notes of the violin.

The last ones in the orchestra.

Even weeks later, the melodies are still coursing through his mind.

Many years later, he will think back on this evening in the concert hall in Osaka.

To the tear on his father's face.

To how fond he had been of him and yet how much he had not understood him.

To the fact that we can never really understand what is happening inside another person, what he feels, what he thinks, what he is planning, regardless of how much we may try and how much we might wish to; that we can, at best, only ever have the faintest trace of a notion of it.

No matter how close we feel, a brief glance from a distance into the labyrinth of another's emotions and thoughts is all we can hope to get.

·   ·   ·

His mother is sitting in the first row, just beside his father and his two siblings.

K. is playing the third movement of a Schubert sonata from memory, all the while observing his family out of the corners of his eyes. As soon as the first notes sound, his father closes his eyes. The stirrings in his expression suggest how much his son's playing pleases him.

His brother and sister are not listening. They never do. This does not bother K.

His mother directs her gaze onto the stage, looking past him and the grand piano to the light-gray wall and the artificial flowers in the background. She wears a faint smile on her face, which he knows all too well. She always carries it with her, like her handbag. She displays it whenever she encounters a neighbor on the street, while shopping, at the school field day.

While he is playing, her countenance remains unaffected.

Music never gets through to her, he thinks, no matter if he plays Chopin or Schubert, no matter if she praises him later or not.

Although she had several years of piano instruction as a child and can still passably sight-read a series of pieces, music means nothing to her. He can hear it in her playing. It is absent all feeling.

K. does not condemn her for that. How could he?

She is not a bad mother. Not at all.

He cannot imagine a better one. Perhaps he is lacking in imagination.

His parents met one another early in their lives. She is the daughter of a doctor. After their marriage, she becomes a housewife and mother. Her task is to raise and tend to the well-being of her children, and she is devoted in her attention to those things.

She only wants the best for everyone. Yet an escape from the hell of good intentions is difficult.

She arranges the necessary tutoring so that the three of them are always among the best in their classes.

She gets up in the morning and gets them ready for the day and for bed in evening.

She cooks the meals whenever the children return home from school or sports and are hungry.

She takes them shopping for new shoes when their old ones have grown too small.

She tends to their wounds whenever K. or one of his siblings falls down and hurts themselves.

Still, he finds her strange.

As she does him.

He can sense this and does not know why.

That she cares so much only makes it worse.

If only she would at least neglect him or visibly favor the two siblings.

But she does not.

It must be his fault.

He is an imposition.

For his siblings.

For his parents.

And, yes, also for himself.

Mother and son are like two instruments created to harmonize with one another, but they do not. One of them is out of tune.

His mother is equally strict with everyone. She makes the same demands of all three of them. She endeavors for fairness, but nothing in families is distributed equally or fairly—not talents, not feelings, not recognition.

Not signs of affection. Not signs of distaste. Not love.

K. plays the final chords of the Schubert sonata. The notes float through the room until even the last of them has quietly disappeared through the closed windows.

K. sees the joy on his father's face.

His mother is sitting next to him, still expressionless. She comes across as if she had not noticed the music had stopped.

Or even begun.

They are an unequal couple sitting beside one another in the first row. With three unequal children.

His family sits before him.

He has no other.

K. cannot understand why he still does not feel a sense of belonging.

I scrolled back to the beginning, read the texts a second time, put my phone on the table, and stared at the wall for a few minutes.

K.'s world.

I couldn't say it was mine.

I had no siblings.

I had no family, not even one to which I felt I didn't belong.

I didn't play piano.

I'd never been to a concert hall.

Brahms' violin concerto meant nothing to me.

Nor did his second symphony.

And yet.

Many lines sounded like I'd written them.

I expressed my gratitude in a short message and asked whether I might read more some time.

I'd paid and set out for home when my phone vibrated a second time that evening.

Three new e-mails from Kento. In the first, he sent me a picture of a cloudless blue sky. Upon closer inspection, I spotted the faint outline of a full moon in the middle of the picture. In the second, a largish file was attached. In the third, he apologized for the length of the texts. I was not to feel obligated, please, to read them or reply to them.

Whatever he'd sent me I didn't want to look at alone in my apartment. Near La Grande Illusion was a sake bar where I liked to sit by myself and drink sake.

The young man behind the bar recognized me and greeted me with an amiable nod. Several customers were sitting at the counter. I holed up on a bench in the farthest corner and ordered a glass of my favorite sake. I still hesitated, looking around first to be sure. The waiter brought the sake and filled my glass. For a moment, I was overcome with doubts about whether I wanted to enter K's world another time.

I drank the first glass in small sips and ordered a second.

Then I opened the attachment.

18

From K.'s World

K.'s brother is outside the door. He is trying to gain entry to the apartment with the key, but K.'s is stuck in the lock from the inside, jamming it.

He rings the doorbell. K. does not answer.

He knocks. "Kento, are you there?"

K. stands behind the door as if frozen and does not budge. For a fleeting moment, he is glad to hear the familiar voice.

"We're worried."

"You don't need to be," K. answers.

"Then open up."

"No."

"Please."

K. does not recall his brother ever having said "please" for something. "No."

His brother rattles the door, but not in a way to suggest he wants to gain forcible entry. He would not manage that without tools either; it was too stable for that. It sounds more like he was trying to lend weight to his request. "Why not?"

"I can't."

"What's so hard about opening a door."

"You wouldn't understand."

"No, I wouldn't. Why won't you at least answer the phone?"

"I need to be alone."

"We've known for a long time that you didn't pass the entrance exam. It's not so bad. Mama says you should try another conservatory. Or try again next year. Then you'll make it for sure."

"Leave me alone. Please."

"What do you have against us?"

"Nothing."

"Then open up."

K. does not answer. His hand moves toward the key without wanting to. The cold metal between his fingers. He is torn. After a few seconds, he lowers his arm again.

"What did we ever do to you?"

Nothing, he wants to reply again, but it does not matter what he says in response. His brother will not understand him. He never has and never will. They are wasting their time.

"Tell me what's going on." His brother is finding it increasingly difficult to suppress his anger. This, too, he knows well.

"What do you mean 'what's going on'?"

"We haven't heard from you in almost two months," his brother retorts, upset. "You don't answer the phone. You don't reply to texts, and you don't respond to e-mails." His rage resembles an earthquake that shakes the ground. K. can feel it from under the door. Like in the past when he would stand outside the bathroom and K. would not open up. His brother had not ever tolerated it when one of his siblings defied his will. "And now you ask, 'What do you mean what's going on?' Come on, are you nuts?"

K. makes no reply.

His brother huffs. "How can you even be so full of yourself, I wonder? Everything always revolves around you and your feelings. Where do you get that? Not from us. No one in the family is even remotely as full of themselves as you are."

He pauses for a moment to catch his breath. "Listen. If it were up to me, I wouldn't be here. You know I've got bigger fish to fry since Fukushima. If it were up to me, you could do what you wanted here. I don't care one bit if you hole up in your apartment in shame, never leave the house, and turn into a hikikomori or not. That's your problem. That's got nothing to do with me.

"But Mama and Papa sent me. They do care. Papa hardly sleeps anymore from worry. They want to know how you are doing. Is that so difficult to understand?"

"No," he whispered, resting his forehead against the door. His heart was thumping, his cheeks burning, his knees trembling. Out of shame, he would have loved to go up in smoke. Like hot steam that simply vanishes in seconds without a trace.

Why can't he be the person he wants to be?

Why can't he be how others want him to be?

How can you live, how can you like yourself if you are not the way you would like to be, because you are not allowed to be the way you would most like to be? He wonders.

"What am I supposed to tell them?"

That they do not need to worry about him, he wants to reply, knowing it would be dumb. Of course they worry, and what is worse: they seek the fault in themselves. They think they have done something wrong, and they blame themselves: each other, and themselves individually. But it is not their fault. They have done everything right. He is solely to blame. For everything. For his breakdown. For his ineptitude. For his failure.

He is a horrible burden.

"That everything's okay. That I'm doing well."

"They won't believe a word I say. If everything were okay, you'd answer the telephone and tell them yourself, you coward!"

"Tell them I'm sorry."

Now his brother is silent.

"Tell them I'm very sorry; that I apologize to them. I know I'm making them very sad. I know I disappoint them, but I can't help it. You hear me? I. Can't. Help.

It." He says these last words so loudly that he is immediately embarrassed.

"Tell them yourself."

"I can't."

"Of course you can," his brother hisses back. "You just don't want to."

Of course he does not understand him. If he did, he would not be standing outside his door now.

"Then tell them to leave me alone. That I don't want to hear from them again and want nothing to do with them. That I don't want to see them and that I don't want to talk to them. That they're too much for me. Always have been and always will be. You got all that? Is that better?"

He hears his heavy breathing on the other side of the door. He sees him there before him, his older brother, who may be half a head shorter but is so much stronger. For whom nothing was ever too much. Who passed every exam. Who became a doctor like their father. Who has never disappointed their parents and never would, either.

They stand facing one another in silence: not a single meter and yet many worlds apart. Minutes pass.

His brother's impatience. His anger. He envisions them as gooey green slime oozing beneath the door. It reeks of sweat and forms bubbles which explode with a loud pop, leaving vile green spatter on the floor. Perhaps he would let him in, K. thinks, if he would not harass him, if he gave him the time he needed. An hour, or even two. The afternoon. The rest of the day.

Perhaps.

Probably not.

His brother is about to leave, but that would mean having to return to Nara without having seen K. How to explain that to his parents? To his mind, it would feel like a defeat. A defeat by K. of all people.

He hears him curse. He shifts his weight from one foot to the other, wavering. He pounds on the door with the palm of his hand. Once. Twice. He utters another curse, and then his footsteps slowly recede into the distance.

Someone in K. wants to open the door. Someone in him wants to run after him and shout: don't go. Take me with you. Please, don't leave me here alone.

But this Someone has long since lost his voice.

He brings nothing but disaster.

He is an imposition, for himself and for others, and he always will be.

I needed a short break and laid my phone on the table. For the first time, I began to realize how far Kento had gone in my presence, the effort it must have cost him to talk with me, to see me, to write me an e-mail. Nothing was self-evident.

I sipped my sake and kept reading:

Message to his parents:

"I'm sorry.

I am neither the son you wished for, nor the one you deserve.

I have disappointed you, and I apologize.

It is all entirely my fault."

He does not get farther. These are the words that have been circulating through his head for weeks, this is what he wants to tell them, but now that he has written it down and sees it on the screen, something within him balks.

He reads them over and over and cannot figure out what about them is wrong.

Still, he cannot send them.

His father is dead.

In the morning he saw and listened to his brother's messages.

The first was ten days old, the most recent one two hours. Between them lay a dozen missed calls and voice messages he does even begin to listen to.

His father has likely already been cremated, his urn interred in the family gravesite. His mother, his siblings, and his two uncles will have stood at the crematorium beside his mortal remains, picking his father's bone fragments from the ashes with chopsticks and placing them into the urn, just as they had done together years ago for his grandmother.

K. is familiar with the funeral ceremony.

Now he had missed it.

He must find his own way to say goodbye.

K. wants to return the call.

He would like to hear a familiar voice, but which one exactly? His sister's, his brother's, his mother's? None of these, he thinks, but the one he would like to hear does not exist anymore.

All day long he holds the telephone in his hand.

It is impossible.

What should he talk about?

He has no words for what he feels.

He has no words for what he thinks.

He is a wordless bubble in danger of bursting at any moment.

Two questions plague him: What did his father die of? Is he to blame?

Was it disappointment at his son's most recent failure?

That is probably not how anyone would ever put it because some truths cannot be captured in words.

They would think it, and he would be able to tell by looking at them: in every glance, in every gesture.

He would hear it, in their voices, in every unspoken sentence.

He remains in bed and will not get up again.

Never again.

. . .

The next morning, I did something I found exceedingly unpleasant and which I had never done in all my years, not even during my mother's illness. I called the office and asked for a last-minute day off. There were urgent family matters that demanded my attention.

Takahashi-san was audibly surprised, despite his attempts not to let it show. I apologized profusely and promised to stay longer the next day and the complete the work I had neglected by the end of the week at the latest.

"K. K." was the name listed on his buzzer. The building entrance was open, so I climbed the stairs to the second floor. Kento's apartment was in the same corridor as the yoga studio.

I waited outside the door and listened. A woman's voice emanated from the yoga room. Somewhere, a telephone was ringing. Everything was quiet behind the door to the apartment. I thought of his brother, for whom he hadn't opened the door.

I wondered whether it wasn't a mistake simply to show up at his door like this.

He was a hikikomori.

He probably thought I hadn't seen his texts.

He probably thought I didn't understand.

I buzzed anyway.

Not a peep from behind the door.

I waited.

Eventually, I heard footsteps. "Who's there?" he asked with a bleary voice.

"It's me."

"Oh." Silence. "What do you want?"

I had no answer to that. I'd followed a feeling, not my reason.

"Why are you here?" His voice sounded neither brusque nor unfriendly. More surprised, uncertain, disheartened.

"I...I'd like to talk to you."

"Ah...hmm...what about?

To this I also had no good answer. Maybe I didn't actually want to talk to him, I thought, maybe I just wanted to be in his company.

"I don't know," I admitted. "Nothing specific."

"It's, uh...now's not the right moment. It's really not. Please excuse me."

"When would be better for you?"

"Uh, well...maybe tomorrow night. Or better yet, next week some time."

I stared at the brown wooden door separating us, at its handle, its lock.

"I'm embarrassed to just surprise you like this. It's very rude, I know."

"Uh huh."

"I definitely didn't intend to bother you. I just wanted to..." I found it impossible to complete the sentence.

On the other side of the door, I could hear him breathing heavily. I regretted having come.

"I'm very sorry," I said. "Please forgive me."

"I'm sorry too," he whispered. "You're not bothering, not at all, but it's still impossible."

After pausing, he added, even more softly: "Maybe later, another time."

Although I knew I should leave, I dragged out the moment. A woman my age exited the yoga studio and regarded me with surprise. She was wearing black tights, looking very athletic. "Nobody lives there."

I nodded, but made no move to leave.

"That apartment's been empty for a while," she said. "Some sort of hikikomori lived there once. The whole hallway reeked. Disgusting. He moved out or died, not sure which. As far as I know, though, the apartment isn't for rent."

I nodded again and still didn't move.

The woman looked at me with a mix of astonishment and distrust. We stood there in silence, and eventually she shrugged and left.

"Please go," I heard Kento whisper behind the door.

"I'm really very sorry," I repeated softly, turning away, and slowly crept down the long corridor toward the stairwell.

I stood outside the building on the street, indecisive. Across the way was a konbini, where I bought myself an iced green tea, leaned against the wall, and wrote Kento an e-mail. I offered another apology for my intrusiveness.

Where are you? he promptly responded.

Outside your building

I looked up at his window and for a brief moment saw the curtains peek open a bit. His narrow face appeared behind them.

Our eyes met. I raised my hand, signaling a tentative wave, and the curtains closed again.

I waited and wondered how long I intended to stand here. Kento only ever left his house late at night, if at all, and it would be hours until then.

For the first time, as the clock ticked away, I felt a sort of infuriation toward him. If he didn't want to talk to me, he shouldn't have given me any insight into "K.'s World." He sought out contact with me, but only on his terms. I was always afraid of being too much for him or asking the wrong questions. I wondered if it were even possible to be friends with a hikikomori.

Nevertheless, I continued waiting.

I thought of Hachikō, the dog who would show up to a certain train station exit in Shibuya every day at the same time, waiting there in vain for his long-dead owner. In memory of his loyalty, they'd built a monument to him outside the station, a dog in bronze.

I was imagining what a monument to Waiting Akiko would look like when my phone vibrated.

A FaceTime call from Kento.

I dug my earbuds out of my pocket and stuck them into my ears.

19

HIS HAIR WAS WET. IT LOOKED LIKE HE'D SHOWERED and in his haste hadn't really dried it properly.

"Hi." He waved awkwardly at the camera.

"Hi."

"I just wanted to say that I won't be leaving the house again today. I'm feeling a bit unwell."

"I'm sorry to hear that." I was glad to see him, even if only on the small display of my cellphone, and wondered if I could cheer him up with something.

"If you want, I could show you on my phone what Shimokita looks like in the early evening. We could take a walk together."

"That, uh … I'd really like that."

I rotated the camera and started off. We walked down the street toward the train station. It was full of pedestrians, many of them out for a stroll to browse vintage stores while others were shopping for dinner. I endeavored to keep the camera steady and not pan back and forth too quickly. I showed him the display windows of some secondhand shops, the showcases of a small bakery with its fruit tartlets and colorfully decorated doughnuts. Outside a grocery store were stands of crates containing fresh fruits and vegetables. Mangos from Okinawa were in season; they looked delectable. A torrent of people walked toward us, scarcely one of them taking notice of me. I had the camera scan from left to right while I watched Kento. At quite a few points, his eyes widened, and his mouth stood agape. Again and again I could hear a soft "ahh" and "ohh."

We did not exchange a single word the entire time.

I walked with him to Sarutahiko Coffee, where men and women our age sat behind the large windows, almost all of them occupied with their phones. Beside the café stood a public piano, where a young man played what sounded like a piece by Erik Satie. I'd have liked to stop, but I wasn't sure how Kento would feel and so continued onward. We crossed the square, and a woman overtook us on her bike, a small child in a bike seat. I turned right into a small alley beyond a construction site.

"Isn't this where your mother's bar is?" Kento asked suddenly.

"That's right. To the right behind the parking lot up ahead."

"Do you ever go there for a drink now and again?"

His question took me by surprise. "Uh...no."

"Would you like to?"

I thought about it. "Maybe... yeah, I would. I walked past it a few days ago, but I haven't had the nerve to go inside. Too much history."

Kento asked me to rotate the camera again. He'd tied his hair back into a ponytail and was tilting his head slightly, which he often did when he was pondering something. "Would it be different if I came along?"

"How do you mean?"

"Not in person, of course, more like this now. You could show me the bar from the inside, and we could pretend I'm sitting next to you."

"Hmm." I imagined holing myself up at the little table in the back corner and having Kento at my side on FaceTime.

"Why not. We could try sometime."

"Why not now?"

I checked the time. The bar opened at six p.m., and it was a little after half past seven. It was probably still empty. "I don't know. Are you sure?"

"It's up to you. I can't answer that question for you."

The temptation was great—the fear of overwhelming him or me or us both no less so.

The glowing red lettering of La Grande Illusion was easy to see in the breaking dusk. With her French wine bar, my mother had fulfilled a dream. The place was at the foot of the train tracks between Higashi-Kitazawa and Shimokitazawa Stations in an unassuming flat-roofed building. There were four other bars alongside it, none of them larger than twenty square meters. Her neighbors served whiskey, shōchū, and cocktails: my mother wine, beer, and liqueurs from France. For weeks, we'd scoured flea markets and junk shops in Tokyo in our search for suitable decorations. We bought Gitanes ashtrays, purchased Pernod water carafes, and haggled a long time for a film poster of *Le Fabuleux Destin d'Amélie Poulain*. Shortly before the grand opening, I also found a cover of *Paris Match* from 1990 featuring Isabelle Adjani, enlarged into a poster. It was incredibly expensive; I spent nearly my entire savings on it, had it framed, and gave it to her. She was very happy.

In the evenings, we'd sit together, thinking about the right name. My suggestions didn't go over particularly well. Liberté was too terse for her; it sounded more like a newspaper than a bar. Chez Masako she found ridiculous. Montmartre wouldn't work at all, nor would Paris Bar. La Vie en Rose and La Grande Illusion were her favorites, but she was afraid both were too long.

In the end, she opted for La Grande Illusion, and for a great deal of money had the name installed above the door in red neon lettering.

The day of her grand opening, a few curious customers from the other bars stopped in. Aside from them, it was very quiet, and she didn't have much to do during those initial months.

Over time, word got around among the somewhat older residents of Shimokita that La Grande Illusion offered very good wine at reasonable prices, and little by little, a group of regular clientele grew from whom my mother was able to eke out a modest living.

The door stood open, beside it a small wooden bench my mother had bought not long after the opening. She'd sit there from time to time smoking when no customers came. Inside, a French chanson was playing that I didn't know.

My heart pounding, I entered the establishment.

A man sat at the bar conversing with the proprietor. She offered me a friendly welcome and didn't recognize me right away. I took a seat in the very back at the small table and ordered a glass of red wine from Languedoc despite it not especially being to my taste. It was, however, the wine my mother had liked to drink.

Hanging above the bar were a few French pennants, on the wall beside me a photograph of the French national soccer team, and next to that another of Kylian Mbappé. Hardly anything had changed otherwise: the same walls painted in dark red, the wood-paneled bar, the antique chandelier with its many crystal orbs and pendants, in which still only three lightbulbs were burning.

The owner brought my wine. I saw my mother standing behind the bar and the customers in conversation. I saw her smoking. I saw her laughing.

Kento held a glass of water, and we clinked, to the extent possible via a screen, while he eyed me anxiously.

"I'm doing okay," I said, putting him at ease. "Thanks for accompanying me."

He nodded in relief. "Can I see the place?"

I rotated the camera again, slowly moving my phone over a panorama and hoping that Kento was getting a good impression of the atmosphere in the bar.

"Who's the man on the poster next to you?"

I pointed the camera back at myself. "Kylian Mbappé. A famous French footballer. That wasn't hanging here before."

"Aha." He thought for a moment. "Why was your mother so taken with France?"

"I've often asked myself that too. The music, maybe. She loved chansons. The wine. The literature. She read a ton of French authors. Probably a mixture of many things. But why exactly I don't know."

"Was she ever there?"

I shook my head. "I believe it was her dream to travel to Paris one day."

We sat for a while in silence. I drank my wine and scooted a bit more into the glow of a floor lamp so that I wasn't sitting in the dark so much. The customer and the proprietor were deep in conversation and paid no attention to me.

Kento refilled his water. "What do you do actually, if I may ask?"

"I work in the accounting department at an ad agency."

"You're an accountant?" He sounded as if I'd said I drove a taxi or refilled the coolers and shelves in a konbini.

"Is that bad?"

"Uh...no...of course not."

"I audit statements of travel expenses. I pay invoices. Issue invoices. Prepare tax documents and now and again help out in payroll accounting, which is where I started. It's not a particularly challenging job, nor is it very stimulating, if I'm being honest, but I like it."

"What do you like about it?"

"I know exactly what I have to do. I'm good at it. The job doesn't pose me any great challenges. My coworkers are nice. The biggest disadvantage is that I'm forced to stay at the office very late, but everyone who works in a large firm has to do that anyway."

He shook his head in disbelief.

"Why does that surprise you?"

"I was sure you were a writer."

"Oh," I blurted out. "Where'd you get that idea?"

"'Koko was a very normal cockroach. She had a mother, a brother, and a sister. She did not have a father.'"

I stared at my screen in surprise. Kento was grinning somewhat sheepishly. If I wasn't mistaken, those were the first two lines of an essay I'd written in junior high school and for which I'd won a prize. I laughed in embarrassment. "Why do you still know the beginning of 'Koko, the Fatherless Cockroach'?"

"'To be precise: she of course had a father—everyone had a father—but she didn't know hers,'" he continued. "'She shared this fate with her siblings, but it didn't seem to bother them. It did Koko, though. And so she began her search for him. She scurried rapidly through the cellar and ran into a mouse. Are you my father? Koko asked the mouse.'" Kento paused briefly. "Shall I go on?"

"Are you reading from something, or do you know it by heart?"

"By heart."

"All five pages?"

He nodded.

"I can't believe it."

When he started quoting the next few lines, I put him off. "That was fifteen years ago. Why do you remember the story word for word?"

"Because Koko's search for her father meant a great deal to me at the time. I asked Ishiguro-*sensei* to make me a copy. I still look at it occasionally today. It's one of the loveliest fables I've ever read."

I was so shocked that I fell speechless. The possibility that something I'd written could be of significance for another person had never crossed my mind before.

"'Yikes the bolt of lightning,'" Kento began, "'was a flash of lightning who didn't want to flash. That was more than unusual for a lightning bolt.'"

"You remember that too?"

Kento nodded. "But only the first couple pages. I used to know it by heart from beginning to end. I haven't read it in a long time."

"You . . . you were the only one in our class who liked my stories."

"You're fooling yourself."

"The others always just teased me about them."

"Because they were envious."

"I can't imagine that being true."

"That's how it was though. I heard them talking about your essays behind your back. They'd never have admitted to your face how good they thought they were. I wasn't the only one who wanted to have copies of Koko. Back then, I sat next to Eriko. She cried when she read Koko aloud. So did Naomi."

I kept shaking myself in disbelief. In junior high school, we'd had a young Japanese teacher, Ishigurosensei, who was enthusiastic about my essays. The way I wrote and my imagination, she said, were remarkable, quite extraordinary, not just for my age. Three of my essays were read over the school's loudspeaker, two others hung up on the bulletin board. While that earned me the recognition of my teacher and some of her colleagues, I had the feeling with my classmates that it only made me more of an outsider. They laughed at me, and for a while, they'd only call me "Koko the cockroach."

"I was convinced you'd become a writer. Absolutely sure. I always used to check the Internet to see when your first book was coming out."

"Are you joking, or are you being serious?"

"Very serious! It wasn't just that you could write very well; unlike the other students who won awards for their essays, you had stories to tell."

His words flattered me. I didn't want him to notice and lowered my eyes. In that moment, I was glad he wasn't sitting next to me. At the same time, I was sorry he wasn't. "That was a long time ago," I said quietly.

"Does that matter? You've either got imagination, or you don't. That's not something someone can learn, so it's also not something someone can unlearn. You have a special gift." He took a sip of his water. When he continued, he spoke almost at a whisper, which made it difficult for me to understand him. "Do you remember what K. was told by his father? His talent is a gift, and with this gift comes a responsibility. He doesn't have the right to squander it."

Hearing these lines from Kento's lips was disconcerting. What's gotten into you? I wanted to ask. You weren't able to live up to that responsibility either. It must have cost him a great deal of effort to remind me of his father's admonition. That was another topic entirely, though.

"I have no gift," I countered instead.

Kento's expression signaled sincere astonishment. "Do you really believe that?"

"I'm sure of it."

"Huh. I don't get it. Did you ever try to publish something and you got rejected?"

I shook my head.

"Why not?

That was a good question for which I had no ready answer. "I likely lack the courage to try."

The thought of writing something that anyone who wanted to could read and then also peddle their opinion about on the Internet was excruciating to me. In the second year of high school, I had a Japanese teacher, an old man, who was about to retire and who didn't like my papers. He found them poorly written and their contents downright repugnant, he declared to the class. They were examples of how we should *not* write. What the young woman teacher had praised, he criticized as unsuccessful and hubristic. One morning, he came to class and read one of my essays aloud and made fun of it line by line. I still recall how I blushed and felt shame. The whole class stared at me. They laughed. Not everyone, but most of them. My face burned, and my hands shook. It cost me the entirety of my strength not to cry, and still a few tears ran down my cheeks, which did not impress the old man.

It'd been the moment of my greatest humiliation, and I'd sworn never to write anything and show it to others again, save for the requisite school papers and essays.

My work as an accountant was even more boring and monotonous than I'd portrayed it to Kento; the world of numbers was predictable, hadn't the slightest thing to do with me, and didn't make demands of me. That's precisely why I chose it for myself. It was the right choice.

"The nail that sticks out gets hammered down," was a well-known Japanese saying. In school, I'd heard it often enough and had known good and well who in class had been its intended addressee. At university in Tokyo and now at the office, I'd tried everything not to be this lone nail anymore.

"Do you not write anymore at all?"

"Just in my journal."

"No stories?"

"No, not really."

He let out an audible sigh. "Why not?"

"Because...because I don't have time." Now I did wish he was sitting next to me. As good as it did me to hear his voice and see him on my phone, the image of a person on a screen was the image of a person on a screen and always would be. Kento was sitting in his apartment a few blocks away. It wasn't the same. Everything else was an illusion.

"Is it really only a question of time?"

"Maybe it just isn't important enough to me."

"I honestly can't imagine that to be true."

"It is, though," I claimed.

"When was the last time you read what you wrote back then?"

"Not since we moved to Tokyo."

"Seriously?"

"Yup."

"So...the author of Koko doesn't read her own stories anymore. Correct?"

"Correct." I sipped my wine and mulled it all over. This evening was riling me up. In conversations with myself, I could ignore questions I didn't have any answers to, but not with Kento.

"Perhaps I'd like to leave everything connected to my time in Nara behind me. My new life in Tokyo should have as little as possible to do with my old life. My journals and short stories from before are stored away in a box in my wardrobe." I was quite obviously disappointing him, but I couldn't help that.

"And ever since I've been working, I haven't really had any time during the week. I'm rarely at home before nine p.m. and too exhausted on the weekend to do a lot, much less write something." I wasn't in the mood to tell him about the many short stories I'd thought up over the past few weeks and written down. It might've been different if he'd been sitting next to me. I was even less intent on mentioning that the thought of writing a book had occurred to me more than once during that period, and I tried not to let it gain much purchase.

"And if you had time?"

"I don't," I shot back, more loudly and intensely than I'd wanted. "Why should I think about things that might be if I had more time if I don't have it? It's not like I can quit. What would I live off of? In my case, the question 'what if' leads nowhere. Things are the way they are. Shikata ga nai."

"Most stories begin with the question 'what if,' don't they?"

"Hm...yeah. Maybe I don't write anymore because I don't want to ask myself that question."

Silence. I felt as if we'd argued. Another one of my mother's favorite chansons warbled from the speakers, and my mood was in danger of tanking once and for all. I sighed and bit my lips.

"Would you excuse me for a moment, please?" Kento asked suddenly. "I've got to take care of something and will call you back in a few minutes. Will you wait?"

"Yes."

He ended the call, and I stared at the black display. The significance my stories had for him moved me. Without my suspecting it at the time, I'd created with my texts little islands for him, and apparently also for other classmates, just as I'd found for me in the public library.

The owner came over and asked if I wanted something else to drink. I ordered a second glass of wine. Now she did recognize me, and we spoke a bit about my mother, and I thanked her for having made so few changes in the bar.

Two new guests arrived, and she turned her attentions to them.

I thought of Kento, and the longer I sat alone at this table, the more I experienced a feeling of gratitude.

In spite of everything, I was grateful to him for asking me these questions.

I was grateful to him for listening to me and taking me seriously.

There was no other person I could imagine sitting with in this bar and having this kind of conversation, even if only on FaceTime.

He possessed the gift for getting me to talk, and I wondered how he managed that. It was not only his ability to listen. There was something else he possessed. I was searching for the right word. Authenticity. That was it.

Kento was Kento.

Maybe he wished he were different, but he never attempted to act like someone else. He couldn't have even if he'd wanted to. He was a hikikomori; he'd long ago given up trying to appeal to others or to conform to their wishes and expectations. He'd decided to be as he was; whether he'd done so voluntarily or not didn't matter to me at this point.

He didn't want to deceive anyone.

He didn't try to maintain any pretense.

He didn't wear a mask.

He didn't live behind a façade.

He lived in a cage or behind a high wall, but not behind a façade.

He wouldn't have even been in a position to erect one. In my world, that made him something special. He radiated a guilelessness and an honesty I knew in no other person. With him, I was sure I'd never be tricked.

Kento was genuine.

After a quarter of an hour, I looked at my phone to see whether I'd missed his call.

When I looked up, I saw his silhouette in the doorway.

The owner invited him to come inside; he said nothing, nor did he move.

I stood up quickly and went to him. "Hi...what are you doing here?"

Uneasy, he looked past me into the bar. I pointed to the bench outside the door, and we sat down.

"I was not expecting you."

"It's really much too early in the day for me, but..."

"You surprised me."

"Is that good or bad."

"Good, very good. I'm happy to see you."

"We've seen each other the whole time."

"True, but that was different, don't you think?"

Kento thought about it, clinging to the bench with both hands, his legs bobbing up and down. "Hm. Yeah, probably..."

"Would you like something to drink?"

He shook his head. "I'm not thirsty." It sounded like: I'm in a hurry. The red neon light from La Grande Illusion spilled onto his face. It looked like he'd applied a much too heavy rouge.

A man and a woman, both staggering, exited the bar next door. Kento observed them warily, his torso bent forward slightly; he looked like he might shove off and run away at any moment.

"Your questions gave me food for thought."

"Is that good or bad?" he repeated.

"Good, I think. Right?"

"Then I'm glad." He shot me a quick look and tilted his head slightly. "What's up with your wedding preparations?"

"Another good question. Well, at the moment, I'm in the middle of getting to know the bride better—or the groom, depending on which perspective you see it from."

"I see."

"I don't want to marry anyone whom I don't know very well and don't like a lot."

I smiled, and he smiled back.

"I see," he said again. "That's definitely a good idea."

"It may still take some time," I added, ruminating.

Voices emanated from the bar onto the street. Another few customers had come. My mother would be glad.

"I like the name of the bar," Kento said abruptly.

"So do I."

"How did she come up with it?"

"I think it's a reference to an old French film with that title. Which she really liked. But I'm not sure."

I drank a sip of my wine. Kento kept his eyes glued to our surroundings and slid restlessly back and forth on the bench.

"Shall we leave?"

"That's up to you."

I paid, and we set out for home. When we passed the public piano next to Sarutahiko Coffee, Kento paused briefly. It was now covered in a tarp, but its contours were still clearly recognizable. He hesitated for a moment, then continued onward.

I accompanied him up to his building and thanked him for the evening.

"May I ask you for something? Could you send me a haiku from time to time?"

"I can go upstairs real fast and get the book. I'm happy to lend it to you."

"Thanks. But I find it'd be nicer if you read them aloud. Only if it isn't too much for you, of course."

I hadn't yet made it home when I received a short voice message.

"In Kyoto too
a yearning for Kyoto
Cuckoo cuckooing

"That's by Master Bashō.

"Goodnight."

I quite liked it, fetched my notebook, and transcribed it on the last page.

I was too churned up to go to bed. I turned on all the lights, had a seat in my small kitchen, stood up, sat down again, got up once more, and prowled through the apartment. I didn't have time to write, I'd claimed. But wasn't time a question of priorities?

What work I did and where I did it were my decisions.

Could I reduce my hours? I knew of no one at the firm who'd done that, not even colleagues with children, and I could imagine Takahashi-san's perplexed face were I to ask him for a part-time position. But I also hadn't tried to either. That, too, was my choice.

From the wardrobe, I fished out the box containing my journals and short stories. The three tales to receive school honors were on top. I immediately skimmed the first one about Koko.

For a fourteen-year-old, I had in fact written it amazingly well; it featured idiosyncratic turns of phrase, and I sensed why my teacher, Kento, and a few others might have liked it so much.

I pulled one of the last bottles of red wine that had belonged to my mother from the crate in the corridor, opened it, and gave myself a generous pour.

What if it were true and I actually possessed a gift?

The gift of storytelling, of fantasizing, of dreaming, whatever I wanted to call it.

If I did, I'd severely neglected it during my time in Tokyo, for whatever reason.

If.

What if…

Kento was right. That's how all stories began.

What if I were braver.

I was only able to find out by attempting to be so.

Or was I taking myself too seriously?

Probably.

Certainly.

At once, I was overcome by a guilty conscience.

But why not?

I had no parents and no siblings, no grandparents and no uncles and aunts whose expectations I needed or wanted to meet.

I had no child that needed to be cared for.

I owed nothing to anyone and was only responsible for myself.

I was free.

The thought was a grand one and, with every second I granted it space, got bigger.

It intimidated me.

"Those who know no freedom will perish in it," Kento had written.

What if he were mistaken?

What if... I gave my notice at the firm and wrote a book with short stories? About the woman with the red scarf on the Yamanote Line, for instance.

About the train conductor who always rides this line because he encounters the spirit of his dead father here and wanted to hear from it that he'd meant something to him.

Or a spirit who's been waiting between Ueno and Aki-habara Stations for twenty years to see his wife again to tell her how much he'd loved her. Before his death, she'd always taken the 7:38 train on this line to work in Ueno.

The Spirits of Yamanote, I could call it.

I found a piece of paper and, without delay, wrote a sentence down that had just occurred to me or that I'd had in my mind for a very long time—I wasn't exactly sure which.

I regarded it, read it aloud to myself. It sounded good.

I added a second sentence, regarded that, read it aloud to myself. I liked it too.

I pondered: I hadn't yet touched my mother's life insurance policy.

Naoko had suggested I fulfill a wish with a small portion of the money: a beautiful Louis Vuitton handbag, for example.

I'd waved her off.

A trip to Hawaii or Bali or Europe? Something for the apartment? A pair of shoes from Gucci or Prada?

I'd have liked to go on a lengthy trip, but I lacked the time to do so. At my firm, no one in my position took more than a week of vacation.

Isn't there anything you need? she'd wondered.

I couldn't think of a thing.

Or something to treat yourself with?

Yeah, of course, I'd replied, but nothing I'd need two, three, or four hundred thousand yen for: more like trifles I could afford as it is.

If that were the case, she envied me, she declared. I was perfectly happy.

Which is not how I'd have phrased it.

Grabbing a pen and a piece of paper, I began writing down every possible expense: rent, groceries, shopping, extras like going out to eat, books, cosmetics. If I lived modestly and earned a little on the side with odd jobs, the money would last at least two years, probably even three, depending on how frugal I was—roughly speaking. Naturally, it'd be bound up with uncertainties. I could fall ill. Need an expensive operation. My landlord could terminate my lease, forcing me to move. None of that was especially probable, though in principle not outside the realm of possibility.

I could afford to quit my job.

I could take time for myself.

I could ponder a third sentence in peace. And a fourth...

Until my conversation with Kento, the thought had been so absurd it'd never even occurred to me.

As if it'd been lurking somewhere inside me, waiting to be found.

Like the seeds of a sunflower buried in the dirt for ages that all of a sudden begin to sprout.

I imagined what it'd be like not having to go to the agency every morning and not having to come home every night until nine or ten.

If I didn't have to add up numbers that held no interest for me, day after day.

If I had time for myself.

What would I do with that time if I couldn't think of a third sentence?

I imagined what it'd be like if I could just travel to France without having to ask for an extra-long vacation to do so.

If I didn't have to ask anyone for anything.

I considered whether my mother wouldn't have wanted that for me.

For a woman of her generation, her own biography had been quite out of the ordinary, not to mention for a woman in this country. Even for a woman my age.

She'd blazed her own trail without bothering about conventions and expectations, no matter if by design, by necessity, or owing to her circumstances.

She could've made other choices. I was convinced she'd understand me.

Whether she'd ever asked herself the question "what if?" I didn't know.

What if I'd never gotten pregnant with Akiko?

What if I'd visited Paris once?

What if...

I had an even harder time imagining how she might have answered those questions.

If I didn't write a book, or couldn't find a publisher for my book, or the publisher couldn't find readers for my book, and the money eventually ran out, I could go back to work in accounting for some large firm at any time. Probably not for one as highly regarded as SunSun Agency—more like at an agency for temps and at a lower salary—but accountants are always in demand.

The risk I was taking was only partly of a financial nature.

It bore a different name: La Grande Illusion.

On this evening, of course, my story would not begin.

But perhaps it could take a new turn, I thought.

Or a new chapter in this finite story would open.

With a simple sentence that sounded beautiful and right to my ears, and then a second, which a third would necessarily have to follow.

I drank another glass of the red wine I didn't actually like.

The next morning, my phone woke me at 6:50. I felt tired and worn down as though I'd worked through the night. Maybe I had too. The aftereffects of the alcohol made my body heavy. I stretched, and every movement hurt. Contrary to my usual habit, I remained lying in bed for a few minutes, staring at the ceiling and reflecting on the previous afternoon and evening.

I wondered whether Kento and I had met before in another life. I was no Buddhist, nor did I believe in reincarnation, but I felt an affinity and a familiarity with him that couldn't have originated in this life. For that to be true, we knew one another far too little.

But maybe it isn't only the question of how well we know someone that decides whether we feel close and connected to that person or not. Maybe, for some people, just a few moments are enough to produce a feeling of spiritual kinship. A smile. Silence at the right moment. A look, a sentence that touches us where no one else can.

On the way to the train station, I bought myself a cappuccino to go, and while I waited, I watched the pedestrians scurrying past me to the station in haste. For six years, I'd been one of them, and the idea of quitting all of a sudden seemed absurd to me. Lying in bed when others were sitting at work. Not knowing in the morning how to fill the hours until evening. No day would resemble the next.

Would I be able to endure that? Probably not. As boring as it may be, work gave my life substance, structure, and shape. I was needed. I was part of a community.

I didn't know what had gotten into me yesterday.

The platform was even more crowded than usual at this hour; a train had been canceled. The doors of the newly arrived Rapid Express opened in front of me, and I stood before a wall of human beings. I shoved my way inside, nevertheless, as others did after me. I could hear the soft groanings of people being squeezed too tightly. I could scarcely move my arms anymore. I felt the warmth of other bodies on mine and became part of a mute, submissive horde that shifted back and forth at every stop like water sloshing in a tub. It stank of sweat, of aftershave, and of a cloying perfume. At the subsequent stop, even more passengers shoved their way inside with such vehemence that the groaning around me grew louder. No one said a word. I was glad to be a few centimeters taller than most people around me, shut my eyes, inhaled and exhaled deeply, and counted the stations.

Four more.

Three more.

Two more.

What if ... is not a question that should concern me, I thought.

Nothing would happen if ...

20

"IS SOMETHING GOING ON BETWEEN YOU AND SATŌ-san or Nakagawa-san?" Naoko looked at me inquisitively.

"The guys from the creative department?" I shook my head vehemently.

"With both of them?" she whispered to me lewdly.

"Stop it, how could you even think that?"

"I've seen you all go out for lunch together occasionally. And just now they secretly gifted you a bottle of sake. I was keeping a close eye on that."

"They were saying thank you."

"What for?"

"Their campaign for the cosmetics firm won a competition for the best slogan."

"I know. 'The world is changing. Are you? Say 'I do' to you.' It's pretty genius too. But what's that got to do with you?"

They were saying thank you because I brought them dinner late at night, I'd normally have replied. Or because I kept them company at the office the evening before they submitted. Because we were goofing off together. A façade, I thought now. Everything's a façade.

Why should I lie to my best friend just to maintain appearances?

"I came up with it."

"You're nuts."

I shook my head.

"I don't believe it. What've you got to do with the creative department?"

"Nothing. I help the two of them from time to time when they're stuck. We go out to eat, they tell me what their campaign is about. Evidently, slogans are my thing. Sometimes I get an idea, sometimes I don't."

She regarded me with a wide-eyed stare and sincere astonishment, laughed, and took a large gulp of beer. "That's amazing. And the two of them don't say a word. Typical for men."

"But this stays between us."

"Why?"

"I wouldn't want anyone to find out. Not at the office or outside. Deal?"

Naoko mumbled "you've got to be kidding me" under her breath.

"This is important to me, please."

She nodded.

I raised my glass for a toast. "Promise?"

"Promise."

She threw me a glance as if pondering what all else she might not be able to put past me.

"If you don't have anything on with them, do you have a different lover?"

"Why do you ask?"

Naoko eyed me. "You've got to be having sex with somebody."

As was her manner, she again spoke so loudly that guests at neighboring tables could understand every word. In spite of the topic, it didn't matter to me today. Let the two women next to us listen and look over nosily.

"Do I?"

"You're twenty-nine!"

"Yes, and?"

"Your best years."

"Who says?"

"I do." She laughed. "We're the same age, and if I go two weeks without sex, I become insufferable."

"I know. I don't."

"I don't believe you."

"How come?"

"Because there's something called lust. Desire. Longing. Don't act like you've never heard of them before. They demand to be satisfied, in you as well as in me."

I shrugged noncommittally.

"It's fine if you don't want to talk about him."

"There's nobody," I now said myself louder than intended.

Naoko looked at me from the side. "In that case," she paused as if about to reveal a big secret to me, continuing

269

with a quieter voice, "I can introduce you to a super nice guy. A friend's ex. Two years older than us. Good-looking, doesn't talk much, and knows what he's doing…" She laughed suggestively. "I swear."

"Leave me alone."

She sighed. "I don't get how you…"

"Different people have different needs, don't they?" I interrupted. "When we go out drinking, you drink more than I do. When we go out to eat, you eat more than I do. Why shouldn't you also need more sex?"

"It's not the same thing," she maintained.

"Why?"

She thought about it. "Okay, maybe you're right. But there's a difference between more or less and none at all."

I knew she wasn't intending to be mean, but I still wasn't in the mood to continue discussing my nonexistent sex life with her in public. It wasn't a topic that interested me particularly.

"Nothing against solo sex," she insisted. "I had a solo wedding after all. But getting off by yourself every night also gets boring after a while, doesn't it?" She grinned at me.

"Depends…," I said with as wicked an expression on my face as possible, just because I wanted to see her amazed, curious look.

"Spill it!"

"You're getting on my nerves."

We drank a sip of our beers and sat in silence for a while. Naoko took a look around the izakaya, and I followed her gaze. Of the guests, there were only a few paired off, which I hadn't noticed before; at most tables, men and women sat among themselves, drinking sake or beer, immersed in conversation.

"What do you think of them?" Naoko pointed to two men leaning against the wall at the opposite end of the room, looking over at us. They might have been three or four years older than Naoko and me. One of them was a bit bigger and stronger, with a round face and short hair. The other seemed a little younger, was lankier, and had a conspicuously receding hairline. Like us, they were probably employees at one of the neighboring offices.

Even if I didn't know them, they seemed familiar. They didn't look any better or worse, any more or less intriguing or boring than most men I stood next to on the train when I went to work in the morning and came home again at night. The sight of them didn't disgust me, nor did I feel myself attracted to them. They didn't interest me as men, but the temptation was great to think up a story about them for myself.

I averted my gaze again quickly. "What am I supposed to think of them?"

"They look very nice, don't they? Not thrilling, I'll admit, but likeable. We could join them. I'll start a conversation, and if we like them, I know a love hotel right around the corner."

"You really are getting on my nerves."

"I'll take the burly one with the round face, if that's okay with you," she went on as though she hadn't heard me. "I like men with round faces. I'll go ahead, and you can join whenever."

271

Naoko made a move to stand up. I grabbed for her arm. "Stay here."

She turned around to me. "What are you so afraid of?"

"Why do you think I'm afraid? I just don't have any desire to sleep with a man I don't even know."

"You'd get to know him first."

I rolled my eyes and shook my head.

"If we don't like them, we'll drop it. We can get up and leave at any time. I know guys like this. It'll be perfectly fine by them. Believe me."

"I don't want to. Stop."

She sighed. "What's so bad about having a little bit of fun?"

"Nothing. But I wouldn't have fun."

"How do you know that?"

"Why do I have to justify myself for not needing to sleep with a man I've only known for two hours?"

"You don't have to justify anything, and you don't have to sleep with anyone you don't want. This is about creating opportunities for a fun night, and in the end, you get to decide what you want. It's very simple. Why does that upset you so much?" In her voice, there was neither irritation nor disappointment, more like mystification about my vehement reaction.

"Tell me instead how I'm supposed to know if I really care for someone."

"Why are you thinking of this question now?"

"No reason."

"It's something you feel."

"Where?"

"Here." Naoko put one hand on my left breast and the other on my stomach.

"And how do *you* know?"

"I read it somewhere."

We laughed.

"Not from experience?"

She stopped to think. "Definitely not. Too much intimacy isn't for me."

"Why not?"

"People who get too close to somebody else make themselves dependent on them. You know I hate that."

"Maybe it might be nice to depend on someone?"

"What's nice about that?"

I reflected, but despite lengthy contemplation, no persuasive answer came to mind.

Naoko ordered another two beers. I emptied my glass and sat in silence.

When was the last time I'd slept with a man? I considered the question for a moment. It'd been during my university studies. The year after the end of my relationship with Daisuke, I'd had two brief flings. The first had been with a fellow student. He was a year younger than me, and we'd sat next to one another in the lecture hall. He'd talked me up, we'd gone out a few times together, and eventually, he'd almost casually suggested going to his place. I'd agreed without exactly knowing why. I hadn't found him unlikeable or even ugly, but I was unable to say I harbored more than friendly affection for him or felt a great desire for him. He'd asked me, and I didn't want to be impolite or disappoint him. Maybe I also just thought this was part of being a twenty-two-year-old who dates a man for a few weeks.

As for the sex, he was even more inexperienced than I was. He tried to play that off with emphatic coolness, which only made it worse. When we undressed one another, he was nervous and awkward in his movements. Half naked, he disappeared into the bathroom for several minutes while I lay on the bed alone, wondering what I was even doing here. Just when I was about to get dressed and leave, he came back.

The whole time, I had the feeling I was standing beside myself watching us: the way he joined me on the bed, the way he tried to arouse me with abrupt and clumsy fondling, the way I let him do as he liked without reacting.

Everything happened very fast; not even an hour later, we were standing out on the street again. I'd hardly felt anything, lust or pain.

Perhaps he'd felt similarly. He didn't show up to the next lecture, and for the rest of the semester, he sat on the other side of the lecture hall and vanished right after class ended. Whenever we happened to run into one another in the corridor, we'd give each other a brief nod and lower our eyes in shame.

The sex that evening was akin to the experiences I'd had with Daisuke. He was my first boyfriend, I his second girlfriend, and we'd both been inexperienced lovers. The first few times were painful and not nice, and each time, I was glad when it was over. Eventually, we learned new things, and it began to be fun—for him more than me, which either he didn't notice or wasn't bothered by.

Daisuke wasn't the sort of person to think all that hard about the needs and wishes of others. Maybe that's why he'd fascinated me so much at the outset. The occasions on which we took our time and he aroused me so much that I forget everything else around me were rare and only nice in that moment. Afterward, I'd always feel uneasy, even while lying in his arms, as though I'd divulged something precious about myself, as though I'd lost control of myself and thereby crossed a line beyond which I had been very alone and very lonesome.

In the summer of that same year, a man at least ten years older approached me at an izakaya. I had sat down at the bar alone, drunk a beer, and had something to eat. He'd sat beside me and initiated a conversation. At first I found him pushy—I found the situation uncomfortable—and only answered his questions so as not to be rude. Soon, however, he made me laugh. He was witty and charming, handsome, and worked as a sales director at a large manga publisher that had printed two of my favorite series. Some of the illustrators and authors I enjoyed reading he knew personally, and he told me some pretty funny stories about them. We met up a few times, always at the same izakaya, drank a lot of sake, which he knew a lot about, and then, one evening, when he invited me to join him at a love hotel, I followed him without giving it much thought. The sake had made me bolder and more curious.

On the way there, he picked up a bottle of white wine and some snacks. The room had a large bathtub and a number of toys for stimulation. He asked if I wanted to watch porn with him, and I shrugged indecisively. Instead, we took a bath, and then he massaged me for a long time. He was an experienced lover who knew exactly what he was doing. He took plenty of time, pampering me in a way I'd never known. Even so, the whole time with him I also felt like I wasn't in my body, but instead floating beneath the ceiling like a spirit, observing us. I watched him undress me. I watched him kiss my breasts in the tub, watched his hands glide over my body, watched him caress me. Nothing he did made me uncomfortable, but I still couldn't surrender myself to him. Whether I wanted to or not: instead of enjoying his touch, I thought about my last class, my household chores, my mother's shopping list, a book I'd read.

I imagined what it'd be like if he were to stop right in the thick of things, as if we were in rehearsals for a play when the director suddenly comes on stage, shouting, interrupting us, telling us it's time to rehearse a different scene.

Let's stop, I wanted to say. This is all a big misunderstanding. We should get dressed, polish off the white wine, and leave. I'm really sorry, it's my fault.

But I was afraid to. I'd consented to go to a hotel with him, he was trying and doing nothing wrong, and to disappoint him now would've embarrassed me.

So I let him do what he wanted.

Afterward, I avoided the izakaya for a long time. When I visited it again months later, the barkeeper told me he hadn't seen my lover for a long time either.

That was six years ago.

I haven't had sex since.

I suspect my libido isn't particularly strong, and I don't feel like I'm suffering because of it or missing out on something. Once or twice a week, I pleasure myself, but that has little to do with lust. It feels more like a controlled release of pent-up energy, just like other people go for a run or lift weights at the gym to relax after a long day at the office.

That, too, happens less often. Most evenings, I'm too tired even for that.

"It's our first time here," I heard Naoko say.

The guy with the round face was standing before her. I'd been so lost in thought that I hadn't even noticed him walk over. His friend was still sitting at the table, smiling at us somewhat ashamedly across the bar. The guy invited us to have a beer with them. Naoko must've given him some sort of sign; I cannot imagine he'd otherwise have worked up the gumption simply to approach us like that. She looked at me inquiringly. I could tell how much she wanted to accept the invitation, and I didn't want to be a spoilsport. We picked up our things and followed him to the table where his colleague was waiting.

He stood up somewhat laboriously and bowed. His face had a slightly red tinge to it, though from alcohol or embarrassment I wasn't sure. His shyness appealed to me.

We took our seats, Naoko made a joke about us, and we laughed. I was impressed how easily she'd dispelled the initial awkward silence.

The shy one was called Obayashi-san and was a more pleasant and more interesting conversational partner than I'd suspected. His voice had a warm quality about it, he spoke in an unusual singsong, and I enjoyed listening to him.

The two worked for a French food conglomerate; he had studied literature for two semesters and had already been to Paris once.

Naoko ordered some more to eat and drink. This round was on us, she said. Her cheeks had reddened. Unlike me, she got red spots on her neck and face after the first glass of beer or wine. She was having a glorious time, and I was happy for her.

The earnestness with which Obayashi-san asked me questions reminded me of Kento. That made me uncomfortable.

I felt the beers, and I felt them making me more adventuresome.

I didn't want that.

Alcohol relaxed me, calmed me, gave me a lightness I didn't naturally possess. I liked the way it tasted, which is why I drank it, but there was a faint line before excess that I had to locate anew each time. If I crossed it, alcohol's effects could have unwanted consequences. *More doesn't help more*, my mother had always said.

Naoko winked at me encouragingly.

Obayashi-san told me about Paris and asked me if I'd been there before.

"That's her big dream," Naoko interjected.

What if...

Without intending to, I suddenly imagined what might happen if I immersed myself in a conversation with Obayashi-san. He might tell me things about Paris I found interesting and, in doing so, grow more likeable to me than I'd thought. I imagined us getting up at some point and going to a hotel with Naoko and the other guy, us entering a room, and him starting to undress me.

Images appeared in my mind I didn't want to see.

It was time for me to leave.

When I rose, the ground swayed for a moment. For a brief second, I believed it was an earthquake, yet Naoko and the other man kept on talking. Not one table, not one barstool slid back and forth, and neither the glasses nor the bottles on the bar clinked. I clung to the chairback, hoping the others didn't notice.

"Where are you off to?" Naoko asked.

"To the bathroom. I'll be right back."

"I'm coming with you." She stood up.

"Do you really want to leave me alone with the two of them?" she whispered to me on our way through the bar.

I nodded.

"They're game, the shy one too, I swear to you. We could get adjacent rooms and switch at some point if you didn't like yours..."

She was even more tipsy than I was, and grinning, and I couldn't be sure if she meant the suggestion seriously.

"I'm afraid I'm not the right person for that."

"Can you at least stay another half hour? Otherwise they might feel compelled to leave too. That'd be very unfortunate."

"I'd like to, but I think I've had too much to drink. I'm not feeling well. I'd like to go home."

She sighed.

When we returned, I excused myself from the two men on account of a headache and nausea. Obayashi-san thought it was because of him—I could see it in his face—and I was embarrassed, but there was nothing I could do now. I said my goodbyes and treated myself to a taxi.

The ride through nighttime Tokyo did me some good. I asked the driver whether it'd bother him if I rolled down the window a little.

The fresh air was pleasantly cool, a premonition of autumn hanging in it. I observed the colorful neon signs reflected in the shiny exteriors and windows of passing cars. After a few minutes, I was already feeling better.

In the rearview mirror, I saw two eyes that keep watching me.

They were friendly eyes, with crow's feet at the edges and wrinkles underneath. I suspected they'd seen quite a bit and was glad that they were still smiling in spite of it.

"Summer'll be over soon," he said with the calm voice of an older man, with a tinge of melancholy in it.

"Do you like the summer?" I asked, surprised.

"No, who likes summer in Tokyo, as hot and humid as it is? Still, I'm sorry it'll soon have passed."

I understood what he meant and nodded.

We sat in silence for a while. His eyes lingered on me often without making me feel harassed by them. Rather, I got the impression they were looking out for me.

He wore white gloves, his hands fixed on the steering wheel, piloting the vehicle through the traffic in Shibuya with great composure; he only needed to brake at the traffic lights.

"Have you been driving a taxi for a long time?"

"Thirty-three years."

"Oh, that is a long time."

"I used to work for Toshiba. But offices aren't for me. Too many people, if you know what I mean. I've been driving the night shift now for thirty years and sleeping during the day. That's the rhythm that suits me. Odd, isn't it?"

"You don't leave the house during the day?"

"No, never, really. The last time was two years ago, for my wife's funeral service."

"Oh. I'm sorry. Please forgive me for asking."

"It's okay."

We continued our ride through the night, and I thought of Kento. Since we'd met outside my mother's bar, he'd sent me a message with a haiku every evening around ten o'clock. Today's was already waiting for me.

I strongly preferred to listen to them at home before falling asleep, but I was in the mood to hear his voice now. I reached for my phone and pressed "play."

"Good evening. I found this haiku today, and you immediately came to my mind."

He cleared his throat.

"The long night;
The sound of the water
Says what I think."

As he did every evening, he paused briefly before saying goodbye, as though intending to give the words the chance to echo within me, to produce their effect. Today the pause was especially long.

"Goodnight."

"Goodnight," I replied softly.

Well, what did I think? There was no water far and wide to reveal it to me. I couldn't hear anything but the sonorous drone of the car's motor and the occasional blinker.

Do you know yourself?

Do you like yourself?

I felt I'd never in my life been farther away from answers to these questions.

I asked the driver if I might open my window all the way and held my face in the wind. It swirled my hair around and scoured my skin. I closed my eyes and thought of little Akiko and how much fun this would've been for her.

Maybe, I thought, we know ourselves better than we think. Maybe there's a voice within me that knows more and can say more than I believe. Maybe I just have to learn to ask it the right questions, to listen to it and trust it, even if it doesn't say what I expect or want to hear.

"Will it bother you if I turn on some music?" the driver asked all of a sudden.

"No."

"Jazz or classical?"

"Jazz."

He tapped around on his phone, and soon thereafter came the thrum of an upright bass and a piano, accompanying a voice that pierced me to my core. It was clearly the voice of a young man, yet at the same time sounded as raw and intense as if he'd already lived at least one lifetime, probably several.

Despite not understanding what he was singing, I got goosebumps.

"Who's this?"

"Early Chet Baker."

The name didn't ring a bell.

"If you don't like it, I'll find something else."

"Thank you, please don't bother. I like it." The voice wasn't beautiful, yet I was forced to listen whether I wanted to or not. Gradually, it took on an oppressive and sinister aspect, and I was glad when the song was over. A jazz trio without a voice part followed, the music of which suited my mood well.

"Miles Davis. *Kind of Blue*," the driver said.

"You know your stuff."

"I've got a lot of time on my hands."

We were nearing Shimokita. Just before we had to exit the main road, I asked him to take a little detour. My tiredness was gone, and I didn't want to go home. If I'd been able to afford it, I'd have ridden with him through Tokyo by night until daybreak, listening to jazz.

He shot me a look in the rearview mirror as if he'd been expecting this request and simply nodded. Two cross streets later, he suddenly turned off the taximeter.

"Oh, that's not necessary, really it isn't," I said, but he showed no reaction. Perhaps I'd said it too quietly as well.

He just continued driving calmly onward.

I'd have loved to ask him to tell me a story.

"Do you have children?" I asked, just to hear his voice.

"Yes, a daughter. You both must be about the same age."

"Does she live in Tokyo?"

"I don't know."

"Oh," I blurted out.

Again, our eyes met in the rearview mirror.

"Shikata ga nai," he said.

"Shikata ga nai," I repeated.

For a while, we remained on the dori leading toward Inokashira, the traffic cleared up, the shops were closed, the streets and sidewalks empty. Only the colorful neon signs blinked and glowed for pedestrians who'd long been asleep at home, lying on their futons.

We turned left, then right, then left again. I liked the aimlessness with which we rode through the night.

"It's after midnight," the driver said eventually. "Around this time, I always stop by a takeaway shop in Eifukucho and eat something. If you like, you can come along."

21

WE PULLED OVER IN A SIDE STREET WHERE THREE OTHER taxis were parked. The driver removed his gloves and placed them neatly on the passenger seat with his cap and uniform jacket. He was half a head shorter than me, with a slender build and thinning gray hair. Now I could see more than just the portions of his face in the rearview mirror. It was narrow, with a little scar on his left cheek. Oddly enough, he had the slightly dark complexion of someone who spent a lot of time in the sun. Maybe his family's from the south, I thought, or from the countryside. I put him in his mid-sixties. His expression was affable and caring not just in the mirror. He introduced himself as Ito-san and asked me to follow him. We walked into a small alleyway full of bars, pubs, and izakayas, the lights of which were out, their doors closed at this hour.

From one old building façade in darkened wood hung a lamp that was still glowing. Someone had made a great deal of effort to lay out a tiny garden in front: a strip of white pebbles, perhaps two feet wide, in which stood a moss-covered stone lantern, a bonsai tree, and a little fountain burbling with water.

The driver opened the sliding wooden door, which noisily rolled to the side in its tracks.

"Heeei irasshai," the proprietor called out, no sooner had we entered the place.

It was even smaller than it'd seemed from the outside, consisting only of a counter with three sides, with four stools at each. Seven men were sitting around the barkeeper, conversing loudly; it appeared they all knew each other well. Most were Ito-san's age; they greeted him happily and eyed me with curiosity.

"Who's that you've brought along?" one of them called out.

I bowed and said hello to them politely, and they greeted me just as politely in response.

We sat down, and the owner handed us two warm towels. The delicious smell of frying bacon and garlic hung in the air, and although I wasn't hungry, I immediately developed an appetite.

I got the impression that five of the men also drove a taxi and met here almost every night. The two others were a good deal younger and sat on the stools in the corners. While not themselves participating in the conversation, they looked as though they were listening intently.

"The one on the left is a porn star," Ito-san whispered to me. "He's been filming in the area here for three years and comes here every night after work. The one opposite him is the inventor of some famous video game. I forget its name. *Glory Days*, or something like that. He can only work at night, he says. He never has ideas during the day. And since he doesn't cook, he comes here to eat. Most places are of course closed at this hour. The other guys drive a cab."

I looked around. A large clock stood on a shelf over the door, its ticking clearly audible, even amid the conversations. The rice paper on the door and the wallpaper were faded, bubbling up in some areas. Empty sake bottles covered in a layer of dust were perched on a plank. Strips of paper were hanging everywhere, with the foods and beverages written on them by hand.

"Those you don't even need to read," one of the men said. "Endo-san will serve you what he wants anyway."

The others laughed.

"Not what I want," the barkeeper retorted, "but what she likes."

"He looks at you and knows what you like to eat," Ito-san said to me under his breath. "No one else can pull it off like he can."

Unsolicited, Endo-san, whom almost everyone here called sensei, set two glasses in front of us, pulled two different bottles of sake from beneath the counter, and poured. Mine came from Niigata Prefecture, and as it happened, I liked the wine from that region best.

"I suspect it's the only place in Tokyo where you can get nonalcoholic sake at this hour," Ito-san said, grinning at me. "Kampai."

"Kampai."

The barkeeper disappeared into a kitchenette behind a curtain where I could hear him slicing and chopping. Something sizzled in a pan. A short while later, he set a small plate with deep-fried chicken wings on the counter before me. They lay on top of a couple of green lettuce leaves and were garnished with a lemon wedge. Ito-san received a dish of rice with several slices of fried pork belly.

My chicken was tender and juicy and wonderfully seasoned. I sucked each and every bone as if I hadn't eaten for days. The barkeeper watched me contentedly.

Ito-san helped himself to a pair of chopsticks and zealously ate his rice and meat. He was one of the taciturn ones in the group.

The men treated me with unquestioning courtesy, as though I were there with them every night. They were full of stories, and I enjoyed listening to them. One of them drove exclusively between eight o'clock at night and six in the morning because he thought his wife wouldn't put up with him otherwise. He told of a passenger he regularly had to drive around the same block at night because the man couldn't fall asleep otherwise. Only when he had nodded off in the taxi first could he find rest at home.

Another had a regular client he'd pick up every morning at six and drive across the city to his office. He could also have taken the train, but the man suffered from claustrophobia and couldn't bear it on the cramped cars. No one but the driver knew of his fear. He still lived with his parents; he couldn't afford his own apartment because he spent more than half his salary on cab rides.

A third driver was a widower like Ito-san and couldn't stomach nights at home alone.

The man next to me claimed he knew he'd die in two years. His father and grandfather had died at sixty-six from strokes. He had an inner clock that revealed to him that his time would run out soon. To get used to the solitude and darkness, he drove a taxi at night. The others laughed, but the man looked serious as he said it.

Did I also sense a clock like that within me? he wanted to know. The others sighed; apparently, this wasn't the first time he'd asked this question.

I thought about it. "Hm, no, I'm sorry, I don't. Maybe I'm still too young."

He shook his head. It had nothing to do with age. Even as a kid he'd known when he would die: at sixty-six and six months.

"And if you do live longer than that, you'll have worried your whole life for nothing," the porn actor interjected. All eyes turned to him in surprise. "It's true," he added, almost by way of apology.

"In my life, I have not spent one day worrying because of that," my seatmate countered. "On the contrary: I found it helpful to know how much time I have. That way I was able to pace myself better."

For a while, everyone ruminated in silence.

My eyes wandered about. I regarded the nondescript clock above the door, thinking: what if there actually were a clock that displayed our probable span of life?

I imagined a world in the near future in which medicine and artificial intelligence were so far advanced that they were able—on the basis of a newborn's genes, prospective life circumstances, compliance with certain standards pertaining to diet and lifestyle—to calculate the year, and in most cases even the quarter, in which somebody would die. Unforeseeable events like accidents, natural disasters, murders, or suicide couldn't be accounted for of course.

The idea fascinated me. What would I do if my clock showed thirty-one and three quarters? Keep going to the office every day for a year and a half longer? Probably not.

While the others resumed talking again, I got more and more lost in my fantasy world. Would I become friends with someone whose clock ran out in a few months or years? Would that be one of the things we'd want to know first from a stranger: What does your clock say? There could be clubs and associations for people whose life expectancy was similar.

The more I thought about it, the more the story fascinated me. I imagined writing a lengthy story about it.

"Where are you in your thoughts?" I startled and saw that all the men were looking at me inquisitively. Someone had obviously asked me a question I hadn't answered.

"Uh...," I replied, embarrassed.

"The bartender wants to know if you've seen one of the actor's films before," one of the men shouted, and the others chuckled.

I felt my neck and check going very warm.

"Uh...I don't think so...I'm sorry."

"Don't listen to them," Ito-san interrupted me. "Sensei only asked whether you enjoyed your food."

"Oh, yes, very much," I said in relief, laughing. "Very much. It was delicious."

The driver dropped me off outside my building shortly before two thirty. I thanked him for the evening, but he was of the view that there was no need for that; he owed me thanks. We bowed to one another, and he gave me his card in case I ever planned a nighttime cab ride in advance—or couldn't sleep. I slipped it into my phone case and said thank you once more.

At home, I hunkered down in the kitchen right away to take notes. Ideas were bubbling up within me; I had no clue where they were coming from so suddenly. I jotted down outlines of them, otherwise I'd never be able to relax tonight.

In my fantasy, that clock was a Japanese invention. Other countries had rejected its use for ethical and moral reasons, but for the Japanese government, its advantages canceled those out. Since resources were getting scarcer and scarcer, did it make sense for a community to waste them on people whose clock registered a very low life expectancy?

Naturally, no one was compelled by law to participate in the program, but practically everyone did anyway. Anyone who refused was an antisocial outlier who placed his interests before those of the community.

I thought of a young woman whose parents had refused to have her life expectancy analyzed when she was a child and who now felt compelled to do so after the fact. Maybe because her boyfriend wants to know before starting a relationship with her...

It was after four in the morning when I went to bed. In spite of my tiredness, it took a while for me to fall asleep.

Naoko's phone call woke me at nine thirty. For the first time in six years, I'd forgotten to set my alarm and overslept. I briefly considered calling in sick, but that wouldn't have been fair to my other colleagues. I asked Naoko to forgive me—I'd be in the office in under an hour.

My phone showed Kento had sent me a brief message at 5:37.

I got ready as quickly as possible and rushed out of the house. On the way to the train, I listened to it.

"Good morning. Today you're getting a haiku to wake up to. I just read it, and it didn't want to wait until the evening. It wants you to have it."

Pause.

"O snail,
Climb Mount Fuji,
But slowly, slowly!"

Again he waited a while.

"It's by Master Issa. I hope you have a good day."

22

I'D FIRMLY RESOLVED NOT TO TAKE NOTES ANYMORE.

Not to ask myself any more what-if questions.

They did no good.

They were a poison trickling into my day-to-day life, slowly diffusing into it and causing a weird effect. In my thoughts, they opened up possibilities that didn't exist in my real life.

They shifted boundaries in my mind I'd thought were sacrosanct.

They were tempters.

In my imagination, they promised me different versions of myself, as if I could select one from among them just as I'd select from among the various kinds of green teas at the supermarket the one I wanted to drink in the moment.

Reality was different.

The Spirits of Yamanote and *The Clock* wouldn't leave me in peace. I caught myself wondering about my colleagues' private lives.

More and more often, I considered what would happen if I were to sit in a café instead of at a desk and continued to write the stories.

I was responding to my e-mails with delays, and I made frequent miscalculations, which I otherwise never did.

This had to stop.

At lunch one day, I asked Naoko whether she could sense a kind of inner clock having to do with her lifespan.

She groaned audibly. "Yet another of those weird questions you've been asking so much lately." We were sitting in a soba restaurant we seldom visited because it was a bit too far away for our brief lunch break.

"What's going on with you? You're worrying way too much."

"I think it's an interesting question," I said, telling her about the taxi driver.

"What I think is interesting is where you hang out at night," she said in surprise, dipping a piece of vegetable tempura into its sauce, relishing it, and reflecting.

"No, I do not hear or feel my clock ticking. And even if I did, what difference would it make? I could die at any moment as it is. A burst blood vessel in my brain. An idiot looking at his phone instead of paying attention to traffic and running me over in a crosswalk."

"That's not the same thing. Imagine if you knew with a likelihood bordering on certainty, because artificial intelligence could calculate that you'd die at thirty-two. Wouldn't that change anything for you?"

"No," she answered impulsively.

"Why not?"

Naoko thought about it longer than usual. "Emi recently told me she wants to go to Bali at some point in her life and stay in a five-star hotel. That's her biggest wish. She's been saving for it for years, looking forward to it, thinking about it when she's not doing well. Lying on a beach in Bali for a week and treating herself.

"So? Will that change her life? Probably not, unless she falls in love with some superrich Chinese man there and moves to Shanghai, which we wouldn't wish on her…"

I couldn't help but laugh.

"Seriously," Naoko continued, "I don't have a dream like that. Whether or not I've been to Hawaii before, walked down Fifth Avenue in New York, or gone shopping in London makes me a happier person at most in the short term."

"Still," I objected.

"For me that's different than a dream I'd like to make come true at all costs because I know I'll die soon. In the face of death, every dream is irrelevant. Otherwise people take themselves and their lives too seriously. Don't you think?"

"Hmm, I don't know," I said evasively.

"You always say that when it gets interesting."

"Do I now?"

She raised her eyebrows, and I wasn't quite sure how she'd meant that. "As far back as I can remember, my parents have talked about taking a trip to Okinawa together someday. A few years ago, they treated themselves to it and argued there so much they didn't speak to each other for a week. My father was constantly calling me: 'Could you tell your mother she ought to...' Just because one time they wanted to live out their dream."

"Your parents are extra."

"That's true," she admitted. "So, tell me what you'd like to do no matter what if your time ran out in a year."

I swallowed my "Hmm, I don't know" and thought about it. "I think I'd want to meet my biological father."

"Oh. Why that all of a sudden?"

"I don't know," slipped out of me then anyhow. "Ever since I learned about my rental father and met him, I've been thinking about him more often. Maybe we look similar. Fifty percent of DNA is from him after all."

"I see. Anything else?"

For a second I wanted to tell her about my stories but changed my mind. It was still too soon for that. "I think I'd like to go to Paris."

"Sure, I wouldn't mind that either. Let me know when it's happening, and I'll come along. Does your happiness depend on it, though?"

"I don't know," I said, unable to suppress a laugh. "Maybe it does, maybe it doesn't. I'd probably only find out once I go there."

She nodded.

An elderly waitress cleared away our dishes. Her hands were trembling. I'd have liked to help her.

Naoko looked at the clock and stood up. "I just had a thought," she said suddenly, and from the way she grinned at me, I guessed what was coming.

"I'd ask Takahashi-san if he wouldn't like to sleep with me at least once."

To relax, I started walking home from the office. It took between one and one and a half hours from Akasaka to Shibuya, depending on how quickly I walked and what route I took. Whenever I wasn't too tired, I'd walk the whole way to Shimokita.

When I was standing at the huge intersection in Shibuya one evening, Kento called me on FaceTime.

"Hi. Bad time?" He grinned awkwardly and waved.

"Not at all."

I crossed the intersection. Neon ads cast their colorful lights across my face; I looked like I was wearing a mask. Kento looked at me without saying anything. After a few paces up Inokashira-dori, I took refuge in an entryway to a closed business.

"It's a little quieter here."

"Where are you?"

"In Shibuya."

"May I see?"

I flipped the phone camera and panned once around myself.

"Oh, oh," I heard him say over and over. "So many people. Even at this time. So much traffic."

"And you?" I asked. "Where are you?"

"At my desk."

"May I see?"

To my surprise, he rotated the camera and circled around himself without comment. The curtains were drawn. I could see a drying rack full of laundry, a shelf full of books, a kind of long side table with two computers on top. Dirty dishes sat in the sink, and books lay open before him. His room was larger and tidier than I'd imagined. He spun around briefly and pointed to a white sheet or blanket. Beneath it, the legs of a grand piano were peeking out, presuming I identified them correctly in haste.

"Thanks," I said.

He directed the camera back at himself. "Did you have a chance to read 'Koko' again?"

"Yes, and a few others from those old stories."

"Will you admit I was right?"

"I wouldn't go that far. But for a fourteen-year-old, they aren't bad."

He sighed audibly and shook his head. "You're too modest."

"Realistic," I countered.

"Modest," he insisted. "Have you ever heard of Jean-Jacques Morceaux?"

"The French author?"

He nodded.

"My mother read him a lot. I think she owned every book he wrote that had been translated. Why mention him?"

"He wrote a novel entitled *La Grande Illusion*. There's also a TED Talk by him about it. It might interest you. If you like, I'll send you the link."

"Thanks, I'd like that."

We remained silent for a while. "Shall we get together in the new few days?" I asked.

"Hmm. Yeah...sure...why not?"

As hesitantly as he said it, it sounded like a no.

"I should let you go and stop bothering you now," he said.

"You're not bothering me."

"You sure?"

"Quite sure."

"Would you mind showing me Shibuya again?"

I rotated the camera. "Shall I take you along on my walk again?"

"Sure, if isn't too much for you."

I held the phone in front me with my arm outstretched as though I were lighting my way with a lantern, and set out. Together with hundreds of people, I crossed the big intersection. They came toward me from the left and the right, from in front and behind, and still we didn't touch one another. Again I could hear Kento's amazement from the phone.

"Not so fast, please," he said, and I slowed my pace. One block more, and it got to be too much for him, and he asked me to turn the camera off.

Right after our conversation, I googled Jean-Jacques Morceaux. There wasn't much information about him in Japanese. He was 80 years old, lived in seclusion in Paris, only rarely granted interviews, and was married to a Japanese woman. He'd published ten novels, and his most famous, *La Grande Illusion*, had been awarded the Prix Goncourt—an important French literary prize, apparently. The book was about a highly regarded French physicist who realizes that the world cannot be explained by science and that to even try was nothing more than an expression of human hubris, that the important things in life aren't quantifiable, that rationality is not a key variable in human behavior—in short, that his view of existence is predicated on illusions. During a speaking tour in Japan, he suffers a grave existential crisis and feels like he's losing his mind. To recover, he spends a week in the onsen of a remote mountain village in Gunma Prefecture where he meets a recluse who shows him the holiest place in the region: a shrine erected in the forest in honor of a stone animated by a spirit. The physicist spends a great deal of time with the onsen owner's daughter and falls in love with her. In that love, he believes he's discovered the real meaning of life. Whether that's the case or whether it's just another of his many illusions the author leaves open at the end.

I was sure my mother had read the novel; it was probably at home on our shelves.

I opened the link to Morceaux's TED Talk. It was recorded in Paris, eighteen minutes long, and ten years old. I'd actually wanted to watch it at home in peace, but the brief blurb made me so curious I couldn't wait. I slipped my earbuds in and kept strolling slowly up Inokashira-dori.

The title of the talk was "What If?"

"The famous French writer Jean-Jacques Morceaux speaks about the inspiration that lies in silence and the source of his creativity."

The video began with an empty stage, in the middle of which lay a red round rug bathed in a bright glow from a spotlight. Everything else was black. A Japanese woman in a loose-fitting black dress stepped out of the darkness pushing a wheelchair in which Morceaux was sitting. He had a large head and curly white hair, was wearing a gray sweater, and held a microphone in his hand. The audience clapped politely. When the applause had died down, he looked around the hall without saying a word. He maintained his silence for so long that the audience gradually became restive. Someone cleared his throat. Others coughed a little. Morceaux put his index finger to his mouth, made a "shhh" sound, and waited until it grew very quiet—and continued his silence. No one moved another muscle.

"Silence," he said eventually, almost whispering. "In silence we find our way to one another. In silence, ideas arise. Anyone who claims silence as his friend receives aid. Anyone who cannot endure it is beyond help." He paused, and I stopped walking. His voice was quiet and firm at once. I understood most everything in the original. Only now and again did I read the subtitles. A power and urgency issued from his voice that even ten years later, ten thousand kilometers away on a street in Shibuya, I could still perceive. I leaned against a building and watched the entire video.

Morceaux spoke slowly and inserted short pauses after each sentence. He related how, as a young man, he'd often enjoyed hiking the French Alps by himself. Back then, he was working as a French teacher in a small town and dreamed of writing a book. His experience, his skill, and his cockiness caused him to become care-less while climbing, and on one trip, he lost his footing on a steep, narrow ascent and plunged fifteen meters into the depths. He survived but couldn't feel his legs. For two days and nights, he lay motionless in the ra-vine, knowing it would be a miracle if anyone found him on this lonesome path. His calls for help went un-heard. To save his strength, he soon fell silent. No one knew he'd gone hiking. By the time someone noticed his disappearance and reported him missing, he'd be dead.

Morceaux described the silence around him as some-thing all-encompassing and terrifying. Sounds—a rus-tling of leaves, the wind, or the call of a bird—were signs of life; silence was an emissary of death. He was afraid of it in the same way he'd been afraid of the devil as a child.

On that first night, he didn't shut an eye, and eventu-ally he began to hear a voice in that silence, with a clar-ity he'd never known. This voice began quietly telling him stories, and they helped him better endure his fear of death and the pain.

Each of them began with the question: what if?

He understood that his previous life and way of think-ing had been based on illusions and, through making up stories, conjured himself into a high which was stronger than his pain and fear and which relieved them bet-ter than all the drugs he'd later receive in the hospital, as though someone had opened a gate or uncovered a spring that never stopped burbling. One image became a sequence of images, one thought a string of thoughts, characters appeared, and he wondered where all of this could have come from.

On the second day, he was convinced he wouldn't survive and tried to make peace with approaching death, but it was impossible. Everything in him bridled against death—not because he was so attached to life, but because he still wanted to write down the stories he now carried.

They were the material on which all of his novels would be based.

On the third day, a Japanese exchange student who also enjoyed hiking remote trails happened upon him. The camera pivoted to the woman behind him, whose face remained expressionless.

She had saved him. It was to her and to his imagination that he owed his life.

While still in the hospital, he began working like mad on his first novel. He'd wanted to keep teaching— he liked the children and his work—but it was no longer possible. He *had* to write down what had preserved him from death; he regarded every other pursuit as a waste of time.

To this day, nothing about that had changed.

"Although a place might appear desolate and empty," he said at the end, "there often reside in it eloquent spirits or even tortured souls harboring their own untold stories—forces and powers we cannot see but can only feel or hear whispering. In order for us to do so, we must be silent and must endure this silence as well.

"I thank you for your attention and would like to make a request as I leave: don't clap when I've finished. Try to listen to the silence."

He gave a brief nod and closed his eyes. His wife ushered him offstage, and for a few seconds, all was quiet. Then, the first person began to clap, others joined in, and the two disappeared into the darkness amid thunderous applause.

At home, I checked the bookshelf to see whether we had any novels by Morceaux. I found *The Silence*, *The Cold*, and *Journey to the End of the World*, but not *La Grande Illusion*. My mother must have loaned it to one of her customers and never gotten it back. I wanted to order it on the Internet, but the title had long been out of print. There wasn't even a copy to be had on the websites for used books. My best chance was one of the many secondhand bookstores in Jimbōchō.

The next day, I broke my resolution not to ask myself any more what-if questions. Naoko and I stayed late at the office, and instead of visiting a bar with her afterward, I took another train on the Yamanote Line.

I thought about *The Clock*, retrieved my notebook from my bag, and started writing down my thoughts. I don't know whether it was because of the monotonous sounds of the moving train or because in the nearly empty train car I could devote myself entirely to my imagination—whatever the cause, one idea after the other popped into my head such that I could hardly keep up with writing them all down. I felt a joy and lightness while doing so that I hadn't felt in a long time.

Even a brief voice message from Kento couldn't interrupt the flow of my writing. Instead of playing it back right away, I waited until I was in bed.

At home, I rolled out the futon, switched off the light, watched the shadows cast on the ceiling by the streetlamp outside the house, and listened to it:

"Good evening, Akiko."
He paused briefly, then inhaled, continuing:

"An autumn evening;
It is no light thing,
To be born a man."

Again, he kept silent for a moment. "It's by Master Issa and a favorite haiku of mine. I hope you like it too... Sleep well... Goodnight... Oh, and by the way..."

Instead of a sentence, I could hear only his long silence, and the longer it lasted, the better I understood what he'd wanted to tell me.

23

DURING THE FIRST YEAR OF MY NEW LIFE IN TOKYO, I'D spent time in Jimbōchō frequently. One bookstore after the other lined the main road and the surrounding side streets. Rolling shelves, crates, and displays full of used books lined the sidewalks. For hours, I'd browse these secondhand shops without looking for anything in particular. Some carried only cookbooks in all different languages, and others specialized in books about film, fashion, art, or atlases and travelogues. Sometimes, I'd get lost in a two-hundred-year-old account by a Jesuit traveling through China or in the biography of a French artist I'd never heard about before. I liked the smell of old books in the stores; they were places for me to dream. Ever since I'd begun working at SunSun Agency, I'd only been once or twice.

I remembered a little bookstore near the train station that carried only French and Greek literature. It was my best hope. My search for it took a while, and when I finally found it, I stood before closed shutters. A sign posted on the locked door by the owners thanked their customers for their years of loyalty.

In the shop next door, the books were stacked on the floor in towers, and its overfull shelves nearly reached the high ceiling. In the very back, an elderly man was sitting behind a computer. He scarcely looked up when I spoke to him. He'd never heard of Morceaux. The books weren't cataloged, so he couldn't tell me for sure if the book might be there somewhere. He didn't think it likely. If I didn't find it up on this floor, I could look in the basement; there were boxes down there that'd just arrived and hadn't been unpacked yet. I walked along the aisles but couldn't divine how things were ordered. Nonfiction titles stood alongside novels, and they weren't in strict alphabetical order either. On the lower level there were nonfiction texts like *Native Birds of New Zealand* and *Spatial Questions in the Theory of Elasticity*; the novels were almost all by Japanese authors. After a while, I gave up.

At the next store, two young men in aprons and white gloves were behind the register, busy with a new delivery. From one of several cardboard boxes beside them, one removed a book, wiped it carefully with a damp cloth, and passed it on. The other checked to see whether it was sufficiently clean and labeled it. So it went, book by book. They performed their tasks so scrupulously that it took them a moment to notice me. The name Morceaux didn't ring a bell with them either, for which they apologized profusely. When I explained to them how important the novel was to me, they set their books aside and began meticulously scouring each shelf. The only thing they found was an edition of *The Silence.*

At the next store, the woman at the register claimed to have one German and one Japanese edition of *La Grande Illusion* in stock; she'd only just held them in her hands. But they weren't on the shelves under "M." That was extremely embarrassing to her, and she began hectically racing through the shop, checking all the different sections.

"I've got it," she cried in relief after a few minutes, handing me an old, dogeared Japanese edition. It must've had a series of previous owners. Riffling through it, I noticed some lines had been underscored and entire paragraphs marked. I hesitated for a moment.

"I'm sorry it's in such poor condition," the saleswoman said. "But it's the only copy we've got, and I don't recall ever having another one. Morceaux is not an especially—how should I put this?—popular author."

"I don't mind. I'll take it anyway."

On the second floor of the bookstore was a vending machine for drinks, in front of which were three high-top tables with barstools. I bought myself a hot lemon soda and paged through the book. Curious what readers before me had marked, I opened to random pages.

Physics, Monsieur Calais thought, is a natural science that studies fundamental phenomena in nature. He had devoted his utmost passion to these phenomena. By researching some of them, he had gained worldwide renown in his field. Now he was forced to realize that he knew nothing about that most fundamental and important—that most enigmatic and mysterious—natural phenomenon: love.

He had wasted his time.

Monsieur wondered how far back into his mistakes he could go. Where was the point at which his life had slipped from his control?

We are time travelers. Courtesy of our memories, we travel into the past, and with our plans, we travel into the future. We shuttle between these worlds. No one lives solely in the present.

The hermit and the physicist stood at the edge of the Shinto shrine, looking through the *torii*, behind which lay nothing but woods and a gray, craggy boulder. The hermit bowed before it.

Faithless, the physicist examined the torii with its two wooden pillars and the doubled crossbeams on top, all painted a deep vermilion. No matter how long he stared through it, he could see nothing but ordinary forest floor, tree trunks, brambles, and a large boulder jutting from the dirt. "You worship rocks."

The hermit nodded. "And you a cross."

Lost in thought, I shut the book and wondered how many people might've held it in their hands before. I imagined what might happen if all the readers of this copy were to meet and talk about why they'd marked certain passages, what the book meant to them. It would probably be a mixed group of young and old, men and women, and we'd realize that we'd all read *La Grande Illusion* and yet each of us had read a different book.

I walked to a nearby café, ordered a matcha latte, and began to read. The story of the physicist generated a pull from which I was unable to escape. I ate a sandwich, ordered a second matcha, and kept reading and reading. Eventually, I made my way home without putting the book down on my walk or on the train. At home, I continued reading while lying on the futon until I arrived at the last sentence late at night. Exhausted, I put *La Grande Illusion* aside.

The world of the physicist's thoughts was foreign to me. He always wanted answers to his questions. He was convinced there was an explanation for everything. I understood the hermit better. I couldn't get many of his lines out of my head. "The world is full of spirits and gods. Some are well-disposed toward us, some are not. Some come to us, and others we must seek out where they reside and try to make peace with them," he'd explained to the physicist.

I thought of the trip with my mother to Kinosaki Onsen. My memories of it were, for me, a sort of spirit that kept plaguing me to this day, more frequently since her death than before. They were a kind of wound that hadn't healed properly.

Perhaps I should seek it out where it resides and try to make peace with it.

It took me a great deal of effort to ask Takahashi-san on short notice for a week of vacation for my trip to Kinosaki. He furrowed his brow, played with his pen, and at first said nothing. Beneath the table, his feet began twitching incessantly. Five whole days were a lot in the middle of autumn, especially in my position and with respect to my colleagues. Had I considered that? He personally was on board with it, but his boss, Watanabe-san, would certainly wonder why someone in his, Takahashi-san's, department wanted to take off an entire week this time of year. That would not reflect well on him, Takahashi-san, if I understood what he meant.

I understood—and shortened my trip to two days over the following weekend.

On the Shinkansen to Kyoto, I sat beside the window and looked out. I'd consciously neglected to bring a book with me to read and resisted the urge to watch cat videos on YouTube or a movie. My phone and earbuds were in the storage rack above me. I didn't want to be distracted.

The sky was overcast with low-lying, silvery-gray clouds. Gray buildings, gray walls, and gray streets flew past me. A train station, then more buildings, walls, streets. Until past Nagoya, the route wove through one large city. I listened to the turbulent air outside, to the announcements before and after each stop, to the conductor apologizing for the disturbance after entering and leaving each car, and still, within me, everything gradually grew more silent.

With each kilometer we covered, I transformed more and more into a time traveler.

By the time I was taking the regional train in Kyoto, I saw Akiko and her mother standing on the platform, boarding the train after me. I took a seat amid a group of schoolgirls and observed the two. Akiko had a window seat, her joyful anticipation overshadowed by a great sadness, which she feared. There was no one there to dispel that sadness, nor anyone with whom she could've shared it.

Her mother Masako was tired and slept.

The train grew emptier with every stop, and eventually, just the three of us were sitting in the train car.

In Kinosaki, I followed them on foot from the train station to the ryokan. We crossed a bridge, walking along the river, passing willows and cherry trees. It was a lovely autumn day, the clouds having yielded to a deep-blue sky.

I'd booked the same accommodation in which my mother and I had stayed. It seemed to me shabbier than I remembered. The carpet was worn and covered in stains, the doors dinged, and along the walls, I could see black and gray marks from luggage carried upstairs carelessly. I'd noticed none of that at the time.

The proprietor bowed politely and asked if I was traveling alone. When I said yes, he scrutinized me with an anxious expression, took my small suitcase, and carried it to a room on the second floor. On the way, he recommended several sights to me I wasn't to miss, described the different public bathhouses, and advised me on the order in which I should visit them. I only half listened, thanked him courteously, and was glad when he closed the sliding door.

The room measured six tatami mats and was almost as large as the one I'd shared with my mother. From the chair in an alcove, one could look out onto the street. No sooner had I removed my jacket, than the nakai-san arrived and prepared me a pot of green tea. She inquired whether there was anything I didn't or couldn't eat and when I'd like to have dinner and breakfast served. After she'd left, I poured myself a cup of tea, sat in the alcove, and did nothing but look out the window. Akiko and Masako lay on the tatami mats in silence, exhausted. From the street, the odd voice carried up to me. It may not have been the silence Morceaux had spoken about, but that didn't matter. Every silence is different, I thought.

The tea was only just lukewarm when I tasted it.

Eventually, I changed clothes and made my way to one of the bathhouses. Akiko and Masako remained behind in the ryokan. Unhurried, I strolled through the lanes and bought myself a mochi with sweet red bean filling and a beautiful *tenugui* for Naoko.

I took my time at the bathhouse too—soaping up more thoroughly than usual with a sponge, sitting at the edge of the pool for a few minutes, and dipping my legs in the hot water before sliding my whole body in. Not until my heart began pounding from the heat did I climb out of the water. My white skin was as red as a lobster.

I returned to the ryokan just in time for dinner.

The nakai-san served a multicourse meal similar to the one we'd eaten back then. Three pieces of vegetable tempura lay on one plate, tuna and hamachi sashimi on another, pickled seaweed, radishes, and cucumbers in small dishes. A quarter of an hour later, she brought a small pot with fish, tofu, and vegetables, served alongside a dish of miso soup and rice.

I ordered a beer. The hot bath had made me thirsty, and after a short while, I ordered a second.

The clickety-clack from the wooden sandals guests wore to walk from one bathhouse to the next echoed up from the street.

For a moment, I thought of Kento. I'd actually intended to call him from the ryokan, but now I was having a change of heart. My life in Tokyo was in another world, one I couldn't reach with FaceTime. It was just the three of us here in this onsen, and that was a good thing.

I observed Akiko and her mother. Only a few years separated Masako and me. At my age, she'd already had a nine-year-old daughter and a sunakku in which she'd had to serve men and women every night—in a manner so affable and stimulating that they'd want to return. I found both things unimaginable.

I could see the two of them sitting at the richly set table, could see how happy she was to be with her daughter in this ryokan, what these two days meant to her. I could see all the things that, at the time, I'd had no ability to see. A part of Masako's world had been invisible to me even though I'd lived in it. Now, I could see that she'd looked forward to this trip at least as much as Akiko had. Her tiredness faded; she giggled and was more spirited than usual. This distressed her daughter. Her mother's gestures and expressions reminded her of those with which she entertained her customers at the sunakku and which Akiko so despised.

I could see Akiko lying on her futon, her eyes open, staring at the ceiling while Masako got drunk and watched one gameshow after another on television, its sound muted. I could see them both and now understood why Akiko had fallen silent, why language had failed her for the rest of their trip, why she'd been unable to find her way out of her speechlessness. They could have stayed another whole week and exchanged not a sentence more.

It was not a kind of knowledge I could capture in words, which didn't make it any less true.

I knelt down on the tatami mats and bowed so low that my forehead touched the mat and begged my mother for forgiveness over and over. For a long while, a very long while, I remained like that.

And I bowed to Akiko. I told her I understood her and that there was no reason to be ashamed.

Everything was fine.

Her mother had forgiven her a few days later.

She should do the same.

It was about time, after all these years.

I remained on my knees until they began to hurt. Then, I was overcome by an extreme weariness, and I stretched out over the tatami mats.

When I awoke, the nakai-san was just clearing away the dishes and spreading out the futon for me.

Her reproachful look.

She probably thought I'd gotten drunk. But I didn't care. I switched off the light, climbed under the covers, and lay there calmly. I listened to myself breathe. I slipped off my yukata and felt desire rise up within me. The darkness aroused me. My own naked body aroused me. I began caressing myself, carefully, timidly. I took the time I needed. My breathing gradually grew faster. I became warm, and at some point, I began trembling more and more intensely. The aftershocks roiled my body for a while afterward. I couldn't recall ever having sensed myself like that while feeling so at home in my own body.

I drew up a second pillow and clung to it. A short while later, I fell asleep.

The next morning, I awoke shortly after sunrise. I put on my yukata and walked to one of the bathhouses. It was just opening, and an old woman and I were the first guests. A natural pool lay beyond the washing room, bordered by a cliff face with a little waterfall running down it. Bamboo grew along its edges, and the rock was covered with moss. I slipped into the water, submerging myself up to the neck, placed a cool rag on my forehead, listened to the birds chirping, and didn't move. Somewhere, a cuckoo called.

It occurred to me that Kento had sent me a haiku neither yesterday evening nor this morning—for the first time in weeks.

Instead, I recalled one he had read to me a while ago.

The long night;
The sound of the water
Says what I think.

There was no need for it to; I myself knew.

I was twenty-nine years old and wanted a different life.

This was no toying around with ideas like last time, no vague notion or mere inkling.

It was a certainty.

How exactly that different life was to look I didn't know.

And how could I?

I'd have to seek it out, and there was no one to whom I owed accountability who could pressure me into doing anything or hurry me along—aside from myself of course. And I promised to be patient with myself.

In my attempts to get to know myself and to understand where and when my story had begun, I may not have made very much progress over the past several months. I might have, however, with the other question Kento had asked me.

I, Akiko Nakamura, was beginning, tentatively, to like myself. At first, I started at the thought, but then it began to appeal. And why shouldn't it? I thought. Why shouldn't it?

On the train ride home to Tokyo, I took a short detour to the small town along whose beach my mother and I had strolled side by side in silence back then. I followed our footsteps from the train station to the sea, a good half-hour walk past closed shops, boarded-up restaurants, and dilapidated houses. At one point a car passed by.

Not until I was on the beach did I encounter other people. A couple my age was sitting on a wall, looking out onto the mirror-smooth surface of the water before them without saying a word. No wind blew, and the waves lapped ashore diffidently as they might in a lake. A woman was pushing a stroller with a small dachshund in it; she'd strapped her baby to her chest. Two fishermen crouched on a jetty, casting their rods and reeling them in again tirelessly. For a while, I joined them there. They took no notice of me. Two buckets full of water sat beside them for their catch. In one of them, a small fish swam in circles.

I had no recollection of the town's bleakness. At the time, I was probably too caught up with myself to notice it. Perhaps, fifteen years ago, it hadn't been so desolate either. I'd have loved to ask my mother now how she'd felt here, if she'd seen what I was now seeing.

I set out on my way back and was glad when I reached the train station.

I slept most of the way on the Shinkansen.

At home, I recorded a voice message for Kento:

"Hi...I'm back...I had a good trip...It took less time than I imagined...to travel back into the past, I mean...it's much closer than I thought...even if it was a very long time ago." I paused, weighing my next words carefully. "I'd like to ask you for a favor. It's hard for me because I know it won't be easy for you to turn down my request. I can only hope you don't feel any sort of obligation." For a moment, I froze because once again I was unsure whether I was even permitted to ask this of Kento. After a few seconds, I continued anyway: "I...I'd like to scatter my mother's ashes, and I know where too: in the ocean. On the beach at Tsujido.

"I don't want to rent a boat for it and don't want an official ceremony. But...I don't know if I have the strength to do it by myself. Could you maybe imagine accompanying me? We could leave early on a Sunday, take the first train, and be back by nine in the morning. The train and beach would be empty, and it's likely we wouldn't see another soul. I know how difficult it'd be for you. No, of course I don't know. Maybe I have some sense of it, just as you might have some sense of what it'd mean to me.

"If it's too much for you, I'll understand. Truly. In which case I'll find another solution. Take your time to think about it. For me, the time has come, but it doesn't matter exactly when.

"I hope you understand my request and don't resent me for it. It's very selfish, I know.

"I look forward to hearing from you.

"Goodnight.

"Sleep well."

I listened to the message a few times and hesitated in sending it.

Some favors you cannot ask of another person.

I had to trust him to say no if he felt like it.

Didn't he say it every day as a hikikomori? Why should he make an exception for me?

I pressed "send."

His reply came minutes later.

"Hi... thanks for your message... I'm glad you had a good trip... I haven't left the house in a long time... I'm working on an essay, did I tell you? I haven't gotten very far yet. If you're interested in it, I'll send it to you when it's finished... That might take a while... I don't really have a haiku I like right now... sorry..."

24

I'D INVITED NAOKO OUT TO EAT AND WAS LOOKING forward to telling her about my decision. It was Saturday night, she'd come to Shimokita, and we were sitting at the bar in one of my favorite restaurants. It was noisy and full. The three cooks were toiling intently before us; each of them knew exactly what he was doing. It smelled like grilled fish and vegetables, like miso and freshly tapped beer. The waitress brought two Sapporos, and one of the cooks served us a dish of edamame and a plate of seaweed salad. Naoko looked around. I could tell from her face how much she liked it here.

We clinked our glasses.

With my heart thudding, I told her about my plans.

"And what do you intend to do after you resign?" Her

voice had a tone of curiosity and uncertainty about how seriously she should take my announcement.

"Don't worry about that. I've got ideas."

"I'm on tenterhooks."

Something in her voice unsettled me.

"First, I'll look for my father. I've got a copy of our old koseki, so it shouldn't be too hard to find him.

"Then I'm going to travel to Paris, walk down the Rue du Faubourg Saint-Antoine, and drink a glass of wine in my mother's bistro. Maybe even two.

"And when I get back, I'll write a book."

Naoko laughed out loud. In her laugh was a mixture of surprise, amusement, and something else I didn't recognize in her.

"A book," she repeated. "And what will you live on? Nobody reads books anymore."

"My mother's life insurance policy will last for two or three years, depending on how frugal I am."

"And then?"

"That remains to be seen."

Naoko shook her head in disbelief. "A book!" She raised her beer glass, about to drink, and set it back down. "What will you write about?" She thought for a moment. "Let me guess: *A Thousand Times Nothing Happened: Tips for a Happy Life without Sex*?

"*Mindful Masturbation: How to Achieve Orgasm with Solo Sex in a Relaxed Manner*?

"*Secrets from the Life of a Woman Accountant*?

"*Bookkeeping for Dummies*?"

I refused to be provoked. "Not nonfiction," I replied calmly. "A collection of short stories."

Naoko looked at me as if I'd lost my mind, then suddenly smiled. "Now I know what you mean. You're thinking up stories."

"Something like that, yeah."

"You're writing down all the fantasies you have but don't live out."

I wasn't sure what she was getting at but nodded anyway.

"I see. Like how to knee the balls of the guy who gropes you under your dress on the train. How you go at it with Nakagawa-san in his office amid the piles of invoices. How you..."

"Stop it," I interrupted her, insulted. "You don't need to understand, but you don't need to make fun of me either."

Naoko rolled her eyes. "Well, aren't you sensitive today."

"I mean it."

Then she turned to face me and gave me a stern look. "So do I. Who do you even think you are? A writer? Where is the Akiko I knew?"

"She is sitting in front of you."

"No. You're somebody else."

"Why would you say such a thing? Just because I'm quitting?"

"If only it were just that," she said coolly.

"What, then?"

"The Akiko I knew would've talked to me before-hand. The Akiko I knew wouldn't have left me in the lurch."

"I'm not leaving you in the lurch," I retorted.

"You think I like this job?" she blurted out. "I became an accountant because I come from a family of accountants and couldn't think of anything better. The work is boring as hell. Checking invoices, paying bills, checking invoices, day after day, week after week, year after year. Variety? Zero. Prospect for a change? Zilch. Twelve hours of work every day, one week of vacation because nobody in our position dares take the second one. Sitting around at the office into the night just because the boss hasn't left yet, because his boss hasn't left yet, although everybody's finished the day's work. Standing in packed trains all squeezed together for an hour every morning, and again at night. What's the point of it all?

"But I thought we were toughing it out together. I thought we'd stick together. I thought you were my friend, who I could rely on."

"And you can."

"I can see that." Naoko took a big swig of her beer and turned her head to the side.

"Then we'll resign together," I said spontaneously.

"Great idea. You want to reveal to me what I'm supposed to do without a generous life insurance payout to help? Become your agent? Do your accounts? Call me when you've sold the first million, then I'll consider it."

She made a move to stand up. I clutched her arm.

"Let me go, I've got to use the bathroom."

"I'm very sorry," I said softly.

Naoko got up and disappeared into the rear of the restaurant. I felt like I was on trial. I hadn't reckoned with such an angry outburst.

We'll still remain friends in spite of it, I wanted to shout after her. We'll still see one another. I don't like you any less on account of this. I'm the same Akiko.

"I hope you've given this a good deal of thought," Naoko said upon returning to the table. Her anger and disappointment had not abated. "No one's going to understand."

Again I'm the nail that sticks out, I thought. At that notion, I felt the fear I knew from my childhood return. There were so many ways to hammer it in. And everybody was happy when they got to hold the hammer.

Had I given it some thought?

"Yes," I said feebly. "Yes, I think I have."

"You 'think'? That doesn't sound very convincing. Akiko, wake up." She took my arm and squeezed it. "Think it over again. You're making a big mistake."

"Am I?"

"Absolutely. Those two or three years will go by faster than you imagine. And then? You'll be broke and without a job."

"I don't know. I didn't come by the decision easily."

"I hope for your sake you didn't," she said, and I could hear the disappointment returning to her voice. "Let's go."

I glanced at the grilled fish and the sashimi. We'd hardly touched them. "Let's talk about something else," I suggested, "and enjoy the food."

"I've lost my appetite," Naoko said.

I asked her not to tell anyone until I'd spoken with Takahashi-san and delivered my letter to him asking for permission to be allowed to leave the company.

She emptied her beer. "I want to go home."

"I'm going to stay."

"Suit yourself." She stood up, removed a five-thousand-yen bill from her bag, and placed it on the counter.

"I wanted to treat you," I said, but she wasn't listening to me.

"See you Monday. Have a nice evening," she said and turned around and left.

I had tears in my eyes.

One of the cooks had been watching us and sent me an encouraging smile.

That helped. I ate a slice of sashimi and relaxed a bit.

Naoko was impulsive, which I liked about her, and she usually cooled back down quickly. I was disappointed in myself for having been so surprised at her reaction. I should've seen it coming.

On the way back, I walked past Kento's building. Most of the windows were dark, but lights were on in his apartment. I stopped. The feeling of being only a few meters away from him and unable to visit him hurt. He'd understand my decision. He'd encourage me and back me up, I was certain of it. I'd have liked to hear that from him now.

You're doing the right thing, Akiko. Don't be afraid. You'll manage.

I called him and asked if he might still want to go for a walk or have a beer outside the konbini.

Alas, no. I hung up and felt even more miserable than before.

A moment later, he called again on FaceTime. I retreated into the shadows of a building and was difficult to make out on the screen in the darkness. He shouldn't see that I'd been crying.

The obscurity didn't seem to bother him, or at least he didn't mention it.

"Just now you sounded...different somehow."

"Hm. Yeah. I had an argument with a friend."

"An argument with a friend," he repeated, while lengthening each word pensively. "That...I'm sorry...sadly, there's not a lot I can say about that...I'd like to..."

Still, the sight of him gave me some comfort. Kento expected nothing of me. In many respects, my world must seem strange to him, yet still I was sure he understood me and, whenever he didn't understand, wasn't judging me.

"I'm irritated with myself. It was my fault."

"Did you disappoint her?"

"Yeah, that was probably it. How'd you know?"

"Isn't that often the reason for an argument? I know my way around disappointments."

I stepped out of the shadows so that he could see me better. "I'd like to tell you something."

He nodded.

"I've thought about our conversations for a long time and have decided to quit my job."

"Oh...oh." He furrowed his brow and put on a serious face. "You are very strong."

"You think so?"

"You've always been."

"Why do you say that?"

"You were always alone."

"So were you."

"I had my piano."

"I had no choice."

"I think you did."

"I don't think so."

"You could have fought back."

"What was I supposed to have fought back against?"

I could hear him breathing in and out deeply. The phone's microphone intensified the sounds even more. "I remember how most girls would talk about you behind your back. I know who smeared dog shit in your school bag, and you did too."

"Of course I knew. It was no secret. But what was I supposed to do?"

"You could've gone to the teachers. You could've told your mother. You could've kept asking the girls to stop, or you could've tried to pacify them with little gifts, like Wako did. Instead, you put up with it."

"So what?" I asked when he didn't go on. It wasn't clear to me what he wanted to convey.

"It takes a lot of strength to put up with misery like you did. Without being broken by it. They tortured you, and you still never became their victim. Only a strong person can manage that."

"Hm," was all I could muster in response. I'd always felt myself to be weak. "Hm," I repeated. "You think so? I didn't feel that way."

"I know. You never complained and never asked for help. I admired you for that."

What Kento was saying turned my world upside down. "I need to give that some thought."

We looked at each other. I had the strong urge to caress the screen.

He smiled. "May I read you a haiku?"

"I'd love that. I like the haiku you pick out for me."

"Soon to be dying
yet giving away no sign
the cicada sings.

"That's by Bashō."

On Monday, I could tell from the faces of my colleagues that Naoko hadn't kept anything to herself. Their quizzical looks, their inquisitive nodding at our encounters in the corridor told me they knew what I was planning.

That afternoon, Takahashi-san asked to chat with me in one of the conference rooms on our level. Through the large windows, the view from the fifteenth floor reached far across the city. Takahashi-san gestured to a chair and served us coffee. He'd never done this before.

We took our seats at the long table and both smiled politely.

"Are you doing well, Nakamura-san?" he asked, his voice sounding more formal than when we usually spoke.

I sat bolt upright before him, my hands placed in my lap, and nodded without looking at him.

"I'm glad." He paused. The soft whoosh of the air conditioner accompanied our silence. "I've heard," he finally went on, "that you are entertaining the idea of leaving our firm?"

"Hm."

"Is there something that displeases you here with us?"

"No, it has nothing to do with that. I'm very satisfied here."

"Then this is simply a rumor?"

"Um...well...no, it's not a rumor."

Takahashi-san let out a quiet groan.

"It's not because of the firm," I said quickly in reassurance. "Everything is my fault. My behavior is quite selfish—I'm aware of that."

He looked at me directly and sighed. "You are the best employee in your department. You are fast and efficient. I can rely on you. If you leave, your colleagues will have to take over your work. That would be an additional burden. You are aware of that, I assume."

I nodded several times in apology. "Yes, and I'm sorry for that. I don't want to inconvenience anyone."

"In these times, it's hard to find good accountants. It's impossible for me to let you leave. You're needed." He took a sip of his coffee and, gesturing to me, invited me to do the same. Hesitantly, I tasted my cup.

For a while we both said nothing.

"I really don't want to cause you any trouble. I regret it very much and didn't make the decision lightly."

Takahashi-san waited a while before continuing. "They say you want to write a book."

I smiled bashfully and nodded imperceptibly.

"A book?" He grinned.

I wished he'd say something I could reply to. What was I supposed to say to a smile like that?

"That's a nice pursuit, for the weekends. I suggest you stay with us another year."

He was acting as though I were a kind of specialist. Any accountant could do my job.

I maintained my silence, and he knew how to interpret that.

Takahashi-san turned to the side and gazed out the window for a while.

"There are colleagues," he said without glancing at me, "who claim you thought up the slogan 'The world is changing. Are you? Say 'I do' to you.'"

"That's not true," I countered, hoping he didn't notice my irritation. I was furious that Naoko hadn't even kept this story to herself. "That is simply a stupid rumor."

"Hm. That's what Satō-san and Nakagawa-san are claiming too," he said pensively. "I wasn't there." He took a pregnant pause. "Be that as it may, it is a great success. Well done. It was rightly honored, and I wonder whether you might like to transfer to the creative department. I could put in a good word for you with Komatsu-san should a position there open up."

"That is extremely generous of you, but I couldn't. I only gave my colleagues a few very general suggestions for the campaign. It was nothing. I'm an accountant. I don't belong in the creative department."

"Hm."

He looked past me. I didn't know what he was seeing or thinking.

Our silence continued.

"Is there something we could do to change your mind? Perhaps an enhanced salary? There is by all means leeway on the upper end."

His question surprised me. I hadn't expected it. "That is extraordinarily generous. I owe you a debt of thanks, but my decision has nothing to do with money." I lowered my gaze sheepishly. I was embarrassed to turn down such an offer. It was ungrateful. I regarded the gray carpet, my black shoes. I shook my head.

"Now and again, positions open up in our offices in Bangkok and Singapore. Would that be something that would interest you?"

Again, I shook my head.

He sighed audibly, discontented. I wasn't making it easy for him and could understand his irritation.

Still, I rose. It was impolite for me to end the discussion, but there was nothing else I could do.

I bowed several times, apologizing again for every inconvenience I caused him or the company, and left the conference room. My eyes downcast, I hurried to my desk.

For the rest of the day, I buried myself in my work. Toward evening, one coworker after the next said goodbye until I was alone in the department. From time to time, I could hear voices in the corridor, the dinging of the elevator. People were still working elsewhere. For a long time, I sat at my desk motionless, staring at my computer's screensaver. It displayed a photograph of a small brook with moss-covered stones in the forest. I closed my eyes occasionally for a few seconds and listened to the water burbling, a few birds, the buzzing of insects.

I clutched my desk with both hands, looking at the keyboard in front of me, the lamp, the two shelves filled with binders and books, the little porcelain cat Naoko had given me once as a good luck charm.

This had been my spot in the world for six years, I thought. How happy I'd been when I'd finally found it. Maybe not happy, but satisfied. That was worth a lot. Now I was giving it up—of my own accord—without knowing where I might find another or what it might look like, or whether I'd feel more at home there.

Had I weighed my choice well? No.

Did I nevertheless feel like I was not making a bad decision? Hm.

Yes.

Which didn't mean that made it the right one.

I packed up my things. After I'd left the office, I recorded a message for Kento:

"Hey . . . I just wanted to say hello . . . Today I had a chat with my boss. I told him I wanted to leave the company at the end of the year . . . He was not thrilled at all, sadly . . . Anyway . . . I'm not sure what I'd expected . . . It'll be okay." My voice grew softer with every sentence, which I didn't like. Before I went on, I took a deep breath and cleared my throat. "On Saturday, I'm going to Inokashira Park. The weather's supposed to be really nice. On Sunday, I'm heading to Tsujido Beach early... I'll take my mother's ashes with me." I briefly considered adding something else but let it stand. He'd indicated with his silence that he wouldn't be joining me. "Anyhow... I hope you're really well... See you..."

On the way to the train, Naoko sent a message with only a single sentence:

"I'm sorry."

Relieved, I replied with a smiling emoji. For me, there was nothing more to say about it.

In Shimokita, at the spur of the moment, I treated myself to a foot massage. The advertising board of a newly opened massage parlor promised fifty percent off this week. I wanted to be pampered a bit to relax a little.

The shop was busy. Of the six seats, only one was still free.

I booked for an hour, paid, took off my shoes and stockings, and sat down in a soft, comfortable chair. A young man pulled up a basin of warm water, took my feet, and carefully lifted them in.

"Is the water okay like this or too hot?" he asked.

"It's just right, thank you," I said, reclining my seat, lying back, and closing my eyes. It was pleasantly quiet: a fountain splashed, what little talking there was was done at a whisper, a jazz piano played in the background, muffled.

After a few minutes, the masseur dried my feet and legs, wrapped one foot in a hand towel, and began to massage the other.

I winced involuntarily.

"Pardon me, is it too intense?"

"No," I said. "It's...I'm not used to it."

He pressed firmly into my soles, rubbed the balls of my feet, kneaded my calves. None of it was tender, yet still I got goosebumps.

When had someone last stroked my skin intentionally, aside from fleeting encounters on the train, with Naoko or Madame Montaigne?

Probably my mother, who frequently used to massage my shoulders and neck when they were tight. That was a long time ago.

The massage was a boon to my feet. The young man was good at what he did; at the same time, I was embarrassed. I felt uncomfortable and couldn't relax. I was glad, in the end, when the hour was up.

At home, I drafted the resignation letter for the human resources department. Since I didn't know how to formulate such an official document, I used a template from the Internet as a model.

Dear Takahashi-san,

With this letter, I kindly request permission today from the company SunSun Agency to be allowed to end my employment with you effective December 31 of this year. The termination of our employment relationship is solely my failure, and I beg pardon should any inconveniences arise for the company.

*Should you consent, I would like to make a formal
apology to you now and to thank you for your
understanding.*
> Yours sincerely,
> Akiko Nakamura

Instead of being relieved, I felt empty and numb. I
felt like crying. I mostly wanted to call Kento, but he
couldn't help me now either.

To hear his voice, I played the message he'd sent me
a few days earlier.

"Good morning...Today I want to read you a special haiku...It was in one of my schoolbooks in high
school...I copied it down...A few weeks ago, I found
the slip of paper in a book as a bookmark."

The pause was so long I thought he'd hung up.

> *"Here on a roadway*
> *where nobody else travels*
> *The autumn evening"*

Silence from Kento, though I could hear him breathing.
Softly, very softly, he said: "That's it."

25

WHEN MY PHONE ALARM RANG, DAWN WAS BREAKING. I was already awake and had hardly slept. My whole body felt heavy and spiritless.

I felt nauseated.

I buried myself beneath the blanket, drew my knees up to my chest, and made myself as small as possible.

The day ahead loomed horribly. Yesterday, I'd been full of confidence, and now I was doubting whether I'd have the strength all by myself to part ways with my mother's ashes, whether I was ready to let go.

Eventually, I hounded myself out of bed and got dressed.

I wrapped the vessel containing my mother's urn in a dark-blue scarf. Made of French linen, it had been her favorite scarf, one of the few things I'd kept. I padded the backpack on both sides with two towels as well.

Shortly before leaving the apartment, I paused for a moment and looked around.

The spot on the sideboard suddenly looked empty, naked, like a cherry tree that had lost all its leaves and blossoms.

At that moment, I realized how much the urn, her photograph, and my offerings had been the focal point of the apartment before, how often over the previous two years I'd sat in silence before the sideboard or talked with the urn during meals, how often my gaze had rested on it.

My half-desolate home, but I didn't have any other.

I believe in spirits. Not ghosts: spirits. I believe that places, objects, and the dead—not just people, animals, and plants—have their own power, energy, or soul, and that we have a connection to them, sometimes stronger, sometimes less so.

Now I was standing in the room, feeling like my mother was speaking to me, not just in words of course—it was a different form of communication. It resembled the kind I'd experienced occasionally over the previous weeks and months on my walks with Kento.

And at this moment, my mother clearly indicated to me that she wanted to leave, that her time in this apartment was finally over, that I should let her go, just as she'd used to tell me without words when she was well or when something displeased her. I'd seen it in her eyes, in her expression and her gestures. It was in the air, and I'd sensed it.

I put on my shoes.

I shouldered the backpack—which was heavy, much heavier than I'd imagined—switched off the light, quietly locked the door to the apartment, and left the building.

After a few steps, I stopped in my tracks.

Kento was waiting on the street.

"Oh . . . hi," I stuttered in surprise. "What are you doing here?"

"Hi," he said back in greeting without answering my question.

"I . . . I'm on my way to the beach."

"I know."

"Uh . . . so . . . I . . . ," I couldn't think of anything else to say.

He wrinkled his brow and gave a faint nod, whatever he intended to convey to me with that.

I took a few hesitant steps toward the train station, and he followed me. We walked side by side in silence. I had no idea how long he'd been standing there, whether he wanted to walk me to the train or join me by the sea. At the next corner, I stopped to remove the backpack and put it on frontways; I wanted to carry her as close to me as possible.

The streets were still devoid of people. Even in the two konbini we passed, the salesclerks were standing alone behind the counter in their uniforms, furtively yawning.

At the train station, I wanted to buy a ticket for Kento, but he already had one.

Only a few passengers were waiting on the platform. We boarded the first car. A woman was sitting there asleep, her head lolled onto her chest.

The journey took nearly an hour, the gray houses of the Tokyo suburbs passing us by. I kept the backpack on my lap, embracing it with both arms, squeezing it tightly from time to time while looking out the window. Kento and I still hadn't exchanged more than our few words of greeting.

We alighted in Tsujido. It was a good twenty-minute walk from the train station to the ocean. On the way, we passed a coffeeshop that was just opening. I bought myself a cappuccino with a double espresso. Kento didn't want anything.

The closer we came to the beach, the more my steps slowed. The path had never seemed so long to me. I stopped in the parking lot behind the dunes. I thought I could hear the surf, though perhaps I was only imagining it. Two joggers ran past us at a quick pace. Kento followed them with his eyes.

He waited. I was grateful to him for his silence.

We stood abreast for a few minutes, regarding the sky, the empty parking lot, the crows gliding away above us. I'd never liked their loud crowing. Now I found it sinister. We walked through a stand of pine trees and came out onto the wide, blackish gray beach. It lay there deserted. In the distance, I spotted a few surfers in the waves and a fisherman. I was relieved we wouldn't attract any attention. The winds were nearly calm, yet the deep thundering of the breaking waves roared over to us. Clouds obscured the sky. The Pacific lay before us, a silvery gray.

We took off our shoes and socks, rolled up our pant-legs, and walked down the beach to the water. As it washed up around my feet, I sank up to my ankles in the soft, wet sand and looked out to sea.

The water was colder than I'd expected. Nothing was as I'd expected.

In nearly an hour, the tide would reach its high-water mark. Kento and I looked for a spot that would be flooded by then. I asked him to help me build a sort of temple structure out of sand that I wanted to fill with my mother's ashes and surrender to the sea.

I took off the backpack, we knelt down and began burrowing. Kento marked out about one square meter and around that erected a wall about one hand high. With both hands, I shaped an inner rampart. In the middle, we built a raised rectangular prominence into which I pressed a round, deep well. Kento looked for stones and shells to decorate the rampart and the plinth. With a few small sticks, he crafted three little gates facing toward the sea. My mother was to begin her journey into the Pacific through them.

It looked beautiful.

I nodded in approval.

The water hadn't yet reached us, but it was coming closer. The waves were ebbing just about a half meter in front of our structure.

I picked up the backpack, my movements growing heavier and slower. Each motion of my hand was hard.

I unzipped the backpack.

I took out the vessel with the urn.

I uncoiled the scarf from it.

I could hear the dull thud of an especially high breaking wave and started. Its edges reached the outer embankment.

I wanted to open the urn and fill the well with the ashes, but I couldn't.

I stood there, paralyzed, staring at our structure, at the urn, at the sea.

I felt my heart beating into my throat.

The feeling that my knees would give out any second.

Kento and I exchanged looks, and I could see in his face that he knew exactly what was happening within me, how much it hurt, could see that he knew my doubts and my pain and that I had no words for it, that he understood the step I'd soon take—and that in his presence I didn't have to be ashamed if I didn't take it.

I knew I could pack up everything, pick up the backpack, turn around, and leave without having to offer a single word of explanation for myself.

That was something very precious.

With a gesture, he offered to empty the urn for me. I shook my head.

Gingerly, I lifted its lid.

The sight of the gray-black ashes.

The thought that this was supposed to have been the person who brought me into the world was absurd.

Or not.

I began to cry: quiet, soundless tears.

Leaning over, I held it just over the well and carefully poured the ashes into the sand. They nearly filled the depression to the edge. I placed the lid of the urn on top so that the wind wouldn't carry my mother away.

Tears were now streaming down my face.

The water rose.

Inexorably, it washed around our structure, channeling its way through the sand, eating away at the outer wall, sloshing over it, withdrawing, returning, reaching the inner one. The calm and certainty with which everything happened calmed me. Gurgling and roaring, it receded and took another run.

The first gate collapsed, then the second.

Now I was crying more loudly and bitterly than I ever had in my life, as though all the tears I'd held back since her death were bursting out of me.

I felt someone graze my hand. Brief though the touch was, it did me good. I regained my composure a bit. I wasn't alone.

And again I could hear my mother. I heard her humming, humming the melody of a song she had sung to me as a small child when I hadn't been able to fall asleep.

I felt something I had no words for.

How can we give a name to what we do not know?

With wave after wave, the sea took my mother with it.

The border of the well crumbled and disintegrated until it gave way.

The ashes began mixing with the water.

A bigger wave came, thinning out the silt, which disappeared into the ocean with the ebbing water forever.

I watched it go and was deeply sorrowful and relieved at once.

The next wave rolled up.

And then another.

And another.

Just a few minutes later, our little temple of sand had been levelled. Gone.

Without a trace.

As though it'd never existed.

Just as my mother had become slighter and slighter in the months before her death until, from one moment to the next, she had ceased to exist—with one difference, I thought:

She *had* left behind a trace.

She had given me the gift of life.

It may not have been a big trace or a significant one, but that didn't matter.

The wind had freshened and was tousling my hair. It'd driven away the clouds, and above us lay a deep-blue sky. The air tasted of salt.

Without conferring with one another, we began walking along the beach in silence.

His bare feet next to mine in the sand. They were pretty feet, long and narrow, with slender toes. I looked back and saw the indentations we'd left behind. Two large ones and two not quite so large ones, lined up as though on a string, side by side in harmony.

The tide had reached its high-water mark, the water was ebbing, and our footprints would remain visible until the wind eventually whisked them away.

This thought appealed to me.

Kento noticed my gaze and turned around.

Together, we regarded our traces in the sand.

I felt for his hand and took his in mine.

When was the last time I'd touched someone intentionally? It must've been my mother's corpse. I'd stroked her face and held her hands. They'd been cold, cold and lifeless.

Unlike Kento's.

After a few seconds, I let go of his hand again, although it was hard for me.

I didn't want to be one of those people who was too much for him.

Before us, the intensifying surf roared.

For a long while, we stood beside one another, looking out at the sea.

ACKNOWLEDGMENTS

When I traveled to Japan for the first time in 1995, my destination was Kobe, which had been destroyed by an earthquake. The city lay in ruins, fires were burning everywhere, and people were staggering about the streets looking for their loved ones.

I was to report on the aftermath of the quake for *Stern* magazine. Those were dramatic and very moving days, and my experiences left a deep impression on me. Never before had I witnessed the destructive fury of the forces of nature, and on the other hand, I was overwhelmed by the strength, dignity, and discipline with which the people there faced their destiny.

Since that time, I've often been in Japan, initially as a foreign correspondent and for almost twenty years now as a writer. In particular, the photographers Greg Davies and Michael Wolf, who both passed away much too soon, and my then interpreter, Hans-Jürgen Classen, helped me quite a bit during my first travels.

Many people were a great help to me in the genesis of this novel, and without their willingness to support me and share their knowledge with me, I would never have been able to write the book as I did. I owe them all a great debt of gratitude.

To unlock the world of Akiko and Kento, I stayed in Japan for many weeks over the past two years.

Sayaka Funada-Classen painstakingly arranged and organized these research trips, helped me as an interpreter in numerous conversations, explained much to me that I would otherwise never have understood, read the manuscript with great care, and pointed out to me many errors and mistakes. For those remaining, I bear sole responsibility.

During the conversations I had in order to better understand a world foreign to me, Emi Yahiro, Naoko Watanabe, Maho Watanabe, Miho Hara, Masako Yonekawa, Tomomi Awamura, and Mai Kobayashi were great and indispensable aids to me as translators and interlocutors.

I would especially like to thank Kanji Izumiya, Ryo Inoue, and Takashi Tamura for the generosity with which they answered my questions and for their hospitality.

In Berlin I am particularly indebted to the artist Sae Esashi-Schild for her many insights and conversational contacts, but also to Kanahi Yamashita, Eriko Yamazaki, Ken Nakasako, Ibuki, and Ayane.

Stephan Abarbanell and Ulrich Genzler read various drafts of the manuscript and continually supported me with their counsel.

With his thorough reading, Willi Boelcke saved me from several major errors. My wife Anna also supported the creative process for this novel with great patience, read the text at various stages, and pointed out to me its inadequacies. In my many moments of doubt, she always encouraged me not to give up, not to lose faith in Akiko and Kento and their stories.

I'd also like to thank a series of people who were willing—and often took many, many hours of time—to tell me, a foreigner, their stories in detail, as sad and painful as it sometimes was. *Arigato.*

Louie Miura, Kohei Yamashita, Yuichi Ishii, Yukiko Inoue, Tomoe Sawano, Yūki Takimoto, Toyo Ito, Ayaka, Mika, Megumi, Alisa, Miyu, Eseru, Tomoya, Madoka, Risa, Yuka, Reina, Kyoya, Shiho, Chinatsu, Chihiro, Souma, Yuki, Shotaro, Satoshi, Tomoko, Mana, Suzuki-kun, Chizuru Wakai, Tomoko Daimon, Naho Tanimoto, Miyako Takeshita, Yuki Iiyama, Makoto Honda, Mariko Adachi, Chiaki Kaneko, Ken Matsuda, Taku Kawauchi, Yoko Sano, Mikino Takahashi, Rei Suzuki, Kimitoshi Nakaya, Tomoko Nagase, Miki Yoshida, Tomi Matsuba, Daikichi Matsuba, Masako Konoe, Kosaku Hidaka, Naoko Hidaka, Shoujun Yoshida, Yasue Nagatomo, Nanoha Higuchi, Mika Kondo, Kaori Nishimaki, Fuyuko Miwa, Mai Suzuki, Miu Kikuchi, and Toby Koyabashi.

GLOSSARY

Agedashi tofu – fried silken tofu in a seasoned broth.
Bento – a dish or box in which meals are transported for school or travel.
Bukatsu – popular extracurricular clubs every school offers in the afternoon after classes and in which participation in Japan is in many cases mandatory.
Edamame – immature green soybeans, traditionally served in their pod as a snack or a side dish. They are sprinkled with sea salt or chili flakes, and the beans are sucked out of the pod.
Futon – Japanese sleeping mattress, in many households rolled out onto the floor at night and stored in a cabinet during the day.
Geta – traditional wooden sandals with elevated soles.
Haiku – traditional Japanese poetic form, always consisting of three lines and seventeen morae (or syllables).
Hayashi – rice dish with beef.

Heeei irasshai – a greeting of welcome that staff in many restaurants use to receive new guests.

Hibakusha – term for survivors of the atomic bombings of Hiroshima and Nagasaki.

Hikikomori – term for people who have withdrawn from society and live in complete social isolation. Many hikikomori do not leave their room or apartment for years. According to official estimates, there are far more than a million of them of all age groups in Japan.

Izakaya – a combination restaurant and pub, with a small food menu and a larger beverage menu.

Kaiten-sushi – reasonably priced sushi restaurants where the fish is served on small plates that circulate on a conveyor belt.

Koban – small local police station that exists everywhere in the country and that serves many purposes.

Konbini – small supermarket ("convenience store") open all day every day. They are on every corner in Japan.

Koseki – most important personal document in Japan: a family register in which all important information is listed, ranging from birth to death. A *koseki-tōhon* is the official, certified copy.

Kushiyaki – grilled meats, vegetables, or seafood served on skewers.

Love hotel – the Japanese version of a hotel that rents by the hour, widespread throughout the country.

Mama-san – term for the female proprietor or person who runs a bar or pub. She is responsible for the entertainment of her guests and for her staff.

Matcha – green tea in powdered form, made from ground tea leaves. It is used in the Japanese tea ceremony, today often drunk with warm or cold milk as a sort of latte.

Mochi – very popular Japanese sweet made from rice flour, often filled with a sweet paste made from red beans (azuki).

Nakai-san – employee in small Japanese-style guesthouses, called ryokan.

Obon – one of the most important Japanese holidays on which people honor their deceased relatives and are visited by the spirits of their ancestors.

Office lady – the female equivalent to the salaryman.

Omamori – amulets or good luck charms promising protection often sold in shrines or temples.

Omikuji – prophecies offered at temples and shrines.

Onigiri – a small snack made from rice wrapped in nori (seaweed), usually filled with fish or vegetables.

Onsen – term for a thermal bath or a town with hotels and inns that have baths fed from hot natural springs.

Otoshidama – gift for children on the new year, usually a small sum of money in an envelope.

Ramen – popular Japanese noodles often eaten as a quick meal.

Ryokan – traditional Japanese inn.

Sake – Japanese rice wine.

Salaryman – term for an employee in a large company with long working hours who is part of a strict hierarchy. They are frequently associated with overwork, stress, and a monotonous lifestyle.

Sensei – respectful expression for a teacher or master.

Sento – public bathhouse, still widespread in Japan and part of daily life.

Shabu-shabu – a kind of Japanese hotpot with thinly sliced meats and vegetables cooked in a broth by the diner.

Shikata ga nai – one of the most common Japanese expressions. It essentially means: There's nothing one can do. That's the way it is.

Shinkansen – Japanese bullet trains that connect the country's large cities.

Shōchū – high-proof Japanese beverage distilled usually from rice, potatoes, or buckwheat.

Soba – buckwheat noodles eaten primarily at lunch, warm or cold. There are many restaurants that exclusively serve soba dishes.

Sukiyaki – Japanese hotpot.

Sunakku – a kind of snack bar or corner pub that serves a regular clientele, always run by a woman, and where small snacks and mainly hard liquor is served, often in connection with karaoke.

Tamagotchi – a virtual pet developed in Japan in 1996. The aim of the game is to keep the Tamagotchi alive by feeding, playing with, and caring for it. The Tamagotchi dies when it is neglected.

Tamagoyaki – Japanese omelet.

Tenugui – a kind of small cotton towel or cloth used for many different things in daily life.

Torii – a gate, usually painted vermilion, that often marks the entrance to a Shinto shrine.

Yakitori – grilled chicken skewers.

Yukata – a kind of robe worn at home made from light cotton fabric.

Yuzu – Japanese citrus fruit, somewhere between a lemon and an orange.

BIBLIOGRAPHY OF HAIKU REFERENCES

177 Ryōka, "Carpets on the grass" ["Decken auf dem Gras"], in *Bambusregen: Haiku und Holzschnitte aus dem Kagebōshishū* [Ōsaka, 1754], trans. and ed. Ekkehard May and Claudia Waltermann (Leipzig: Insel, 1995), 40–41. English translation by Daniel Bowles.

177 "Oh, butterfly, oh!" ["Ach Schmetterling!"], in *Ihr gelben Chrysanthemen! Japanische Lebensweisheit: Haiku*, ed. Heinrich Tieck, freely adapted from the Japanese by Anna von Rottauscher (Vienna: Verlag W. Scheuermann, 1940), 9. English translation by Daniel Bowles.

190 Masaki Yūko, "In a former life" ["In einem früheren Dasein"], in *Haiku: Gedichte aus fünf Jahrhunderten*, ed. Masami Ono-Feller and Eduard Klopfenstein (Stuttgart: Reclam, 2022), 311 [no. 301]. English translation by Daniel Bowles.

190 Iida Ryūta, "Father, mother – dead" ["Vater, Mutter – tot"], in *Haiku: Gedichte aus fünf Jahrhunderten*, ed. Masami Ono-Feller and Eduard Klopfenstein (Stuttgart:

Reclam, 2022), 288 [no. 278]. English translation by
Daniel Bowles.

259 Bashō, "In Kyoto too," in *Bashō: the complete Haiku of
Matsuo Bashō*, trans. Andrew Fitzsimons (Oakland, CA:
University of California Press, 2022), 237 [no. 638].

282 Gochiku, "The long night," in *Haiku*, vol. III: Summer–
Autumn, ed. Reginald Horace Blyth (Tokyo: Hokuseido,
1960), 357.

301 Issa, "O snail," in *Haiku*, vol. III: Summer–Autumn, ed.
Reginald Horace Blyth (Tokyo: Hokuseido, 1960), 250.

306 Issa, "An autumn evening," in *Haiku*, vol. III: Summer–
Autumn, ed. Reginald Horace Blyth (Tokyo: Hokuseido,
1960), 353.

330 Bashō, "Soon to be dying," in *Bashō: the complete Haiku
of Matsuo Bashō*, trans. Andrew Fitzsimons (Oakland,
CA: University of California Press, 2022), 238 [no. 642].

337 Bashō, "Here on a roadway," in *Bashō: the complete Haiku
of Matsuo Bashō*, trans. Andrew Fitzsimons (Oakland,
CA: University of California Press, 2022), 339 [no. 916].

ABOUT THE AUTHOR

Jan-Philipp Sendker, born in Hamburg in 1960, was the American correspondent for *Stern* from 1990 to 1995, and its Asian correspondent from 1995 to 1999. In 2000 he published *Cracks in the Wall*, a nonfiction book about China. *The Art of Hearing Heartbeats*, his first novel, became an international bestseller, and was followed by two sequels, *A Well-Tempered Heart* and *The Heart Remembers*. He lives in Potsdam with his family.

ABOUT THE TRANSLATOR

Daniel Bowles teaches at Boston College. His translation of Christian Kracht's *Eurotrash* was long-listed for the 2025 International Booker Prize, and he was awarded the Helen & Kurt Wolff Translator's Prize in 2016 for his translation of Kracht's *Imperium*.